Traces of You

John

Elaine

Live - life to the fullest
love - unconditionally
laugh - simply because
it cleanses the
soul

Raymond Goode

1

Dedication

Nicole Barden…My last love letter;

You are the epitome of what it is to be called a woman. I have seen the beauty of the world through your eyes. For that moment that I will carry with me throughout eternity; I am FOREVER IN YOUR PRESENCE.

Goode, Raymond D.

ACKNOWLEDGEMENT

First of all I would like to thank Al, Angelena, Bo, Brandon1&2, Brittney, Chirlyne, David 1&2, Dexter, Eric, Greg, Holly, Jacky, Jessica, Jr., Keith, Kimberly, Lynette, Marcus, Margaret, Marica, Marisha, Monica, Myles, Najai, Neverett, Patricia, Ronald 1&2, Ruben, Sonia, Stacy, Tarez, Taryn, Tasha, Towanta, Tayshone, Tealaza, Tera, Terrell, Thomas, Tiffani, Toeka, Tyrell,, Wandrell, Yvonne, Zenobia and Zokee; Whose lives are an inspiration to me and who I hope and pray feel the love and respect that I have for them in *"Traces Of You"*. I am truly blessed to have had the chance to capture a small glimpse into your lives and pray that I have given you world the traces of you that is definitely worthy of your approval.

I would also like to thank:

T.J. Snyder: (Google as I like to call him) for your huge contribution to the information that I could not find at times.

Bianca Brown: Thank you for your unrelenting efforts to see my vision to the max.

Robert Townes: Thank you for your constant guidance in seeing all the things that I could not see and encouraging me when I thought the chips where down. (We go see stars together).

Jewell Brown: Thank you for going above and beyond in the call of duty so many times. (Get your business off the ground. I got your back.)

Shaunda Davis: Thank you for your late night conversations and redirection when I lost sight on myself.

Lisette Torres: Thank you for being my first love. I will never forget how deep our love truly was. You will always have a special place in my heart no matter how far I go or what becomes of my life.

Angel Sims: Thank you for all of the emails and texts (Batman has actually done it…Gotham has a new hero).

Margaret Wade: Thank you for the God-given skills that you have contributed.

Goapele: Thank you for your inspirational song which has pulled me closer to my dreams.

To my military personnel: *Disclaimer*: To all the names I've forgotten please charge it to my brain and not my heart…You all know how I get down and I love you all.

Houseworth, Sgt. Dejesus, Rodriguez, Brown, Hunt, Besseliu, Tucker, Love, Muse, Peaches, Rob, Jamison, Robles, Broadnaux, Riddick, Greene, Grice, Rudd, Townsend, Coleman, Richardson, Hill, Nelson-Tillmon, A-Z, Woody, Pierce, Young, Ortiz, Mcneese, Gordon, Graham, Bailey, Tappin, Coles, Hall.

I would like to thank God, Allah, Buddha and any other forces for keeping me together when my mental state of mind was unconscious. I would like to thank my family and friends for continuously giving me support and encouragement. I would like to especially thank my Grandma Mattie Goode/Moore for continuously believing in my dream and encouraging me to continue on my path without judgment. For your everlasting love and wisdom that you have provided to keep this family as tight of a family unit as it is…This book is devoted to your life. I love you Grandma.

Last but certainly not least. I would like to give a special THANK YOU to my family. The people that know me like no other and has loved me since day one.   *Disclaimer: I apologize in advance if I have left anyone out. It was not intentional and my heart is with each and every one of you*.

Thank you Mattie Goode/Moore, Steve Goode Sr. and Jr., Lynette Goode, Lakesha Goode, Shaniece Goode, Takeysha Goode, Mykala Kenney, Michael Kenney, Donald Goode, Melvin Goode, Judy Goode/Cox, Nicole Goode, Micheal Martinez (Tater), Tayshone Perry, David Perry, William Goode Jr. (Lil Will), Trinity Goode, Toren Goode, Ashley Cox, Shantae Goode, Daneka Dickerson, Marsha Goode, Raquan Goode, Markie D. Goode, Bridget Goode, Lorenzo Goode (Lo), Gary Goode/Payne, Tony Goode/Payne, Anthony Payne, Michael Payne, Sydney Moore, Tyshaun Goode, Latrell Goode, and Amajah Goode.

To my family that has passed away I have not forgotten about you and through me your legacy lives on. I would like to THANK YOU for the contributions you have made to my life and our family as a whole. This family is continuously reminded of the very essence of your memories in every song that is played, every step that is taken and every prayer that is sent up. The children that you have provided give this family a glimpse of you whenever we look in their eyes. I love you all Joyce Goode, William Goode Sr., Lorenzo Goode Sr., William Fox (Maryland), Gladys Pryor, and Linwood Pryor.

TABLE OF CONTENTS

FOREWORD

Life is a meticulous journey comprised of assorted emotions and correlating circumstances synchronized by a series of irreplaceable moments. Moments cannot be reproduced or reduplicated! I can imagine the confusion such a statement evokes. Allow me to demonstrate. Close your eyes and try recreating the moment you first felt reading this commentary. I'm pretty sure you can recall how you felt and what you thought at the time. However, you will not be able to replicate your original reaction to this analysis because; your initial opinion only exits within the past tense. Here is another example. Attempt to duplicate the same level of excitement and skepticism you initially felt when receiving a copy of this very publication. Unless you own a time machine capable of instantaneously transporting you into the past; it would be impossible to experience those very same emotions you felt the first time you received this book. This task is impractical because your initial opinion has come and gone. At this very moment, the thoughts you expressed sixty seconds ago have become memories stored within your subconscious only retrieved as a point of reference validating your perspective. It is virtually impossible for this publication to get a second chance to make a first impression upon you.

Moments are created by people, places, and external variables which act as unsuspecting participants inadvertently influencing every aspect of our existence. Moments are authentic, impatient, and unpredictable. A true moment will not wait to be acknowledged. It simply emerges, fulfills its purpose, and disappears like a thief in the night. Moments just happen! I've known Raymond Goode for twenty years. I will never forget the moment I observed our friendship evolve into brotherhood. Over the course of time our brotherhood has experienced a variety of pivotal moments. I recall the moment Raymond discovered his purpose in life through a passion for writing. I remember the moment Raymond realized that he could intrigue our minds and captivate our emotions by utilizing his God-Given talent as a novelist. The majority of our lives we never get the opportunity to appreciate the precious moments which collectively contribute to our existence. Moments have the ability to come and go as they please. Raymond has accomplished the impossible task of extending the duration of a single moment. He has immortalized a moment by providing a collection of detailed narratives which explain the present and predict the future, by considering the individual circumstances related to past experiences. It is extremely rare that we get that opportunity to appreciate life's most precious moments before they slip away. The Moment is Now. Traces of You.

Robert L. Townes III

Renzi

PREFACE

Traces of you have meant so much to me. This project started as a way to mentally free myself from the everyday craziness of life. It invokes happiness in me when I can make another person's answers come to life. As I interviewed these 50 people; it amazed me how much people wanted to reveal the happiest parts of their lives. When I finished interviewing each person they began to reminisce on the very moments that made them joyous and those are the moments that I truly tried to captivate in my book. My life has become a voice for the "little" people who cannot or have not been heard by the outside world. I saw intimate details of people lives. When I interviewed gay people; some showed me the fear that they have of being comfortable in their skin around others and some displayed the strength gained after expressing love to oneself in its rarest form. While interviewing older people; I fell in love with the way their eyes would light up at the opportunity to reminisce on the past rather than the future. I saw innocence in each person and not the superficial world around them.

I have utilized every single quote and song that I have heard, book that I've read, or situations I've been in. *Traces of You* has defined more than just the people that I interviewed but to my friends and family it defines traces of me as well. I have learned that we as people are all the same lump of coal. We are all cut from the same cloth. We all share the same emotions of being afraid, shocked, mad, angry, and sad but love and only true love is the cure to all of the above.

In conclusion; *Traces of You* is my legacy and I would like to thank the powers that be for allowing me to be one of the blessed ones to be able to pursue my passion. Speaking on behalf of the characters within this publication: We would like to Thank you for reading our stories and welcome to "Traces of You".

INTRODUCTION OF AUTHOR

Born and raised in Richmond Virginia, Raymond Goode graduated from Meadowbrook High School in 1996. At this time, Raymond Goode was overwhelmed by the need to serve others, which continue to shape his life today. In an attempt to placate this need, he enlisted in the Navy after his time with the Army. Despite 7 years of military/civil service, a deep-seated desire to serve still flowed within him.

Raymond dedicated 2 years of his young life to the public by serving the state of Virginia in the Bon Air Juvenile Corrections Center in Bon Air, Virginia. This background in service and interactions with troubled youth prompted his transition to qualified mental health professional, serving multiple organizations in a variety of positions so that he could teach youth to "believe" so that "they will achieve". The most recent steps of his dedicated journey have led him to become an author. *Traces of You* is the first of many works to come.

Raymond's earliest writings consisted of love letters as well as an autobiographical analysis of his then relationship. With any writer; the development of one's work is dependent upon age, life experiences, and maturity. From writing love notes in crayon during his early years of "puppy love" to composing a journal during a recent bout with depression, writing has always been his outlet to share his ideas with the world. To him, writing fulfills all of the emotional support of a lover and a friend. It provides love, encouragement, guidance, an ear to listen and a shoulder to cry on.

One's relationship with writing is always capable of growth and transformation just as a friendship with a person. Through a lifelong relationship of growth and exploration and a

13

journey through the medium of love letters, songs, poetry, monologues, skits, and short stories; he has arrived at this phase of his journey…the love story. Now he writes to share the knowledge gained from this journey with the world, revealing traces of himself along the way.

Described by those closest to him as a chameleon due to his ability to adapt and change; Raymond is dedicated to giving all of himself physically, mentally, emotionally and spiritually to the reader. In 2010 he eschewed all of his worldly possessions, becoming homeless, in order to become a slave to his art, his passion, his muse so that he may produce his best work. Above all; he is an idealist, in love with love.

In the author's words, *"Love in its rarest form is accepting, loving, and being yourself completely before loving someone else"*. The epitome of Love; a rarity in itself, is Raymond Goode.

Bianca Brown

"BB"

Chapter One

"The best and most beautiful things in the world cannot be seen or even touched; they must be felt with the heart"

"Al"

Al scrolls his finger down the list of stores on the mall directory. Louis Vuitton, Dolce and Gabbana, Moschino, Brekka, Argentovivo, Church's K. Boards, Voyage, Prada and Mercedes Benz. He begins to walk around the first level of La Rinascente mall; stopping to gaze at the five floors. He steps on the escalator heading to the second level. He eyes a young Italian woman walking his way. They catch each other's eyes

"Hey, how are you doing?"

She says nothing and continues to walk. He chuckles to himself and enters the Louis Vitton store.

"Hello sir, how can I help you?"

"Benito; I'm not sure what I'm looking for but I want a classy look," Al says reading Benito's name off his nametag.

"Well I'm sure we can assist you with all your needs. Look around and I'll check on you in a few," Benito tells him.

Al walks through the aisles and sifts through the 3 for 135$ tie rack. He picks out a navy blue and black tie and holds it up in the mirror.

"I see you have good taste," Benito say complimenting Al on his selection. "If that is your choice I have the perfect suit for you."

Benito walks towards the suits hanging on the wall. He sifts through the rack and stops at a navy blue and black

15

pinstriped suit. He walks towards the shirt rack and pull out a solid colored gray shirt. Benito directs Al towards the dressing room and opens the door allowing him to enter.

"Thank you Sir," Al says as he steps in the dressing room shutting the door behind him. He holds up the shirt and tie in the mirror

"Damn good choice" he thinks to himself flipping off his shoes and unbuckling his pants. He takes his clothes off and puts on the outfit noticing that the pants are too long. He steps out the dressing room where Benito is stands waiting and holding the measuring tape in his hands. He leads Al to the short stand facing the mirror wall. Benito stretches the measuring tape from Al's belt to his feet.

"You're nobody till somebody love you
You're nobody till somebody cares
You may be king, you may possess the
World and its gold
But gold won't bring you happiness when
You're growing old
The world still is the same, you never change it
As sure as the stars shine above
You're nobody till somebody loves you
So find yourself somebody to love," plays in the background.

"You chose a great suit, this is one of Louis Vuitton's best," Benito tells him.

"Thank you; this is um…um…Deam Martin right? You're Nobody until Somebody loves you right?" Al says tapping his finger to the tune.

"You have good taste in music. In our country the old saying is Sicilian first and Italian second. We are very proud of your culture, no matter how bad the situation is, it's never serious," Benito says laughing and slapping Al on his leg.

They both look in the mirror staring at the cuff that Benito has just hemmed. Benito stands up and adjust the tie around Al's neck.

"I think that you will like this sir," he says.

Al fixes the tie tightly and stares at the suit in the mirror.

"How long do you think it will take to tailor it?" Al asks.

"Forty five minutes to an hour," Benito replies.

"I'm heading to the rooftop for a drink; I have a plane leaving in two hours. Can you have it ready in one" Al asks.

"Yes Sir, you have my word," Benito replies writing him his receipt.

Al exits the store and walks to a poster of CEO Vittorio Radice; the mastermind behind La Rinascente's mall makeover. As he reads the quote under the poster he reaches in his bag pulls out the watch that he has bought from Armani Exchange. He glances over the label that reads, *Self-winding watch with date display and Centre seconds, eighteen carat pink gold case, transparent sapphire case back, water resistant to twenty meters.* He snaps the watch out the box and looks at the engraving on the back: *Audemars Piguet Millenary.* "A real man should always wear a watch" he thinks to himself placing the watch on his left arm and fastening it. He takes the elevator to the seventh floor. He steps off the elevator and walks over to a picture of a woman dressed in plaid with a double image of her wearing red in the background. "Esposizione Rhodia Albene Rinascente" he reads the quote off the picture.

"You have good taste in art," he hears a woman behind him say. He turns around looking her up and down observing her long legs heading up to her short skirt.

"Apparently I have good taste in women as well…my name is Al," he says reaching out his hand.

"My name is Vittoria," she says laughing and taking his hand looking him up and down seductively. "This doesn't look like your first time here" she says.

"Observant, but I see something new every time I come," he tells her.

"Well; let me tell you about this beautiful city," she says walking towards the window. "You are actually facing the Piazzo Duomo Square…and right over there," she says pointing to the left; "is the Vittorio…the world's most famous and largest galleria…and to the right of that is the II Duomo…the world's largest cathedral…and right over there is the La Scala the most famous opera house," she tells him.

"You sound like a tourist guide" he replies as they both laugh. "Can I buy you a drink?" he asks.

"It's not like that, I just love my city and I think that people should take pride in what they love…especially if it's their city…and yes I would love a drink," she answers.

He stops the waiter walking past and orders two glasses of Barabaresco wine.

"Well tell me…what do you do? You are very beautiful," he asks her.

"Thank you; I am a Victoria Secret model and I also attend the Instituto Di Moda Burgo which is a fashion school in Milan. What do you do?" she asks.

"I own a chain of stores across the U.S." he tells her.

"Your stores must do very well," she says rubbing her hand down his arm fondling his watch. "Very nice taste," she says looking at his watch. She finishes off her glass as the waiter returns with their orders.

"I don't usually drink but I think tonight deserves a toast," he says clinking his glass with hers.

"I have to tell you the truth, I am a little tipsy" she says accidently spilling some of her drink on him. "I'm sorry" she says grabbing her napkin and wiping his blazer off.

"Don't worry about it," he responds continuing to allow her to wipe him down.

"How lucky can one guy be
I kissed her and
She kissed me
Like the fellow once said
Ain't that a kick in the head?
The room was completely black
I hugged her
And she hugged back," she begins to sing Westlife's "Ain't that a kick in the head," as she looks in his eyes.

"I have a room close by…if you wouldn't mind joining me I could use the company," she says teasing him and rubbing his face lightly.

"Sweetheart; any other time I would jump on that offer but I have a plane to catch real soon but I would love to take a rain-check for when I come back," he tells her.

She writes her number in lipstick on his forearm. "Just to be sure that you remember me" she says leaning over to kiss him on his cheek. "I got the drinks" she says walking away.

"Damn," he whispers to himself walking her walk away. He checks his watch and dashes to the elevator. He picks up his suit and exits the mall. He flags down a taxi tells him to head to the airport. He sets his suit on the hook and sticks his ear-buds in turning on music.

"When you're dreaming with a broken heart
The waking up is the hardest part
You roll outta bed and down on your knees
And for a moment you can hardly breathe
Wondering was she really here
Is she standing in my room?

No she's not
Cause she's gone, gone, gone, gone, gone
When you're dreaming with a broken heart
The giving up is the hardest part
She takes you in with her crying eyes
Then all at once you have to say goodbye
Wondering could you stay my love
Will you wake up by my side?
No she can't
Cause she's gone, gone, gone, gone, gone" John Mayer's
"Dreaming with a Broken Heart" plays.

He checks his email and clicks on the one marked from his girlfriend. "*I hate you*" it displays. He reads it over and over thinking of how it ever got to this point. He texts back, *I love you baby…always remember that first and foremost. I realize that I hurt you deeply but in turn I hurt myself the most. I still remember the day I asked you to marry me…looking up at you was like looking at an angel…when you said yes it felt like I had a pass into heaven. I don't know why I do the things that I do but I never intended to hurt you. It seems like I always fight so hard to get you back just to fuck it up all over again. I can't ask you to go through that process again and it feels like my apologies are becoming empty to you. But I am sorry…that comes from the heart. Even if my actions don't prove it; listen to my words. I love you baby"* he reads the message over and over. He presses send.

Chapter Two

*"Love is composed of a single soul
inhabiting two bodies"*

"Angelena"

"Start spreading the news
I'm leaving today
I want to be a part of it
New York New York
These vagabond shoes
They are longing to stray
Right through the very heart of it
New York New York
I want to wake up in that city
That doesn't sleep
And find I'm king of the hill
Top of the heap"

Frank Sinatra's "New York, New York" is playing from the speakers suspended from the Roman Arena. Angelena loops her arm around her boyfriend's arm and rest her head on his shoulders.

"This is a beautiful night," she says rubbing on his arm.

"Truly a beautiful night" her boyfriend responds.

"How 'bout a carriage ride?" she asks pointing towards a Clydesdale horse pulling a gold and black buggy down the cobblestoned road.

"Sure," he replies putting his arm around her. "Dear Sir," he yells out.

21

"Bon Jour," the driver yells out slowing the horse down and stepping off the buggy. "Would you two lovebirds like a ride?" he asks in his thick Italian accent.

"Yes Sir," her boyfriend responds as the driver pulls the small steps out allowing them to climb aboard. He holds his hand out assisting Angelena on the buggy.

"Thank you," she tells the driver as they sit down.

The driver raises the steps and climbs aboard. He whistles and clicks his teeth together as the horse neighs and moves forward.

"This is a romantic night," she says cuddling next to him.

"First time in Verona?" the driver asks.

"First time in Italy," Angelena replies.

"Enjoy" the driver says continuing to whistle at the horse.

"I love you" Angelena says looking at her boyfriend.

"I love you too" he answers leaning over to kiss her.

"You two like Frank Sinatra?" the driver asks as Frank Sinatra's "Moonlight in Vermont" plays.

"Pennies in a stream
Falling leaves
A sycamore
Moonlight in Vermont
Icy finger waves
Snow trails down a mountainside
Snow light in Vermont"

"OOOO...I love Frank Sinatra," she exclaims singing along with the song.

"I love when you sing," he tells her.

"No you don't; but I'll take the compliment," she says laughing and punches him lightly in the chest. "You can be so mean," she tells him jokingly.

"You know I love when you sing…if you could really sing then I probably would love it," he says as they both laugh again.

"This is Juliet's balcony," the driver says slowing down. "And that is the lovely Juliet" he continues while pointing towards the bronze statue of Juliet. "It is said that if you rub the right breast then you will have good luck," the driver says looking at Angelena's boyfriend. "Very good luck" he says smiling.

"Let's go rub her breast," he tells her.

"Boy you silly," she says as they climb out the buggy.

"Dream
When you're feeling blue
Dream
That's the thing to do
Just watch the smoke rings rise in the air
You'll find your share of memories there
So, dream when the day is through
Dream and they might come true
Things never are as bad as they seem
So dream, dream, dream" Michael Buble's "Dream a Little Dream" plays softly as they walk to the statute.

"It's cold out here," Angelena says shivering.

"I got you babe," he says removing his jacket placing it around her.

"Thank you Sir," she says as he swirls her around in a circle.

"Dream a little dream of me," he says twirling her out and bringing her back into his arms.

"Wow, I didn't know you knew how to ballroom dance," she says.

"There's a lot you don't know about me," he says leaning in to kiss her.

"My mystery man," she replies kissing back.

23

"As long as you know that I'm your mystery man," he says releasing her and walking towards the statute.

"I thought you would be all over those breasts by now," she says sarcastically.

"Be quiet," he tells her reaching up to touch Juliet's right breast.

"Don't go overboard you perve" she says jokingly.

"I can't if you don't be quiet," he says laughing.

"What did you wish for?" she asks.

"Good luck," he replies as she reaches up to grab her breast.

"Well I wished for the same thing," she says smugly.

"Come on before the driver decides to leave us," he tells her placing his hand in hers. "I love you," he tells her.

"I love you too," she tells him as they climb aboard the buggy.

"Beautiful?" the driver asks.

"Beautiful," they both reply in unison.

"The Armando Best Western," her boyfriend tells the driver.

"I see trees of green…red roses too
I see them bloom…for me and you
And I think to myself
 What a wonderful world
I see skies that are blue
And clouds of white
The bright blessed day
The dark sacred night
And I think to myself
What a wonderful world" Louis Armstrong's "What a Wonderful World" is playing as they step off the buggy and walk into the hotel.

"I love this hotel," she says as they walk towards their room.

"I need a shower," he tells her while opening the door.

"I need a drink," she replies running to the kitchen and opening the cabinets.

"Make me one too," he says entering the bathroom. "I really do love this shower," he yells out to Angelena as he presses his hands on the glass doors.

Angelena pulls out the containers of food from The Twelve Apostolic restaurant that they had eaten at earlier. She takes a few bites and proceeds to grab the Gin, Tequila, Rum, Vodka, Sour mix and Peach Iced Tea to make her famous Long Island Iced Tea. She presses the remote control to her IPOD docking station.

"Every breath you take
And every move you make
Every bond you break
Every step you take
I'll be watching you
Every single day
Every word you say" The Police's "Every Breath you Take" begins to play.

"You know this is my stalker song for you," she yells to him while he is in the bathroom.

"Huh?" he yells back.

"I said," getting louder, "THIS IS MY STALKER SONG FOR YOU" she yells again.

"Good stalker song," he yells out turning off the shower.

"Here's your drink" she says passing him the cup and playfully slapping him on his butt.

"Hey" he says wrapping himself with the towel.

"Hurry up…let me get in," she tells him as he squeezes past her and she shuts the door behind him.

"Lights out, sucker punch, siked out
Caught a love wave
Rode it then I wiped out
Two ships just passing in the night now,
Offshore, looking for a light house
Reveal you said that it was painless
Down and out
Drowning in a sea of my anguish
Funny, you always said hope floats
Comprehended but I can't cope so I
Gotta find my way back, way back
To you baby"

She hears her boyfriend switching to Jaheim's "Find My Way Back". He walks around the room pulling out his duffel bag. He pulls out three bags of rose petals and shakes them out leading from the bathroom door and around the bed. He places scented candles on the dressers and align them on the floor. He lights the candles and reaches in the bag for the box of Aqua Digio by Armani that he's bought for her. "I love this smell on her," he whispers as he takes the top off and sprays the rose petals. He picks up her True Crime book, "In Cold Blood," by Truman Capote. *"I don't know why she reads this stuff"* he says placing it on the dresser closest to the side of the bed where she sleeps. He hears the shower turn off and quickly dim the lights.

"I didn't mean it
When I said I didn't love you
I should've held on tight
I never should've let you go
I didn't know nothing, I was stupid, I was foolish

I was lying to myself"

Mariah Carey's "We Belong Together" fills the room. He watches her step out with the white towel wrapped around her body. Angelena looks around the room tightly clutching her towel. She begins to hyperventilate and cry. She looks at him and shuffles over pressing her body into his. He reaches around her and squeezes her tightly into him. He releases his grip and leads her to the bed. He lays her on her stomach and removes the towel from around her body. Reaching for the massage oil; he sit on her back and drips the liquid on her.

"Mmmph," she moans as he begins to massage her.
"I love you," he whispers in her ear.
"I love you too," she replies turning over to meet his eyes.

He kisses her softly positioning himself to nibble on her breasts.

"Baby, baby, baby,
From the day I saw you
I really wanted to catch your eye
There's something special bout you
I must really like you
Cause not a lotta guys are worth my time
OOO baby baby baby it's getting kinda crazy
Cause you are taking over my mind
It feels like oooooohhhhhh," Alicia Keys "You Don't Know my Name" begins to play.
She feels him enter her "Mmmmph" she moans out loud.
"It feels like ooohhh
You don't know my name
And I swear it feels like ooohhh"

"You don't know my name" she begins to sing quietly.

27

"Angelena" he whispers in her ear.

"Say it again" she whispers back.

"Angelena" he says and she feels his pace quicken.

"Say it one more time" she says feeling his body tighten against hers.

"Angelena" he says as his body begins to shake against hers.

She reaches up and pulls him close to her as they fall asleep in each other arms. Angelena wakes up to him lying beside her *"Awwwww"* she thinks to herself reaching over to pick up her True Crime book. *"He knows me so well"* she says out loud turning to the page where she last left off. A glint catches her eye and she shakes the book. A two carat platinum ring falls in her lap. She taps him on his back.

"Oh yea...about that," he says groggily, "I had it all mapped out last night...but when you walked out with that towel I couldn't control myself...so what you think?" he asks taking the ring and placing it on her finger.

"Thank you," she says kissing him and cradling his face with both hands "Yes baby yes...Thank you" she says over and over hugging him tightly.

Chapter Three

"A Woman's Heart should be so hidden in God that a Man has to seek Him just to find Her"

"Bo"

Bo rides around L.A. California with the top down on his blue Mercedes coup. He turns up the c.d. that he has purchased from the Orphaned c.d. store on West Sunset Blvd.

"Somebody told me that this planet was small
We used to live in the same building on the same floor
Never met before
Until I'm overseas on tour
And peeped this Ethiopian queen
From Philly taking classes abroad"

The Roots "U Got Me" plays from his speakers as he reminisces about his days in Virginia where he saw the group in concert at the Friday's at Sunset event. He lights the joint that's lying in the ashtray and turns into the Omni hotel. Bo enters the hotel and take the elevators up to the third floor where there is a deluxe workout room and settles on a stationary bicycle. He puts his ear-buds in and searches for Pandora Radio on his cell phone.

"Bust it; la di da di, who like to party
Like Slick Rick the Ruler but I'm cooler than a ice brick
Got soul like those afro pick
With the black fist
And leave a crowd drippin like John the Baptist
It's the cause of that "Oh Shit!"

The skits I kick
Flows like catfish and got many emcees on the black list," he
raps along with BlackThought on "Mellow my Man."
    Bo starts bobbing his head to the music as he watches
CNN on the 42 inch T.V. suspended on the wall. He abruptly
removes his headphones as the reporter reports about the capture
of the Barefoot Burglar after a shoot-out with the cops. *"Damn; I
wanted that nigga to run forever"* he says to himself. He finishes
his workout and heads to his room located on the eighth floor. He
enters room 849 and walks to the window to look at the pool.
"Damn that shit looks refreshing" he says to himself as the door
opens and his girlfriend walks in carrying bags from the Sax and
5th Avenue store.

    "Damn baby…you could just buy a few things…you had
to go shopping huh?" he jokes with her as she leans over and
kisses him.
    "I'll be ready in a minute" they both say at the same time
and bursts out laughing.
    "Hold on babe…you know I take showers quicker than
you" he tells her.
    "Hell naw nigga and anyway I'm going first regardless,"
she says defiantly.

    They stare at each other briefly before both making a dash
towards the shower. Bo leaps on the bed attempting to jump to
the other bed; she clips him in mid-air and he fall face first on the
bed. She runs to the shower and in desperation he tries to grab
her clothes and misses. She slams the bathroom door shut and he
hears her laughing. He chuckles to himself as he turns on the
television to the Utah Jazz game where Eric Maynor is shooting
a three pointer.

"Hey babe; this that dude from VCU that I was telling you about," he yells towards the bathroom.

She rushes out in her bath towel and looks at the TV.

"Oh yeah; I remember him, damn babe that could have been you if you was a REAL point guard," she says jokingly walking towards the bathroom.

Bo grabs a pillow and throws it at her which she dodges in a quick move. He falls asleep and is awaken by her tapping on his shoulder.

"Go head babe…I'm done," she tells him.

He walks to the bathroom bobbing his head to Redman and Method Man's "Do what you feel."
"Just do what you feel
And never follow," he raps out loud.

Bo dries off quickly and walks out to grab his suitcase as she passes him a blunt to light. He lights it and snaps the price tag off of his navy blue Sean John wife beater. He dresses in his Nike shorts and brand new Nike flip flop slide on's. He opens his small carry case and lotions himself while spraying on Calvin Klein's Obsession cologne. "Ouch" Bo yells out in pain cracking his knuckles.

"What's wrong?" she asks him.

"I just cracked my sprained wrist" he says.

"Big baby…that's why you're not in the NBA," she says smartly.

"Come on let's go smartass," he tells her.

She taps out the remainder of the blunt and puts it in her purse. They each grab a room key ensuring that they both have one in case they are separated. They exit the hotel and get in the car. He lets the top down on the coup, puts on his Coogi sunshades and drive off.

"Soooo…what did you buy?" she asks him.

"Listen" he says turning up the radio.

"Step in the realm
You're bound to get caught
And from this worldly life
You'll soon depart
Yo, I walk across this world that deceptive
Beats are perfected,
The ghetto's infested
With more destruction my vocal eruption" The Roots "Step into the Realm" plays out the speakers. They both sit in silence as the palm trees make shadow silhouettes of their bodies. Bo reaches in the glove box for his yellow armband that he kept from his first VCU game as a starting freshman. He pulls into the Beverly Hill tennis club. The valet attendant opens their door and they enter the event "Evening at the Fiesta". He orders two cranberries and vodka's and locates two seats in the stand near the tennis court. Bo stretches his arm around his girlfriend and she leans over to kiss him. The sisters; Venus and Serena, walk out the double doors onto the court. Tonight is their charity ball to raise awareness on breast cancer. The crowd stands and applauds the superstars.

'Damn, Serena got a phat ass" he thinks to himself as they sit back down.

"You probably thinking about Serena's ass" she says reading his mind.

"Naw babe…nothing like that," he says laughing.

"Tits and ass…is that all you think about" she says laughing at him.

He puts his arm around her shoulders. "Only your tits and ass…only yours" he tells her. The match proceeds for three hours but goes by fast as they gulp down four more drinks.

"Let's sit out here for a little while," he says as the match ends and people start walking out.

"Why" she asks.

"Because it's chill out here," he says referring to the stars spread across the sky.

"It's close to midnight
Something's evil's lurking in the dark
Under the moonlight
You see a sight that almost stops your heart
You try to scream
But terror takes the sound
Before you make it
You start to freeze
As horror looks you right between the eyes
Cause this is thriller, thriller night" Michael Jackson's "Thriller" plays from the ballroom of the tennis club.

"You think we can hit that blunt real quick?" he asks her.

"Hell no; you see all these white folks in there," she says laughing.

"Come on…I know it's small as hell," he laughs with her.

She thinks for a minute and reaches for her purse. She sits back up and notices that he has a lighter in one hand and Helzberg box in the other.

"What's that?" she asks

"A lighter" he responds jokingly.

"No dummy; in the other hand…you know I'm intoxicated," she says laughing.

He begins to stutter as he does only when he gets nervous.

"Y-y-you know it's a whole lot of artificial things in the world. There are only a few things in t-t-this life that I've ever trusted completely, God and well…my intuition. I've never been wrong about those things. I believe God is the almighty and I believe that once I let a person in my heart then they have to be there forever. I trust you like I trust my God and I want to make the perfect unity with you. Will you complete the trinity with me?" he asks with tears in his eyes.

"Me, you and God…I like that trinity…yes baby of course I will," she says leaning over to hug him.

Chapter Four

"Love isn't Something you Find; Love is Something that Finds You"

"Brandon 1"

Brandon sits in the lobby of the Red Lion hotel in downtown Seattle Washington. He sips on his Heineken and chases that down with a cranberry and vodka. He observes the arraignments of different bottles of liquor on the circular bar…Ciroc, Belvedere, 151, Hennessy and many more. He watches the bartender pour a drink from a green bottle, put a siphon on top and proceed to burn a sugar cube. As the cube melts; the waitress pulls off the siphon and the man drinks it down in one gulp.

"White people are crazy," Brandon says to himself. He walks towards the elevators and presses the 18th floor. Riding up; he pulls a small pouch out of his pocket, dips his finger in it and brings the powder to his nose. He inhales deeply and feels the drip in the back of his throat. *'Shiiiit I love the way that drip'* he whispers snorting back. He reaches his floor and enters room 1849.

His girl is lying on the bed in her blue Victoria Secret thong and bra set. She is watching Drop Dead Diva on Lifetime. He jumps on her back and kisses on the back of her neck.

"What time are we leaving babe?" he asks.

"Let me take a quick shower and then we can get out of here," he replies.

He gets in the shower and hears her turn on "All The Way Turned Up" by Souljah Boy. He quickly takes a shower and jumps out.

"Hey babe take that song back" he yells out.

He puts on his black and yellow Blac Label tee with the matching pants. He walks out the bathroom and sees her wearing white booty shorts, red shirt, and red and white striped high heels. He puts on his butter colored Timberlands and reaches for a cigarette while calling the front desk to reserve a cab. They exit the hotel and decide to head towards the Trinity Club the clerk has suggested.

They arrive at the club which is already packed and can hear "This is Why I'm Hot" playing loudly from inside. Brandon pays forty dollars for each to enter the V.I.P line. They head straight to the bar and orders two cranberry and vodka's and two shots of Jose Cuervo. His girl excuses herself to the restroom. He notices a group of females at the table in front of him. D.J. Unk's "Walk It Out" begins blaring through the speakers and the females start jamming in their seats.

Brandon notices the brown skin female wearing a tight Abercrombie and Fitch shirt; stand up and start walking it out at the table. *"She do it with no hands, now stop, pop, and roll"* D.J. Unk blares through the speakers. The female starts booty popping and he is frozen over how her hips move from side to side. He takes his shot of Jose Cuervo and tenses up as the liquid burns the back of his throat. His girl arrives back at the bar.

"My bag, I couldn't wait but let me get you another shot," he tells her.

She grabs her shot glass and takes it back in one motion. "Well get two of them nigga," she yells to him. They both burst out laughing and he grabs her hand pulling her to the middle of the dance floor. Young Money's "Bedrock" comes on and the crowd screams in approval. She starts grinding on him and he places his hands on her back and bends her over. She starts grinding on him even harder.

"Look at how she walks
MMM-MMM…she know she bad
Do-do your thing baby,
I aint even mad" blares out the speakers and as if right on cue, she takes a few steps, bend over and shakes her ass for him. He feels a hard-on and starts laughing. "You stupid" he jokes with her.

They walk back to the bar and order two more shots of Jose Cuervo. Brandon excuses himself to the bathroom and steps in the last stall pulling out his small bag of cocaine. He inhales a big line in each nose.

"Goddam let's do this shit!" he yells and walks out the bathroom as the D.J. begins to play techno music. He walks towards his girlfriend.

"What the fuck is this?" he says to his girl as she throws her hands up in bewilderment. They both grab their shot glasses.

"Make a toast baby," she tells him.

"To you and nothing else," he yells out.
She smiles and they take their shots slamming the glasses to the table.

"Come on let's walk, I saw some other clubs on this strip," she tells him.

They start walking and Huey's "Pop, Lock and Drop it" comes on.

"Toot that thang up mami, make it roll
Once you pop pop, lock it for me girl get low
If yo mama gave it to you baby girl let it show
Once you pop, lock, drop it for me
Maybe we can roll, oh"

She lets his hand go and puts on a show all by herself. The guys start looking and Brandon sees guys with their girlfriends

37

turn to stare. When she starts to "drop it" he puts his hand over his mouth and laughs. *'Get it Girl'* he thinks to himself. She stands up, pokes her butt out and turn to look at her small audience.

She walks to Brandon, grabs his hand, and says "Now we can go". They exit the club and she puts her hand inside of his. A light rain begins and he begins to feel emotionally different. There is a guy with a drum set and another guy with a cordless microphone singing:

"Love
There are so many things I got to tell you
But I'm afraid I don't know how
Cuz it's a possibility
You'll look at me differently" the guy begins to sing.
She notices Brandon crying.

"What's wrong baby?" she asks.

"I don't know, but right now…right at this moment…I don't, I've never felt stronger about a person in my life. I can't explain,' he says.

"Try" she urges him on.

"This trip would have been empty without you…ever since I met you it's like I'm found…for the first time in my life…I am happy."

"That's just the alcohol talking" she interrupts.

"Baby just listen," he says quieting her down, "I need you like I need air…I need you like…like…marry me," he asks.

She puts her hands over her mouth, "You don't mean that," she says.

Brandon grabs her hand and looks her in the eyes, "Will you marry me?" he asks.

She feels herself beginning to cry, "Yes baby…Yes."

Chapter Five

"Love is when the other person's happiness is more important than your own"

"Brandon 2"

"There they go right there," Brandon says pointing to Tayshone and his girlfriend walking through the airport.

"Tayshone...Tayshone...What up nigga," Brandon yells waving his hand in the air.

"What up nigga," Tayshone responds turning his Miami Heat basketball hat backwards. They give each other their secret handshake.

"We were watching that game...you did yo thing nigga," Brandon says referring to Tayshone's triple double against Europe.

"Yea you know nigga...this is why I'm hot" Tayshone replies cockily, "Let's get the fuck out of here".

Brandon picks up their bags and they exit the airport heading towards the ten passenger stretch limo.

"Damn nigga...is this how you do it?" Brandon asks.

"Nigga...that's how Padrino's do," Tayshone replies referring to Padrino's Limo Service.

A short whit guy walks over and opens the door. Tayshone and Brandon get in the limo behind their girlfriends.

"Damn I'm glad y'all could come down," Tayshone says opening the mini fridge and pulling out four shot glasses and a bottle of Patron.

"You saw me getting off nigga," Tayshone says pouring everyone a shot.

Brandon presses buttons on the ceiling until the sunroof opens. "Yo…Drake been on his shit," Brandon says reaching in his pocket pulling out a mix c.d. and inserting it in the c.d. player.

"Yeah,
I remember me and Dee used to talk about
This kind of stuff all the time,
Like what its go be like when
You get close to your dreams
I didn't know much then, but I could
Probably tell you a little something now,
Mr. Big dreams no tolerance cut you out
The house and haven't holla'd since
Get bored quickly, he stay grown so the
P-a-tron had to get poured quickly
Ex-girl trippin I can't drop her" Drake and Goapele's "Closer to My Dreams" begins to play.

"See…see," Tayshone says tapping his girlfriend, "I told you he be on that pretty boy shit," Tayshone says referring to Brandon's light skin complexion and wavy hair.

"Nigga please…you the pretty boy," he says pointing to Tayshone's diamond studded watch and chain.

"Nigga…this ain't shit," Tayshone responds taking off his chain and placing if over Brandon's head. He also slides off his watch and passes it to him, "Now you shining," Tayshone gleams.

"My nigga," Brandon says excitedly and stands up through the sunroof.

Tayshone stands up beside him. "Glad you here bro," Tayshone says giving him their secret handshake. Tayshone points to the club called Mansion. "Nigga…that's where we going." Tayshone says as the limo stops in front of the club and paparazzi begin snapping pictures.

The limo driver gets out and walks to their side opening the door. Tayshone grabs a second chain out of his pocket, slides it over his head and fixes the shades on his face. "You know I still gotta shine," Tayshone says as they all step out the limo posing for the cameras. Their females step out and stick out their legs as reporters continue to snap pictures. "Come on nigga…let's get in" Tayshone says as they walk on the red carpet and enter the club.

"Shawty wanna thug
Shawty wanna hump
And oh I like to touch ya lovely lady lumps
She wanna like the rapper" Lil Wayne's "Lollipop" plays throughout the club.

They walk amidst the security guards who escort them to the V.I.P area. They sit on the plush orange chairs and the waiter brings them a bottle of 42 below vodka.

"Compliments" the waiter says placing the cocktail tray on the table.

"Who you suckers think you trippin with
Yes I'm the boss
745, white on white, that's Rick Ross
I cut em wide, I cut em long, I cut em fat
I keep em coming back, we keep em coming back
I'm in distribution, I'm in Atlantic
I know Pablo, Noriega the real Noriega
He owes me a hundred favors" Rick Ross's "Hustlin" remix begins to play.

Brandon grabs the bottle and fills up all the glasses. He leans over and kisses his girlfriend. "You good baby?" he asks her.

"Yea…enjoy yourself…I know you ain't chilled with your friend in a while…I'm good," she replies.

41

Tayshone walks over and grabs the bottle. "Come on nigga…let's walk," he says as they take short steps from the V.I.P area to the regular floor.

"Look at that bitch right there," Brandon says pointing at the exotic dancer dancing on stage in a pink and blue one piece bikini set. "Damn" Brandon says gawking as she does a upside down split on the pole.

"Shiiiit…soon as we get out tomorrow without the girls, we go see all this and more," Tayshone says dapping him up.

"You don't know me
Don't be a groupie keep it moving
Nigga you don't know me
Cuz the truth is really
You don't know me
You be hating and I see why
Cause you don't know me" T.I.'s "You Don't Know Me" starts playing through the club.

Brandon grabs his blue bandanna out of his pocket and begins C-walking to the middle of the dance floor. He throws up his set with his hands and begins spelling CRIP out with his feet. Three guys walk to the middle of the dance floor and begin BLOOD walking. They start throwing their set up and dance amongst themselves staring at Brandon. Tayshone walks beside Brandon and raises the bottle to his lips looking slyly.

The guys continue to throw up their BLOOD signs and Brandon spells out six popping five dropping with his hands. One of the guys stops dancing and stares at them talking to his friends. Tayshone sticks his middle finger up at the three guys. The guys start walking to them continuing to throw up gang signs. As they get close three security guards step between them.

"Keep on moving guys" security says to the men.

"Guess y'all money ain't strong enough to fuck with us," Tayshone says to the guys as they retreat to the V.I.P section.

"Fuck them niggas" Brandon says sitting down.

"Y'all know this shit would look bad on me if something happens...the league would kill me...let's get the fuck outta here," Tayshone says passing Brandon the bottle.

"That's what's up nigga, let's get the fuck outta here" Brandon agrees.

"I gotta holla at you later" Brandon tells his girlfriend as they gather their stuff.

They walk out the club and see the three guys staring at them. Tayshone flashes them the peace sign and Brandon throws up his set and quietly mouths "Fuck You" in their direction. They get in the limo and head towards South Beach.

""Turn that up," Brandon's girlfriend says grabbing the bottle and taking a sip.

"I got your back boy
We were high
We were low
But I promise I will never let you go
Said I got I got I got I got your back boy
Keep my swagger
Keep it looking good for ya
Keep it looking hood for ya shawty
If you don't know
I got I got I got I got your back boy" T.I. and Keri Hilson's "I Got Your Back" plays through the limo. The girls begin to sing and dance along with the song.

"Let's chill at the beach," Tayshone tells everyone.

"Cool with me nigga" Brandon says putting his arm around his girl reaching for the bottle.

"Stop at the beach bro," Tayshone tells the limo driver.

The driver turns in the parking spot and gets out; he opens the trunk grabbing a blanket out of the trunk. "Here you are Sir," he says opening the door for them.

"Thank you," Brandon says reaching for the blanket.

"Woooow," the females yell out as they take their shoes off and run through the sand.

"Ooooh…it's like that," Brandon says kicking off his shoes and taking off his shirt revealing his black wife beater.

Brandon chases his girlfriend and playfully slams her into the sand falling on top of her. She lifts his chain up and allows it to flop on her chest.

"You shining huh" she says.

He lifts the chain over his head and places it around her neck.

"Now you shining," he says leaning down to kiss her.

"You having fun seeing your friend?" she asks.

"Hell yea, that's my nigga right there. I love him to death. I would do anything for him," he tells her.

"I know baby, I just hope that one day you will feel the same about me," she says.

"Baby, I already do. I want you to be my wife. I don't have much but I have a lotta love. I want you in my life. Let's do it…just me and you," he tells her.

"Yes baby yes…I would love to marry you," she says leaning up to kiss him.

"Let's roll, we'll tell them later," he says lifting her up.

They walk back to Tayshone and his girlfriend sitting on the blanket. They hear Jagged Edge's "Walked Outta Heaven" playing from Tayshone's IPHONE.

"I'm rolling down a lonely highway
Asking God to please forgive me
For messing up the blessing he gave to me

I see
Everything clearer now
The nights is black as; black as it's ever been
Without my girl, imma lose it
I pray that he would just shed his grace on me
I need just to be back with my baby
Feel like I just walked right outta heaven"

"What up nigga, let me holla at you," Brandon says as Tayshone passes him the bottle.

Tayshone stands up and walks with him.

"Weeeeeee" they hear the girls yell in the background.

"I guess she told her," Brandon says.

"Told her what," Tayshone asks.

"I just asked her to marry me," Brandon tells him.

"Shut the fuck up nigga; seriously…I just asked my girl to marry me at the game earlier," Tayshone responds.

"Shut the fuck up my nigga; we go be the best man at each other's wedding" Brands tells Tayshone giving him a hug.

Chapter Six

"Master a Formula and then Learn a New One"

"Brittney"

"Will you marry me Brittney?' he asks over the phone.

"What did you say? I can barely hear you," she says walking to find a better connection.

"Can you hear me?" he asks.

"I can hear you know…what did you say again?" she asks.

"Will you marry me?" he asks again.

She stands dumbstruck looking at the phone.

"Did you ask me to marry you? Hello…hello". She says looking at the phone noticing that there are no bars left. "Damn" she curses turning off the phone and placing it in her backpack.

Brittney pulls out her 2010 San Fermin pamphlet that reads *"Running with the Bulls; Pamplona Spain"*. She pulls out a pill bottle of Motrin to combat the hangover from the previous night; as well as a bottle of Crianza wine. She has read that it is customary to bring two bottles of red wine for after the run to make Calimocho's; the famous drink that is made after the *"Running of the Bulls"* event. She looks over the pamphlet memorizing the lyrics to Rezo San Fermin which is the saying the bullfighters shout out before the event begins. *"Well shit, if I forget I'll just mouth the words with the person standing beside me"* she thinks to herself.

She pops the Motrin in her mouth and tilts the bottle of wine to her lips. "I feel better already" she says to herself taking another drink. She puts the bottle back in her bag checking her watch *"almost time"* she thinks to herself pulling out her camera and flipping through the pictures. She stops at a statute of bulls running over top the statues of people appearing to be hurt on the ground. She zooms in closer on the bull with blood on his head and laughs at the people who are lying on the ground. She checks her watch again and sees that it's almost noon. She stand up and stretches reminiscing on the prior night when the Spanish man told her that first timers should not run but observe.

"I don't know what the fuck he was thinking," she says bending over to tie her Air Max run light sneakers.

She stands up and checks her outfit; white t-shirt, white trousers and tugs on the red handkerchief that is tied around her neck. She tightens the red scarf around her waist and begins to run in place to stretch out her muscles. She takes another drink from her bottle and follows the crowd who are dressed in their customary red and white running of the bull's colors as well.

"Yea baby; let's get it in" she says jumping up and down excitedly.

She positions herself in the crowd and can barely hear the president speaking over the loud speaker. She chimes in when the crowd chants their motto.

"A San Fermin pedimos, por ser nuestro patro'n, nos guie en el encierro da'ndonos su bendicion" she begins to chant with the crowd.

By the time the crowd finishes the cadence she is surprised that she knows all the words. The crowd chants down 5,4,3,2 and she hears the sound of the txupinazo inaugural rocket symbolizing that the event has started. Someone quickly passes her a banderilla to stab the bulls with. She recants back to the special on CNN that reported that spears were banned by PETA because of cruelty to the bulls.

"Fuck that," she says clutching the spear in her hand tightly. "Arrrrgh" she yells at the top of her lungs as the crowd gives their signature as well.

She moves with the crowd pacing herself. She follows the crowd to the right when they go right and soon finds herself close to the front of the pack. She looks back and sees people in the crowd jumping on ledges. She continues to run with the crowd in full steam. The crowd comes to a fork in the street and she follows the smaller crowd that has run to the left. She turns again to see a bull in short distance from the people behind her. She sees people on their balcony cheering and edging the runners to jump so they can catch them and pull to safety.

She runs, jumps on a chair, half turns and throws her banderilla at the bull. She hops on the balcony and is hoisted up by the crowd. She looks down at the spear that is lodged in the bull as it swerves crushing the chair that she was just in.

"Yea baby yea" she says jumping up and down excitedly as the crowd pats her on the back cheering her on.

She yells with the crowd and hears a loud roar signifying that the bulls have entered the stadium. She bends over placing her hands on her knees breathing deeply. The people continue to congratulate her. She stands up and they help lower her back down to the street. She reaches in her bag unscrewing the top off the wine.

"The hell with that Calimocho shit" she says taking a drink. "I just did some matrix shit" she says remembering how she turned and threw the spear seconds before the bull crushed the chair she was in.

She sits on the bench and takes a long drink before reaching for her cell phone and turning it back on. *"Now I got full bars"* she thinks to herself dialing her boyfriend back.

"Baby...I just ran with the bulls...yes I will marry you," she says as the phone battery goes dead.

Chapter Seven

"Faith makes all things possible...Love makes all things easy"

"Chirlyne"

Chirlyne walks to the newsstand amidst the crowd and grabs a cop of New Orleans free press. She looks at the musicians dressed in their white and black ensemble's playing saxophones, flutes, drums and other instruments. She finds her way to the bench admiring the marching band. She opens the paper and begins to read the obituary section about the death of Edward Rudolph Bradley Jr. (June 22nd 1941-November 19th 2006) Occupation: Journalist...A great man is being honored for his award winning work on CBS new Television. Mr. Bradley Jr. covered the Fall of Saigon, anchored his own news broadcast; Sunday Night with Ed Bradley, first black to cover the White House. *"Wow; this is an interesting man"* she thinks to herself continuing to read about his Peabody award, National Association of Black Journalist lifetime achievement award and his nineteen Emmy's. She skims down to the section about jazz funerals. Her boyfriend returns holding out two boxes and passes one to her.

"What is it?" she asks.

"They got all these great stuff to eat at. Emeril's, Mother's, Commander Palace, and Gumbo Shot. I know you like Italian food so I got some Creole Italian gumbo," he tells her.

"Sounds good" she says opening the box and taking the fork he is holding.

"What you reading about?" he asks.

"Mhmmmm" Chirlyne grunts taking a bite out of the gumbo, "I was reading about this parade that's going on. I've never heard of this before," she says picking up the newspaper. "It says that when a prominent member of the community or respected musician dies they have a jazz funeral for them," she explains to him.

"Now that's cool. I just hope that when I die someone at least plays an eight track for me," he says laughing.

She looks at him confused. "What is an eight track?" she asks in her heavy Haitian accent.

He laughs even more, "I'm sorry; I forgot that you're not from the states," he jokes with her.

He begins to explain but is interrupted by a solo trumpet. They look around and see people quietly standing and some crying. They both stand and he walks to a couple to ask about the performance.

"They say that's Wynton Marsalis. I don't know who he is but he sure can blow," he says returning. The band picks back up with an upbeat tempo and they sit down as the crowd continues to follow the band.

"What's in this?' she asks stuffing another forkful of gumbo in her mouth, "Don't tell me…I taste crabmeat, sausage and chicken," she replies.

"Don't forget the crawfish. What would gumbo be if there was no crawfish," he says as they sit in silence enjoying their food.

"I'm about to call home and check on my kids," she tells him.

He grabs her hand. "The kids are fine. Just relax and enjoy the day," he tells her.

"Okay" she says looking at him and putting the phone back in its case.

"I like your outfit" he compliments her.

"You do?" she asks standing up to give him a better look.

"Yes…the yellow sash around the earth tone brown looks real sexy on you," he says rubbing his hands over her thighs.

"Thank you," she says as he throws their trash away and they make way towards the car.

He walks around the passenger side and opens the door for her.

"Thank you," she says sliding her hand down her dress. "What?" she asks quizzically.

"Nothing babe…just using my imagination" he says slamming the door shut. He gets in and starts the car.

"Lying in my bed
I hear the clock tick
And think of you
Caught up in circles
Confusion is nothing now
Flashbacks
Warm nights
Almost left behind
Suitcase of memories
Time after time"

He reaches over to change the station.

"Hold on…I like that song," she says.

"Whatever the lady likes; the lady gets," he replies turning up Cyndi Lauper's "Time after Time."

"You can change it. I can listen to it later," she tells him.

"Baby its cool," he says turning the radio louder.

"Then you say
Go slow
I fall behind
The second hand unwinds
If you're lost
You can look and you will find me
Time after time" Chirlyne sings to herself.

"Where are we going?" she asks as they head downtown.

"I got a surprise for you," he tells her.

"What is it?" she asks.

"Surprise…helloooo," he responds laughing.

She notices that he turns down Chef's Highway and into She-She's lounge.

"A strip club?" she inquires and begins to laugh.

"Well…I heard you say you wouldn't mind learning how to strip so I thought we might as well check out the competition," he says chuckling.

She smiles to herself as he parks. "Is it safe?" she asks looking at the group of guys sitting on an old school El Camino.

"Yea babe, don't be so paranoid," he says turning off the car.

"The boy JB was a friend of my mine
Till I caught him in my car trying to steal my alpine
Chased him up the street to call a truce
The silly mutherfucker pulled out a deuce-duece
Little did he know I had a loaded 12-gauge
One sucker dead, L.A. time front page
Cuz the boyz in the hood are always hard
You come talking that trash we'll pull your card
Knowing nothing in life but to be legit
Don't quote me boy, cuz I ain't said shit" Eazy-E's "Boyz in the Hood" plays from the guy's speakers.

"Are you sure it's safe?' she asks again following him as he pays for them both to enter the club.

They walk thru the crowd and find a seat on the couches. The waitress walks to them wearing a g-string and no top.

"Can I get y'all order?" she asks.

He stares at her breast and Chirlyne pinches him lightly on the stomach.

52

"Yes, I'll take a sex on the beach," she tells the waitress.

He laughs and orders himself a Hennessey and coke.

"This is crazy," she whispers to him.

"Yea I know," he responds pulling out a cigar.

"Can I taste that?" she asks reaching her hand out for his cigar. She inhales deeply as she has watched him do and begins to cough violently.

"No baby; you supposed to just hold the smoke in your mouth," he says laughing as she passes the cigar back.

"Sorry…is all that I can say
Years go by and still
The words don't come easily
Like sorry
Like sorry
Forgive me…is all that you can say
Years go by and still
The words don't come easily
Like forgive me…forgive me
And you can say baby
And baby can I hold you tonight" Foxy Brown's "Sorry" begins to play.

"I love this song," she says reaching for the drinks from the waitress. She stands up and moves side to side allowing her ass to shake in his face. He places one hand on her thigh and reaches for his drink with the other. Chirlyne sits in his lap and begins moving back and forth.

"Goddam" he whispers in her ear rubbing his hand between her legs.

"Let's take it back," the D.J. yells in the microphone.

"Man I met this chick so fine
So bad, she make me sick some time

I just had to fuck this bitch one time
I met her in the galleria shopping, buying
Gifts for some guy she dating, still shot
Second anniversary and I'm congratulating that
But man she had an ass so phat
You couldn't palm it with Shaquille hands
It seems to me she had the whole world in her pants
Walked behind her whispering love songs
She started smiling so I handed her this bathing suit
And told her to try it
Replied, while with these light brown eyes
I'm shopping for a lady about your size
She put it on so I paid for it
Then I told her she could keep it
And then I walked out the store, it's our secret
But peep it
Made it down the hall, she came running
I don it
Make a mack move and girl chased me
And shortly thereafter, exchanged our fuck faces
It's tasteless
But honey must of missed being treated
Like something more than a nigga just tumbling and dudes beating
Her ass behind the silly shit
And I can see it in her eyes she was sick of this
Let's see the sights, it's me tonight
Let's leave stuck home pacing
Blowing up your pager, exchanging fuckfaces"

"Oh shit" he says pulling her closer to him. She laughs and puts both of her hands behind his head as he rubs his hands on her stomach and breast.

"You must be used to be all the finer things
Infatuated by what money brings

54

It seems to me like you hoes will never change
So all that's left for us to exchange," Devin Da Dude sings from
Scarface song "Fuckfaces".

The song play plays off and she sits beside him checking her phone. *"Hi mommy; just checking on you"* she reads her oldest daughter's text. *"Mommy is okay...I love you and I'll call you soon,"* she texts back

"Let's get out of here. I just wanted to stop by for a few." He says as they finish their drinks.

"Okay" she responds finishing off her drink that's melting with ice.

They exit the club and get back in the car.

"You are so beautiful tonight," he tells her

"Thank you," she replies smiling.

"I got something I want you to hear" he tells her turning the car on and switching c.d.'s to Bruce Springsteen's "Secret Garden".

"She'll let you in her house
If you come knocking late at night
She'll let you in her mouth
If the words you say are right
If you pay the price
She'll let you deep inside
But there's a secret garden she hides
She'll let you in her car
To go drivin round
She'll let you into the parts of herself
That'll bring you down
She'll let you in her heart
If you got a hammer and a vise
But into her secret garden, don't think twice"

Chirlyne turns the music down. "It's something about you that drives me crazy. I don't usually put myself out there but it's something about you that keeps me happy. It's like you can see me, all parts of me, all the little things. My children are the most important thing to me, but lately my thoughts stay focused on you. It doesn't matter what I'm doing…working, watching TV, or cooking…my thoughts continue to stay with you. I don't know where I stand with you, but I know where you stand with me. You pay attention to me and that makes me want to know more about you," she says as a tear falls from her eyes.

"Baby, I don't know what it is about you, but you make me want to push myself more. I love exactly who you are. You have two of the most beautiful kids I've ever had the pleasure of being around. I want them to be a part of my life just as bad as I need you to be in my life. You have become the air I breathe. The "M" in me; you are everything that I dreamed of…you are my secret garden. I need the total package, not just you but your two girls as well. I love you…I choose you," he says putting his hand in hers and squeezing. "It's you I choose" he leans over and kisses her.

"Baby…I choose you" she replies letting out a silent breath.

Chapter Eight

"The way to Love anything is to realize that it may be lost"

"David 1"

They walk down the pier and are greeted by the local native.

"Bula; My name is Tui" the man says in his thick Fijian accent.

David introduces himself and his girlfriend. Tui grabs their bags and helps them both aboard.

"Okay" Tui says slapping his hands together. "Today we will be seeing some Barracudas, Jacks, Unicorns, Manta Rays, and over a thousand school of fishes. If we are lucky enough we will get to see a reef shark floating past. Well let's get suited up and we can take off," Tui tells them as they pull away from the pier. "Welcome to Fiji Nai'a…sooo where are you folks from?" he asks.

"Richmond VA," David says zipping up his wet suit.

"Nice; so what is this, newlyweds, anniversary, or just a cooool getaway?" Tui asks.

"The third one…just a cooool getaway," David jokes with Tui.

"Well we gon' make this super cooool," Tui responds slowing the ship down. "Welcome to Gotham City…This is the most famous place in the world to see the strangest and most unusual species," he tells them.

Tui passes them both a snorkel making sure their fins are properly connected. They jump into the water following their guide.

"Feels good no?" Tui asks.

They both say yes in unison. He slides his snorkel over his face indicating that they should do the same before taking a plunge into the water.

"I hope the sharks can't smell my cologne," David says before following Tui.

"What?" she says shaking her head in disbelief and following him.

Tui points to a school of blue and white fish floating past. As Tui swims off; David pokes his finger through the school watching them float off and regroup. He points to his girlfriend and gives her the thumbs up. She points to the sun that is rippling through the water making shadow silhouettes over her arm. Tui points to a school of grey and white saw tooth barracuda's floating past followed by a school of unicorn fish.

Tui signals that he is going to let them look around swims off. David turns, pushes his girl and swims off quickly. She chases him around a reef blasting through a school of fish that is in front of them. She grabs his fin and pulls him back slowing hem down. He turns around and pretends to be punching until she grabs his knees sending them both tumbling in the water. They both laugh and allow their bodies to float upwards looking out the ocean. He raises his hand and she does the same giving each other a high five. She swims over top of him and puts her hands together symbolizing the "I love you" sign. David pulls her close to him and gives her an Eskimo kiss by rubbing their noses together. He sees Tui signaling to them that it is time to go. They follow him back to the surface and board the ship.

"So tonight
Gotta leave that nine to five up on the shelf

58

And just enjoy yourself
Groove
Let the madness in the music get to you
Life ain't so bad at all
If you live it off the wall
Life ain't so bad at all
You can shout out all you want tooooo
Cause there ain't no sin in folks getting loud
If you take the chance and do it
Then there ain't no one who's gonna put you down
Cause we're the party people night and day
Living crazy that's the only way" Michael Jackson's "Off the Wall" plays through the sound speaker.

"Oh oh oh," David says and starts flopping around in his fins doing his best Michael Jackson impersonation.

She grabs her camera out of her waterproof bag and begins videotaping him. David calls Tui over and they attempt to dance in unison together. Tui goes back to steering the boat laughing as she snaps a picture of him. Tui restarts the engine and continues to head towards the pier. David sits down and stretches his arm around his girl.

"This is perfect," his girlfriend says.

"Not yet but we getting there," he tells her as Tui returns with a tray of strawberries, cherries, mango, and blueberries.

"You know; blueberries are low in sodium and high in dietary fiber and potassium," David says picking up the bowl of blueberries and putting one in his mouth.

She looks at him weirdly. "For one, I'm impressed that you know that, for two, I don't know why you know that," she says laughing at him. "You are definitely quirky but that's what I love about you," she says reaching over grabbing a blueberry and popping it in her mouth.

They hear Tui turn up the music.

"Just a small time girl
Living in a lonely world
She took the midnight going anywhere
Just a city boy
Born and raised in South Detroit
He took the midnight train going anywhere'

"Hey Tui; turn that up some," David yells out to him."This is 'Don't Stop Believing by Journey," he tells his girlfriend.

"You love this song too?" she asks him.

"Hell yea…this my jam," he tells her.

"A singer in a smoky room
The smell of wine and cheap perfume," they both begin to sing in unison.

"For a smile they can share the night
It goes on and on and on and on"

They both start stomping their feet on the deck.

"You are so stupid," she says leaning over to kiss him.

"We will be docking soon love birds," Tui announces over the intercom.

She grabs David's Neff shirt with a picture of a blue bear growling. "I love this shirt," she says.

David folds his hands like a bear and begins growling.

"What is wrong with you?" she says laughing uncontrollably.

They dock and are helped off the boat by Tui. "I hope y'all enjoy the rest of your stay and welcome to beautiful Fiji."

"Thank you" they both respond walking down the pier.

"This place is beautiful," he tells her taking off his sandals and sitting on the edge of the pier. "You see the way the water ripple over top of each other, and the way the sun shoots right over the trees," he says pointing towards the orange glowing sun illuminating over the trees. "This place is nice," he says folding his arms behind his head and leaning back. "I saw you shutting it down out there in your little wetsuit."

"Down, down, down I be the baddest girl around," she starts singing by Drake.

"You see; that's what I mean, I know I can't be around people long because I get bored and have to do something stupid. But around you; it's like you accept all that about me and give it back. Honestly, I think you're about as crazy as I am," he laughs and pushes her lightly.

"Shut up," she says playfully slapping him in the chest.

"But this is the place I want to start a new life with you. I thought of doing this a thousand different ways. I thought of training a fish to pop up in the water and bring the ring to me, or get one of your high heels cut at the bottom and hide the ring in there…professionally of course. But the best way is simply just the simplest," he says pulling the ring out of the inside pocket of his trunks. "It's not a lot but it comes from my grandmother and it means that I want to connect with you in a very special bond that can't be broken." David holds the ring in the air and she cuffs both of her hands together. He sits up and sees tears in her eyes.

"Yes baby…Yes," she says leaning over to kiss allowing their tears to intermingle.

Chapter Nine

*"Love is when someone gives you a piece of their soul
they never knew was missing"*

"David 2"

"Let us pray for our youth who will be playing a key role in this year's International Ecumenical Peace convocation. The World of Council of Churches has been playing a role since 1948 in Amsterdam where it was declared that *"War is contrary to the will of God"*. The mission in this global movement is to find imaginative efforts to overcome violence through cross community work and to build bridges between communities drawn into violent conflict and to bring reconciliation. The council of youth will focus on these seven cites and their themes. **Rio De Janereio**-Becoming a citizen again, **Belfast**-We want peace, **Boston**-God among children, **Kingston**-Together against violence, **Durban**-No magic formula for peace, **Suva**-Where rivers meet and finally, **Columbia**-Voices for peace…praise god," Ramiero Cantalmessa; preacher to the Napal household, tells the congregation.

David looks over the bulletin…10am (session 1), 10:45 (Coffee), 11am (Group), 12:15 (Liturgical input), 12:30 (Eucharist), 1pm (Lunch), 4pm (Tea/Coffee), 4:15 (Session 2).

David glances at his watch that reads 10:40. *"Good because I sure could use a cup of coffee,"* he thinks to himself.

"Let us all rise," Reverend Cantalamessa says as he leads the church in prayer.

"Amen," David says in unison with the rest of the congregation. He leans over and shakes the hand of the people standing beside him.

"Are you staying for the rest of the service?" the gentleman beside him asks.

"Yes Sir; of course," he replies shaking hands.

"Praise God," the man says.
"Praise God," he responds.

David exits the chapel making his way through the lobby occasionally stopping to shake hands. He pushes through the double doors and is met with different languages of people walking past."*God is good*," he thinks to himself walking towards the Scotland flag. "*In my defense, God defends me,*" he reads the motto to himself. He; for some strange reason, thinks of Chubby Checker's "The Twist" song.

"Come on baby
Let's do the twist
Come on baby
Let's do the twist
Take me by my little hand
And go like this
ee-ohh twist baby baby twist
ooo-yeah just like this
Come on little miss and do the twist
My daddy is sleeping and mama ain't around
My daddy is sleeping and mama ain't around
We're gonna twisty twisty twisty
Til we turn the house down
Come on and twist
Oooh-yead just like this
Come on little miss and do the twist"

He closes his eyes, getting lost in his own thoughts, and begins twisting back and forth.

"Mrgh, Mrgh," he someone clearing their throat as they walk behind him.

David opens his eyes embarrassed; remembering where he is. He steps in the restroom and washes his hands. He adjusts his Polo shirt ensuring the buttons are lined up with his belt buckle as he was taught in the marines. He steps out the bathroom looking for the closest coffee table. He walks through the crowd looking at the different vendor's booths. *Peace among the Peoples, Peace in the Marketplace, Peace in the Community, Peace with the Earth.* David walks past a table and hears "I'm a believer" by the Monkees.

"Then I saw her face
Now I'm a believer
Not a trace
Of doubt in my mind
I'm in love,
I'm a believer and
I couldn't leave her if I tried"

He eyes a female softly singing to herself. He pauses for a moment admiring her beauty before walking to her table.

"Hi; how are you doing," he says chuckling. "What is your mission?" he asks.

"Well; Peace on Earth means having Peace with Mother Earth. Human beings are called upon daily to take responsibility for nature. Today's challenges in regard to ecology, climate change, and natural resources make it urgent to consider views and actions," she says passing him a pamphlet. "This gives you an overview of different ways a Christian should care for creation and what people of faith like you and me can do on both the personal and collective level," she says as he flips through the pamphlet. "What do you do?" she asks.

64

"I work for an alternative school in Richmond Virginia helping children have a better chance at life. I instruct the woodshop class providing them with a useful trade that will help them later in life. It feels good to help others," he tells her proudly.

"I understand exactly how you feel. That's what we are doing on a global level. People helping people; we can't do it alone, it's a collective effort," she responds.

Fascinating is a word I use for the unexpected. In this case I thing "Interesting" would suffice," David says giving the Dr. Spock sign.

"You're also a Trekkie," she says excitedly returning the sign.

"I see you like the Monkees," he says pointing at her radio.

"Well, we Christians do like music," she says laughing. "I saw you twisting over there," she says and they both laugh.

"It's the time of the season
When love runs high
In this time
Give it to me easy
And let me try
With pleasured hands," David sings out.

"Time of the Season…the Zombies…I love that song," she says. "It's the time of the season for loving," she belts out as they both laugh again. "What are you wearing…you smell nice?" she asks.

"Old Spice," he tells her.

"It smells good," she responds smiling.

"Would you like to accompany me to dinner?" he asks.

"Well…I'm not sure," she says hesitantly. "Let me ask you a question…tell me one thing you love…I mean more than anything else on this earth?" she asks.

65

"God" he says without hesitation
"Then yes…I will go out with you," she says smiling.
"Tell me something you love?" he asks.
"Led Zeppelin," she says.
He smiles.

Chapter Ten

"Choose your Love... Love Your Choice"

"Dexter"

Dexter sits up in the bed reading the pamphlet on Lincoln's bedroom. He reads that it was decorated in a nineteenth century style four years ago and this was the very bedroom that was used as his office first which later became the bedroom suite and was called the Blue Room. He continues to read about the famous Lincoln dream.

Lincoln had awakened from a bad dream hearing noises coming from out of a different room. Lincoln got up and checked the East Room seeing people crying. He asks the closet guard what had happened and the guard replied that the President had been shot. Lincoln awoke and told all the guards and wife about his dream. Later that night Lincoln was shot in the back and killed. *"I sure as hell don't want to see the ghosts of Lincoln that is supposed to haunt the White House,"* he thinks to himself chuckling.

Dexter picks up the welcome letter that he received from the White House,

Dear Sir,
You and your spouse are cordially invited to spend one day and one night at the White House for your services that you have provided to your city and country.

He reminisces of all the kids that he's helped received their GED and enter college. "All that hard work paid off and I am

67

actually being rewarded for my part in this world," he says out-loud.

"What you say honey?" his wife asks sleepily.

"Nothing, go back to sleep," he whispers rubbing her shoulder.

He stands up and looks at the oak, gold and white bedroom. He slips his feet in his sandals, touches the chandelier and walks into the bathroom. He puts the lid down on the toilet, sits, and carefully observes the bathroom. He nods his head in approval and reaches over to turn the shower on. He exhales deeply, undresses and steps in the shower. He allows the water to run over his face and starts sing softly,

"Jesus is real
I know the Lord is real to me
Jesus is real
I know the Lord is real to me
Sometimes when I'm feeling low
Nowhere to go
Jesus comes along and He makes me strong," he sings along to John P. Kee's "Jesus is Real".

Dexter pumps his fist in the air giving praise to his almighty God. He lathers up while dancing in the shower.

"I can feel him in my heart
Feel him in my soul," he continues to sing.
"For I know…wooooh ooooooh oooooooh
Jesus is real"

He stops singing and pulls the shower curtain back. He looks out and sees his wife finishing his song.

"I told you too many times that you are not the singer of this family," she says before shutting the bathroom door.

"But I look better than you," he yells out.

"Ha-Ha…even you don't believe that," she yells back at him still laughing.

He turns off the shower and steps out wiping the fog off the mirror before saying real low, "Yes I do". He pulls out his shaving kit and carefully trims his mustache that resembles a squirrel's tail. He loves the way that he's shaped it so that it curls around his cheekbone. He puts on his boxer and step out the bathroom as she enters behind him.

"No you don't," she says closing the bathroom door behind her.

Dexter grabs his bag and places it on the bed and kneels down to one knee clasping his hands together to pray.

"Dear Lord it is you and only you that has placed me in this position. Through you all things are possible. I believe that in my heart, mind, body and soul. Give me the strength to carry on even when the camera and lights are gone. I am eternally grateful…Amen." He praises God by shaking his head up and down. *"Thank you God,"* he finishes and stands up.

He reaches in his bag and pulls out his pink, blue and white bowtie. He picks up the dark suit that his wife has laid across the bed for him. He grabs his haberdasher, folds the brim up on the right side and places the hat on top of his suit.

"Yea Dexter…now that's nice," he says to himself. He gets dressed and glances at the itinerary for the day. Breakfast 9:00am…he glances at his watch that displays 8:49.

"Honey, we have to hurry. We can't be late at the White House," he yells through the bathroom door.

She steps out the bathroom fully dressed. "As I always tell you dear, I'm ready dear," she says putting on her earrings.

Dexter laughs and pulls out his bottle of Grey Flannel cologne by Geoffrey Bean and sprays himself down. They stand beside each other admiring their outfits in the mirror. He reaches on the bed grabbing his haberdasher and stands at full attention in the mirror. She reaches in her purse, pulling out her camera and begins snapping pictures of the both of them.

"Okay dear, maybe today you look better than me. Let's go" she says laughing.

"You know I love you" he says pulling her close to him.

"Yes dear, I know," she says as he leans over to kiss her.

They exit the bedroom and walk down the long corridor looking at the art work on the wall. They stop and observe a water-colored portrait of President Obama poised as Captain America running from the White House. He stops in front of another portrait with the quote: Think…Maybe…I'll. He ponders over those particular words trying to figure out the deeper meaning.

"Honey, honey, come look at this one right here," she calls out to him.

Dexter walks over and looks at the portrait of the White House at night time lighted with a blue background.

"This is absolutely beautiful," she gasps. She reaches in her purse and pulls out her notepad to write down the artist. She writes down; Jell-O World by Liz Hickok.

"I'm going to look up some of her work when we get back home," she tells him as they enter the dining room dressed down with the White House's fine china.

"Ohhh sooo looong
For this night I prayed
That a star
Would guide you my way
To share with me this special day
There's a ribbon in the sky for our love," Stevie Wonder's "Ribbon in the Sky" is playing in the background.

They sit at the table and the cook greets them and sets down their plates of food with a tall glass of orange juice in a wine glass.

"That's Sam Kass," she taps him as the cook walks away.

"Yes I know; I heard that he's supposed to be up for Senior Policy Advisor," he tells her.

The door opens and in walks the president. They both stand to their feet as he shakes their hands.

"I was heading towards a press conference and wanted to stop by and shake the hands of the people that are making a difference in our community. It is truly an honor to meet the both of you. It is your drive and ambition that is what this country needs to make us as a people run smoother as a unit. I will catch up with the both of you later and welcome to the White House." The President finishes extending his hand before walking out.

"Wow, I can't believe that we just met the President," Dexter says as they settle back down in their seats. He places his right hand over his heart. "You hear me Elizabeth...I'm coming to join you honey," he jokes in his best Fred Sanford voice.

"Don't be acting up in the White House," she says playfully hitting him with her napkin.

They eat and are greeted by their personal escort who welcomes them and escorts them out the side of the White House. The limo driver opens the car door and they all get in.

"I hope you both are enjoying you stay. We are very excited to have you two as our honored guests. We will be providing a tour of the city; first stopping by the Washington Monument," their guide tells them as they ride down the driveway and out the gates.

"Look" Dexter says pointing out the window. "There's ABC, C-SPAN, CNN, NPR, and THE WASHINGTON POST," he points out to his wife.

Their guide reaches over and turns on the mini television in the limo. Dexter rolls down his window and waves his hand as they ride past. The limo driver stops in front of the monument and they both get out the car while a small crew of cameras are nearby snapping pictures.

"Sir; the President sends his best and wants me to tell you good luck," the guide tells Dexter.

Dexter turns to face his wife, "I know I said that this is the best day of my life but it would not be special if you were not here to share this occasion with me. You've seen all the things that no one else has. You've seen all the times that I just didn't think that I had the strength to go on. I thank God everyday for the last thirty four years and I can't think of one day that's been better than the other. I've treasured every step of the way and if I had to do it all over again there is absolutely nothing that I would change. I'm asking...no I'm praying that you will remarry me just so we can reach for another thirty four years," he says awaiting her response.

"I have watched you grow into this sort of superman that you have become. I am truly proud of the person that you have become. I have no down times...only up...the down times where what was needed to enjoy the good times. It is a pleasure...no an honor to be married to you for the next thirty four years," she responds.

Dexter half turns towards his guide and gives a thumb up.

"Sir," the guide calls out, "The President and entire world just watched this moment," he says pointing at the cameras that are focused on them. "The President wants me to tell you that he's sitting in front of the television giving you a thumbs up sir...Congratulations."

Chapter Eleven

*"Love is an Energy which exists of itself…
It is its own Value"*

"Eric"

They stand on the balcony looking down at the black stage. Lights began shooting out the back of the stage with fog that weaves in and out of the lights. Eric exhales weed smoke out of his mouth and slowly inhales it in his nose before taking another puff. The spotlight beams on the drummer and ?uestlove begins playing. The crowd goes wild as ?uestlove pauses to pick out the back of his hair with a black-fisted comb.

"Yea baby…play that shit," Eric yells out.

?uestlove looks in his direction, points his drumstick at him and begins to play. The lights shine on the microphone and Blackthought emerges from out the fog. He grabs the microphone and begins to sway back and forth to the music. ?uestlove stops playing and points his stick at Blackthought. "Is y'all feeling that shit Amsterdam?' he yells and the crowd erupts in a frenzy.

Eric sips on his Long Island Iced Tea. "It sure is a lot of white people here," he says.

"Amsterdam dear, Amsterdam," his girlfriend responds sarcastically.

"Shut the fuck up," he says joking with her.

"You shut the fuck up," she says back jokingly.

73

"We would like to thank the Paradisio for having us here tonight; you see…hold on hold on ?uest…let me give them some real shit…can I give y'all some real shit?" Blackthought says to the crowd.

"Fuck yea," someone yells.

"Okay, okay, I'm going to give you some of Blackthought's thought's…you see black and thought are two powerful words together…to be able to stand in yourself is being black…to be able to express yourself is thoughts. So when they are together it is the thought of the black man…equalizing Black Thought…Yooooo drop that shit," he yells to the band.

"It's been a long time
Since I been back around the way
It's been a long time
Let it spin let it spin let it spin
Since I been back around the way
It's been a long time
Long time long time
Struck by the luck of the draw
Real life preservation
What I'm hustling for
My name is Blackthought
The definition of raw
I was born in South Philly
On a cement floor, I had nothing at all
Had to knuckle and brawl, they swore I fall
Be another brick in the wall
Another life full of love that lost
That's silly, this Philly

Y'all really ain't stopping
The boy with the pen like Willie on top of the hall
Pure soul is what the city most popular for
Hear the tones that will ease you

Smooth
As Bunny Sigler's soundtrack
Keeping your head bopping and all
It's something in the water where I come from
They used to sing it on the corner where I come from
Making something out of nothing
Because everybody fifty cents from a quarter
Where I come from
Yeah
The streets ain't timid but I feel at home in it
Gotta see a couple of people I ain't got at
In a minute
Yeah you can take a brother outta South Philly
Can't take it outta him really
I forever represent it," The Roots begin to play "Long Time".

"Goddamn cuz," Eric yells turning around facing the guy that just bumped into him spilling some of his drink on his shirt.

"My fault man, you good?" the white guy asks.

"Yea, don't worry about it," Eric says turning back around looking at his shirt. "Goddamn…I just got this shirt today," he says using a napkin to wipe off the front of his Christian Audiger T-shirt. "And I forgot my fucking watch. You know how much I hate when I forget that shit," he says throwing his hands in the air in disgust.

"I got you babe," she says reaching in her pocket pulling out his watch.

"Seriously; I was ready to slap that nigga for fucking up my shirt like this," he says taking the watch from her and putting it on.

"We'll soak it when we get back to the room. Now I know that's Blackthought. What's the drummer's name again?" she asks.

"That's ?uestlove; remember, he was the drummer on Jay-z's Fade to Black tour," he responds.

"Oooooh…that is him…I thought he looked familiar," she exclaims.

"We like to give a shout out to one of the most skilled rappers of all time…Guru…rest in peace brother," Blackthought says as the crowd throws up peace signs and lighters. The band begins to play Guru's "Feel the Music".

"Times like this make me clench my fist
Then I'm caught up in the midst of the musical bliss
Guru blow a kiss to the ladies in my corner
Caress the mic and kick my game like I wanna
Respect is due, praise me like the altar
The crew we're as true as they come son
We come from ill life experience, and take rap serious
Feel the music," Blackthought raps deceased Guru's part.

"If you got a blunt in your hand hit it twice for Guru," he says and walks to the edge of the stage holding his hand out to a fan that passes him a blunt. Blackthought hits the blunt twice and passes it back to the fan.

"Only in Amsterdam can you do that shit," Eric says to himself. 'I am feeling right," he leans over whispering to his girlfriend.

"What is this weed called again?" she asks.

"Sour Diesel…and I can definitely taste the sour part," he chuckles passing the blunt to her.

"All I know is I'm definitely on point right now," she responds.

"Let me see what you know about this," Blackthought says and the band erupts in a rock-style melody. People start jumping up and down.

"Yea," Eric yells out.

"What is this?" she asks.

"Panic at the Disco…this song is 'I Write Sins not Tragedies'…it's one of my ringtones," he says pumping his fist in the air.

"I'd chime in
Haven't you people heard of closing a goddamn door
No it's not much better to face this kind of thing
With a sense of poise and rationality," Eric sings with the band.

"Eric; I'm not feeling well. I don't know if it's the weed or the drink. Can we go get some air?" she asks fanning herself.

"Cool," he says walking in front of her making his way through the crowd. He feels her bump into his back. "Are you okay?' he asks, half turning to look at her.

She nods her head up and down and makes a motion with her hands signaling for him to keep moving forward. He slides his hand back grabbing hers.

"I got you," he tells her.

"Now how could we come all the way here and not give a special ups to the late great Bob Marley," Blackthought yells in the microphone.

The band begins to play a soft beat. "Kinky reggae," the white guy standing near Eric yells out.

"Kinky Reggae; now we all know what Kinky Reggae is right," Blackthought asks Eric leads his girlfriend out the building.

"Wow…look it's snowing in Amsterdam…Now I know that's rare," he says releasing her hand.

"That is probably rare," she begins to say doubling over and throwing up.

"Damn…how much did you drink?' Eric says taking the cup out of her hand pouring the contents out.

"Don't throw that away" she says in-between dry heaves.

77

"You fucking stupid. You not go keep drinking and you out here throwing up," he responds empting the contents in the snow.

Eric flags a taxi and helps her in. "Art Gallery hotel," he tells the driver and falls back in his seat.

She puts her arms around his and rests her head on his body. "I love you so much...I hope I didn't destroy your night," she says in a slurred voice.

"I love you too but don't be throwing up on me...my shirt already fucked up by that nigga bumping into me," he warns her.

"Oh Eric," she says playfully slapping him on the chest. "You love me right...tell me you love me," she slurs.

"Be quiet and go to sleep," he tells her as she begins to snore.

"Come on babe" he says nudging her with his shoulder.

"Are we here already?" she says continuing to slur her words and falling back on his chest.

Eric pays the driver and nudges her harder, "Wake up; come on," he says in a demanding voice.

"Okay baby...ok," she replies as he helps her out the car.

He puts his arm around her helping her in the hotel and elevator. She crashes into his arms resting her face in his chest. The elevator stops on the fourth floor and he assists her into the room. She falls on the bed and curls up grabbing a pillow.

"This is a nice room, this is a nice hotel, this is a nice city, wait a minute...where are we again?" she asks.

"Shut up and go to sleep," he says.

"I didn't mess up your night did i...are you mad with me?" she asks.

'You goddamn right you fucked up my night. You couldn't hold your liquor and I couldn't see the rest of the show tonight…but," he says sitting on the edge of the bed, "You've held me down through far worse times than this and some of the ways that you took care of me have been far worse than this. I know I argue a lot but the truth of the matter is that it's all about you. I know that even when I argue; you're the only person that I want to argue with. I love you and every time you ask me the answer is always the same whether I say it or not," he hears her snoring and turns around. "I love you and I want to be with you forever," he says kissing her on the cheek. He hits the blunt and brushes the hair out of her face. "I truly do love you," he whispers rubbing her head.

Chapter Twelve

"When the Power of Love overcomes the Love of Power then the World will know Peace"

"Greg"

Greg sits in first class reading a book of quotes from W.E.B Dubois.

"Excuse me Sir…can I get you anything?" the flight attendant asks.

"Yes please; how about a Johnny Walker neat," he tells her.

"Neat?" she asks.

"Yes Ma'am, no ice," he replies.

"Okay sir, I'll be right back," she says walking off.

He puts his headset on allowing the sounds of Duke Ellington and John Coltrane's "In a Sentimental Mood" to play. *"Now is the accepted time, not tomorrow, not some more convenient season. It is today that our best work can be done and not some future day or future year. It is today that we fit ourselves for the greater usefulness of tomorrow. Today is the seed time, now are the hours of work and tomorrow come the harvest and the playtime,"* he continues to read from W.E.B Dubois.

Greg grabs a pad and pen out of his briefcase and reflects on his friends who are wasting time and expect nothing out of life. He begins to write.

My black people get so downtrodden by their situations and surroundings that they become complacent and become a product of their environment. I wonder where the dreams of our great forefathers such as Martin Luther King Jr., Marcus Garvey and W.E.B Dubois have gotten lost.

He continues to write as the flight attendant places his drink on the tray.

We have gotten lost in the mix…the mix of the pudding as Bill Cosby would say.

He sits back and laughs at what he just wrote, "Damn…I need to start writing my own book," he says under his breath. The song switches and Ghostface's "All I Got is You," begins to play:

"Yo dwelling in the past, flashbacks when I was young
Whoever thought I'd have a baby girl and three sons
I'm going through this difficult stage I find I hard to believe
Why my old Earth had so many seeds
But she's an old woman, and due to me I respect that
I saw life for what it's really worth and took a step back
Family ain't family no more, we used to play ball
Eggs after school, eat grits cause we was poor
Grab the pliers for the channel, fix the hanger on the TV
Rocking each other pants to school wasn't easy
We survived winters, snotty nose with no coats
We kept it real, but the older brother still had jokes
Sadly, daddy left me at the age of six
I didn't know nuttin but mommy neatly packed his shit
She cried, and grandma held the family down
I guess mommy wasn't strong enough, she just went down
Check it out, fifteen of us in a three bedroom apartment
Roaches everywhere, cousins and aunts was there
Four in the bed, two at the foot, two at the head

I didn't like sleep with Jon-Jon he peed the bed
Seven o clock, plucking roaches out the cereal box
Some shared the same spoon, watching Saturday cartoons
Sugar water was our thing, every meal was no thrill
In the summer, free lunch held us down like steel
And there was days I had to go to Tex house with a note
Stating, "Gloria can I borrow some food I'm dead broke"
So embarrassing I couldn't stand to knock on they door
My friends might be laughing, I spent stamps in stores
Mommy where's the toilet paper, use the newspaper
Look Ms. Rose gave us a couch, she's the neighbor
Things was deep, my whole youth was sharper than cleats
Two brothers with muscular dystrophy, it killed me
But I remember this, mom's would lick her finger tips
To wipe the cold out my eye before school with her spit
Case worker had her running back to face to face
I caught a case, housing tried to throw us out of our place
Sometimes I look up at the stars and analyze the sky
And ask myself was I meant to be here…why?

He awakens from his daze as the plane makes a bumpy landing. The waitress has already gathered his drink and set the tray in its upright position. He unbuckles his seatbelt, grabs his briefcase, and says goodbye to the flight attendant.

"Watch that bumpy landing next time," Greg says jokingly with the pilot as he turns his Blackberry on.

"Hey mom…just landed…yea it was a bumpy flight but my Johnny Walker kept me warm," he says talking on the phone to his mother.

"Boy you better stop all that drinking," she tells him.

"It was only one drink," he says laughing.

"I don't know what I'm going to do with you boy," she tells him.

"Okay mom…I see my driver so I'll call you later…love you," he says.

"Love you too," she replies.

He shakes the guy's hand that is holding a sign with his name on it "Salam Wa Aleikum," Greg says.
"Wa Aleikum Ah Salam," the driver responds.

The driver takes his bag and they make their way to the vehicle. Greg looks at a reflection of himself checking out his Steve Harvey's dress pants and shirt. *Image is everything-make lasting impressions without even saying a word,* he thinks reminded of a phrase that Steve Harvey quoted.
"Thank you Steve Harvey," he says fixing his collar and checking his breath before inserting a piece of gum into his mouth. He hears a beep and checks his text message. *'You really got a hold on me'* he reads from his mother. *'Percy Sledge, come on mom, you gotta do better than that. A change is gonna come'* he texts back. *'Awwww, Sam Cooke…come on son…you gotta do better than that…love ya'* she responds.
The limo stops in front of The Institute of International Research. The driver opens the car door for Greg and passes him his bag. "Salam Wa Aleikum," the driver says.
"Wa Aleikum Ah Salam," he responds walking through the crowd. He shakes hands with an Arab wearing the customary shemagh and thobe.
"Let me ask you Sir…why do Bedouins wear black in the summer?" Greg asks.

"Survival in the hot deserts has always been a problem, even in the days of Moses. Black retains our perspiration which creates a dampness that cools us off. You know a famous quote of the Bedouins is me against my brother, my brother and I against my cousins, then my cousins and I against strangers…it is the loyalty based on our families," he tells Greg.
"Thank you for enlightening me; that is very interesting," Greg responds walking into the building.

He is shown to the conference room where other interns are waiting. He introduces himself, sits and retrieves his Blackberry. *'Got here early...this place is historical'* he texts his mother. *'Small fish in a big pond now'* she responds back. *'Well you know this my third time here so I guess I'm at least a mid-size fish now hahahahaha'* he sends back. *'I'm proud of you mid-size fish'* she texts back. *'Something has been weighing heavily on my mind...I'm going to ask her to marry me'* he texts. *'Whoa big fish...that's a major move and you've been with her for how long...do you love her?'* she texts. *'With all my heart I swear I do'* he text. *'Greg; you know I stand behind every decision you've ever made...you have made me sooo proud and you are being blessed by the hands of the almighty each and every day. I pray daily that God continues to opens more and more opportunities for you. I think you've made great decisions and you have my blessing'* she responds. *'Thank you...forever mine right?'* he text. *'OJay's...hahahah...Forever Mine...come on son...you gotta do better than that'* she responds. *'They starting mom. I love you'* he sends. *'I love you son'* she texts back.

Chapter Thirteen

"If you Love Life; Life will Love you Back"

"Holly"

Holly taps her boyfriend on the arm. "Look over there,,,that's Charlize Theron from the Valley of Elah and that's Kirsten Dunst from Spiderman…and over there is Helena Christenson the model," she exclaims pointing out to her boyfriend.

"Hellooooo there Madison Square Garden…New York New York…so good they had to name it twice," Chris Martin from Coldplay yells in the microphone. "Well I wanted to give New York a piece of New York," he says as the band begins to play Gerard Kenney's "New York New York,"

"It was a really nice night for a good street
Or a robbery
But I always knew in my hometown
That would never happen to me
I kept walking around trying to make up a sound
Bout what it's like to be
In the city of lights on a rag time night
It's something more than free
Good old New York New York," Chris Martin looks around as the crowd bellows out the lyrics to the song.

"New York New York…it's great to be here promoting our new album Viva La Vida or Death and all his friends…we are doing three concerts and we all know that New York is a place of dream," the crowd erupts in pandemonium. "Thank you for having us New York," Chris Martin yells out.

"This is my favorite group," Holly says tugging on her boyfriend's sleeve. He puts his arm around her and squeezes her tightly.

"Thank you for making this song No 1 in the U.K. and in the U.S.," Chris Martin says as the band starts drumming "Vida La Vida." Chris grabs the microphone and starts bouncing to the beat. Holly begins to clap with the beat. "Yea baby," her boyfriend yells out. Smoke bombs are set off on the stage giving the background a yellowish bluish color.

"I used to rule the world
Seas would rise when I gave the word
Now in the morning I sleep alone
Sweep the street I used to own

I used to roll the dice
Feel the fear in my enemy's eyes
Listen as the crowd would sing
"Now the old king is dead
Long live the King!"
One minute I held the key
Next the walls were closed on me
And I discovered that my castles stand
Upon pillars of salt and pillars of sand
I hear Jerusalem bells a-ringing
Roman cavalry choir a-singing
By my mirror, my sword, my shield
My missionaries in a foreign field," Coldplay begins to play "Vida La Vida".

Holly picks up her cup out of the folding chair and takes a sip. "Too weak," she says reaching for the bottle of Amaretto.

He holds out his cup and she pours some in his. She pulls out an American Spirit cigarette. "I got you…I saw this in a movie," he says snapping the Bic lighter on his jeans sparking a fire.

"A real ladies man…007 bond huh," she says leaning over to light her cigarette. He does one move fanning the flame out. He pulls out his new IPHONE and begins taking pictures of Coldplay.

"Don't forget me," she says stepping in front of the camera. She puts her hand on her hips and pokes her butt out.

"I'm videotaping baby," he tells her.

"Well this is Shay-Shay. I got four baby daddies and once my check come in I'll be able to get my new weave in," she says doing her best ghetto imitation.

"I'm go put that on Youtube," he tells her.

She jumps on him. "Don't do that," she says seriously.

"We'll just have to see how you act," he jokes back with her.

She passes him a cigarette and he slips his hand in hers as they bounce back and forth until the song plays off. They sit down as the band continues to play. Holly takes a sip off her drink and look into the sky.

"This is truly a beautiful night," she says snapping off a piece of her fruit pop tart. "My favorite drink, my favorite food and my favorite man," she says.

"You're favorite man?" he asks quizzically.

"My only man," she says squeezing her arm between his.

"I better be," he says.

"You are," she responds wrinkling her nose. She kisses him and rest her head on his arm. "I love you," she tells him.

"I love you too," he tells her.

"Come up to meet you, tell you I'm sorry
You don't know how, lovely you are

87

I had to find you
Tell you I need you
Tell you I've set you apart

Tell me your secrets
And ask me your questions
Oh let's go back
To the start

Running in circles
Coming up tails
Heads on a
Science apart
Nobody said it was easy
It's such a shame
For us to part
Nobody said it was easy
No one ever said it would be this hard
Oh take me back to the start," the band begins to play "The Scientist".

        "I love this song," Holly says rubbing her hand up and down his arm.

"I was just guessing
At numbers and figures
Pulling the puzzles apart

Questions of science
Science and progress
Do not speak as loud as my heart

Oh tell me you love me
Come back and haunt me
Oh and I rush to the start

Running in circles
Chasing our tails
Coming back as we are

Nobody said it was easy
Oh, it's such a shame for us to part
Nobody said it was easy
No one ever said it would be so hard
I'm going back to the start," the crowd erupts and cheers as the song plays off.

"Cone one; let's walk around, at least we can be close to the streets when it's time to go," he tells her.

They pack their chairs and sling them on their backs. They grab their drinks and interlock hands walking away from the crowd.

"I'm starting to feel good anyway," Holly says slightly slurring her words.

"Come on; lets walk for a minute," he tells her.

They walk down the sidewalk listening to the music blasting from the systems of the cars riding past.

"Damn…the city that never sleeps huh…it's like you got alternative music on one side of the street and hip hop on the other. I love this city, New York New York; so good they had to name it twice," she says.

"Action (not a bag a mout')
Sweet (lovin make de gal bruk out)
Action (not a bag a mout)
Sweet (lovin make de gal bruk out)

You think are so fine
(Big shot nuh work yuh man watch de time)
Stop playing with my mind
(Oman nuh inna joke when she well waan de wine)

You call me on the phone
(One hour worth a talking angel come down)
And now I want you home
(Ital jockey gal me nah use no stone)" Nadine Sutherland and Terror Fabulous's "Action plays out of someone car's stereo. Holly begins to dance and he takes the chair off her arm sliding it on his back. She leans over to kiss him continuing to dance to the song.

"Come on let's go," he says grabbing her hand as the car pull away from the light.

They walk until they reach the Hampton Inn Manhattan hotel. They get on the elevator and she slouches against the rail.

"Baby…I feel so good tonight," she says seductively walking over to him. He puts his hands under her shirt feeling her skin. She begins to kiss on his neck as he slides under her bra. He moves his hands back and forth, *'Mpmmmmm,'* she grunts and pulls up his shirt licking his chest.

"Damn baby," he says taking his hand out and slapping her ass pulling her closer to him.

She begins to breathe heavily in his ear. "Baby" Holly says quietly, slowly, dry humping his mid section. The elevator rings she hurriedly fixes her clothes. They enter their room and she runs and jumps from one bed to the other landing on the floor. She goes to the window and pulls the curtains back.

"Tell him in need him
Tell him I love him
It'll be alright
Tell him
Tell him
I need him
Tell him
I love him

It'll be alright" she begins to sing Lauryn Hill's "Tell Him" softly. A light drizzle of rain begins to fall on the window pane.

"This is the perfect night,' she says turning to him.

She walks to him and sits in his laps wrapping her arms around him. She squeezes him tight and he squeezes her back tighter. He picks her up and lays her on the bed. He begins to kiss her and sits her up taking her shirt off. He leans over and kisses her breast through her bra. She lifts her arms as he slides his hands behind her back and slowly slides off her bra. He unbuckles her pants and she lifts her mid-section allowing him to pull off her pants and underwear. He begins to enter her and she stops him.

"Get a condom baby," she tells him.

"Is that what you really want?" he asks looking in her eyes. "Whatever you want…I got you…I'm right here for you. I'm the man that you need…I will never leave you alone. When you grasp out at night it will be my hands that you feel. In the still of the night it will be my voice that you hear," he says as she slightly begins to release her grip allowing him to slide more inside of her. "It's my soul talking to yours…you are the first thing I think of when I wake up and the last thing I think of when I go to sleep," he says sliding in and out of her real slow. "The crazy part is…you are in my dreams as well," he says and she allows her body to relax. She releases her hands and places them on his back. He begins to move in and out of her slowly.

"I love you," she says looking in his eyes.

"I love you," he responds as she pulls him closer to her.

Chapter Fourteen

"You Can't Love Anyone Fully If You Can't Love Yourself to the Fullest"

"Jacky"

"Look mommy," her son says tugging on her arm and pointing at the Metropolitan Simone Bilovar Park sign. She pays the cab fare and walk towards the entrance.

"I see it baby…I see it," Jacky replies reaching in her purse for their one day pass.

"Thank you ma'am," the attendant says ripping up their ticket and passing half back to her.

"Slow down," she commands her son as he burst through the turnstile.

"Picture ma'am?" the photographer asks waving his camera in front of them.

"Yes," she responds picking up her son and holding him close to her.

"Say Queijo," he says in his Portuguese language referring to cheese.

"Queijo" they both say in unison.

Her son jumps from her arms and run towards the stand selling funnel cakes and cotton candy. He presses his face against the glass.

"Don't do that," Jacky scolds him pulling him back. "Would you like to have one?" she asks picking him up.

"Yea," he replies.

"Yes," she says correcting him.

"Whooosh," her son screams as the vendor spindles strands of cotton candy on the spool.

"Thank you" she says paying the vendor.

"You want a bite mommy?" her son asks putting the cotton candy in front of her mouth.

"I would love a bite; you are growing up to be a very polite young man…thank you," she says taking a bite. She puts him down and grabs his hand.

"Who is that mommy?" her son asks as they walk to a granite statute of a man with a big face and curly hair.

It reads on the inscription, *'Simon Bolivar Escultura Libertado en el par…Que Simone Bolivar de Begota,'* she sounds out in her best Portuguese.

"He looks scary," her son says grabbing her hand.

"What do you want to get on first?" she asks as they walk through the opening of Salitre Magico theme park.

"Ferry wheel," he says pointing excitedly to the Ferris wheel with Samsung printed on the side of it.

"Ferris wheel," she corrects him. "Ok Ferris wheel it is," she says reaching for his cotton candy. "Thank you," she responds passing it back.

"You're welcome," her son says.

They both flash the employee their wristbands and locate an empty seat.

"Raise your hands," the man commands checking the safety bar across their laps.

"Ooooh…I know this song," she says beginning to dance in her seat.

"I would like to reach out my hand
I may see you, I may run
You know what they say about the young

Well pick me up with golden hands
On may see, on may tell you to run
You know what they say about the young" Rusted Roots "Send
Me on My Way" plays off the Ferris wheel.

"That sounds like the Lion King song…Woah," her son
yells as the Ferris wheel begins turning.

"Look baby we can see to the other side of the country,"
she says pointing over the trees. "Look…there's the paddle boats
right there," she points out.

"Are we go paddy mommy?" he asks.

"Yes baby…right after this," she replies.

"Yaaaay," he yells out as the Ferris wheel goes around
again and stopping at the top. "Mommy…mommy it broke," he
says beginning to cry and claw at her in fear.

"No baby, they are just letting people off…see," she says
pointing towards the group of people getting off at the bottom.
"See…here we go again," she tells him as the ride lurches forward
stopping at the bottom.

"Push down and up," the woman bellows over the loud
speaker.

"Paddy boats…paddy boats," her son says taking off
running.

"Hold on baby…slow down," she says jogging to the
booth behind them.

Jacky pays for two life jackets and safety hats. The vendor
helps to fix their safety vests and walks them to the paddle boats.

"Red or blue ma'am?" the man asks.

"Red, red, red," her son yells out.

"Well you hear the man," she says as they step into the
boat. "Okay sweetie, you just put your feet on the pedals and start
turning like this…" she says demonstrating as the man unleashes
the chain. They match each other's speed until they reach the
middle of the pond. " I want to talk to you later," she tells him.

"Okay," he says struggling to turn the pedals.

"Look at the ducks," she exclaims as a flock of white ducks glide past quacking.

"Daffy Duck, Daffy Duck," her son yells out.

"Yes baby; Daffy Duck," she says helping him to paddle back to the dock. "We are going to eat and come back…okay baby," she says as he nod in approval attempting to pedal faster than her.

"I win," her son yells as they dock and the man assists them out. They exit the park and flag down a taxi.

"Adante Ma Non Troppo Restaurant," she tells the taxi driver in her best Portuguese voice.

"Downtown Candelaria it is," he responds in his best English pressing the button to turn the fare on. "How do you like South America?" he asks her.

"I like it a lot…it is a very beautiful country," she says as her son leans over resting his head on her lap. "Very much so," she says quietly rubbing her son's head and leaning over to kiss him. The cab driver turns up the music.

"All my good life I've been a lonely man
Teaching my people who don't understand
And even though I tried my best
I still can't find no happiness
So I got to say
Stop that train" Bob Marley's "Stop that Train" fills the car.

"Here you go ma'am," the cab driver says stopping in front of the restaurant.

"You wake when you smell food don't you champ," she tells him as her son pops his head up upon arrival.

They walk inside the restaurant and are seated by the window. Jacky assists him in the booster seat and picks up the menu. She orders the four cheese pasta and a Brahma beer.

"What would you like big boy?" she asks him as he points at the chicken fingers and fried. The waitress walks away and returns with her beer.

"Look mommy the bottle is curved," her son says.

She allows him to shape his fingers around the curve of the bottle. "Hold on baby," she says excusing herself away from the table. "Hey baby…nothing just sitting down eating with my son…no I haven't talked to him yet…I know he likes you a lot but I want to make sure that he understands that I'm not trying to replace his father…I think he will be excited I'll call you later…I love you," she says hanging up the phone and returning to the table.

"Why yo friend ain't come mommy?" her son asks.

"Why didn't my friend come," she says correcting him. "He didn't come because I thought that we could be alone…just me and you buddy," she responds rubbing his head.

"I wish he could have come…I like him," he says grabbing his cup of juice.

"Mommy has something very important to talk to you about," she says nervously tapping her beer bottle on the table. "Me and Mommies' friend have been spending a lot of time together and we care about each other very much…and he treat you good…he treats you good doesn't he?" she says rubbing his forehead.

"Unh huh," he responds slurping the rest of his drink out of his cup.

"We have been talking about us getting closer…a lot closer," she says nervously.

"Is you gonna marry him…excuse me…are you going to marry him?" he asks wide eyed.

"Well we been talking…" she says as her voice trails off.

"Yaaaay," he yells out interrupting her and raising his hands.

"Yaaaay," she says quietly pumping her hands in the air along with him.

Chapter Fifteen

"Since Love grows within You, So beauty grows.
For Love is the beauty of the Soul"

"Jessica"

They stand outside looking at the "Welcome to Las Vegas" sign taking pictures. Jessica sees some of the famous Las Vegas dancers walking across the strip. She likes their attire of red and yellow rhinestone slide skit skirts with the silver brassieres and matching tall flower hats.

"Excuse me…excuse me," she calls to them. "Can I take a picture of y'all please?" she asks waving her camera.

"Yea sugar," one of them replies. They all step back and arch their legs forward in unison. Jessica snaps three pictures and thanks them.

"I bet you wish you could have been in the middle of them," she says jokingly with her fiancé.

"You never know; by the end of the night maybe I will be. You know what they say…what happens in Vegas stays in Vegas," he says putting his arm around her.

"Yea you're right; make sure you know that saying goes both ways," she responds rolling her eyes.

They get into the Dodge Prius that they rented for the weekend and head towards South Las Vegas Boulevard otherwise known as the strip. She takes pictures of the Mandarin Oriental, The Palazzo, Wynn, Planet Hollywood, Paris, The Venetian, and the world famous MGM.

"Let's head to the room se we can get ready for tonight," he tells her.

He pulls into Bally's hotel allowing valet to park the car. Jessica gets out and stands on the moving sidewalk lit up with neon bright lights.

"Baby I love this thing right here," she says standing on the moving sidewalk.

"You are so lazy…you hear music they are playing?' he asks quieting her and cocking his head to the side to listen.

"In Napoli
Where love is king
When boy meets girl
Here's what they say
When the moon hits your eye
Like a big pizza pie
That's Amore
When the world
Seems to shine
Like you had too much wine
That's amore"

He grabs her hands and starts singing in his deep baritone voice while swinging her side to side. She loves when he starts singing. He pulls her close to him and she lays her head on his chest as he croons softly in her ear.

"Scuzza me
But you see
Back on old Napoli
That's Amore" he continues to sing "That's Amore" by Dean Martin. He grabs their bags and enters the hotel heading to the room. She showers first, dresses and looks in the mirror. She admires her green halter top and mid white shorts. She spreads

baby oil down her long black legs coming up slowly still looking in the mirror.

"Damn, 42 and I still got," Jessica says out loud. She sends a text to her eldest son back at home that is looking after his younger brother and sister. *'Mommy is okay, love you all, and take care of your brother and sister. I love you all very much'* she finishes and presses send.

She slides on her white and green sandals and digs in her bag until she finds her bottle of Eternity by Calvin Klein. She sprays herself down and snaps the top back on the bottle.

"I'm ready," her fiancé says entering the room. "Damn you are looking delicious tonight," he says eyeing her up and down.

"Well I taste better than I look," she replies half joking and half serious.

"Let's get out of her before I get in trouble in this hotel room," he responds opening the hotel door.

They exit the hotel and he turns on the radio.

"I got your love
You need to look no further
Don't you know that
Don't you know that
After my love
You'll never need another
Don't you know that
Don't you know that" Luther Vandross's "Don't You Know That" fills the car. He turns the radio up and they both start singing in unison.

"Without a doubt
You are my sweetest inspiration
Don't you know that
Don't you know that"

He turns into the Las Vegas Hilton where the lights illuminate Maze and Frankie Beverly's names.

"Ooooh baby...I always wanted to see them live," she yells out.

He valets parks and reaches in the glove box for their tickets. They walk into the Hilton which is known as the last remaining great showroom. He gives the host his last name and they are escorted to their table. They sit and she starts bobbing her head to the music.

"Can you hear that?" she asks listening to the background music and starts singing.

"I wait for a day
A sweet gentle sway
Rocks your love right my way
You send me swinging" Mint Condition's "Swinging" is barely heard over the loud chatter of the patrons. The spotlights start flashing green, red and blue colors into the crowd. The curtain opens and out walks Frankie Beverly and Maze. Frankie allows the band to play before grabbing the microphone.

"I hear we have a special couple in the crowd tonight...I actually have a very special guest for you all tonight...I would like to bring up a very special friend of mine" Maze says to the crowd and calls out Jessica's fiancé's name.

She stops clapping and cannot believe her ears that she has just heard her fiancé's name called out.

"Excuse me baby...that's my cue," he says standing up. Jessica is in awe watching him walk to the stage and give Frankie Beverly a hug. Frankie passes him the microphone.

"Tonight is a very special night for me...that's my fiancée sitting over there...raise your hand baby...tonight I want to sing something very special for her tonight," he says as the crowd edges him on. Jessica starts to blush as he tells the band what song he wants. "Baby...I'm going to try this tonight because I know that it's your favorite song," he says looking at her. The band begins playing and he starts moving from side to side.

"There's a time of the day
When the sun's going down
That's the golden time of day

It's a time that the sun
Turns a gold all around
That's the golden time of day

At the end of the day
When the wind is soft and warm
Don't it make the flowers sway
When the sun settles down
And it takes a lovely form
That's the golden time of day" he begins to sing Maze and Frankie Beverly's "Golden Time of Day".

   "Baby I love you and I praise God daily that in ten more days you will be my wife. I love you and I want to thank Frankie and Maze for this Golden opportunity to express my love for you," he says passing the microphone back to Frankie to finish the song. He blows a kiss to Jessica while walking off the stage.
   "Thank you God…thank you for sending me someone who love me," she says to herself looking in the sky.

Chapter Sixteen

"Hate is a form of Love that has not found a way to express itself logically"

"Jr."

Jr. stands in the crowd leaning over the balcony. He hits the blunt and leans back, "Nigga we in Brazil with all these phat ass bitches and shit...who would have ever thought we be doing this shit," Jr. says to his friend stretching out his arms.

"This shit is crazy," his friend says hitting the blunt.

"Look at that shit right there...what the fuck is that...it looks like a tiger," Jr. says pointing at one of the floats floating past playing Jay z's "A Star is Born".

"I seen Mase do it, I seen Ye do it
X came through, Caught lighter fluid
Still I came through it, Clap for em
But I'm the blueprint, I'm like the map for em
I dropped another classic, made Puff pass it,
Nobody could touch back when Puff had it
Wayne scorching, I'll applaud him
If he keep going, pass the torch to him
50 came through, like hurricanes do
I thought I'd finish his ass at Summer Jam two
I had the Illmatic, on bootleg
Shit was so ahead, thought we was all dead
Wayne did a millie, 50 did a millie
Ye too, but what Em did was silly
The white boy blossomed after Dre endorsed him
His flow on Renegade

Fucking awesome, Applaud him"

Jr. eye's two females dancing to the music. "Yo look at those bitches," he says pointing at the two Brazilian females. One of the girls notices them watching and eyes them seductively.

"Damn them bitches is fly as hell," his friend says grabbing his dick.

Jr. holds the blunt out to the females beckoning for them to hit it. One of them looks at them, laughs and whispers in her girlfriend's ear. Her girlfriend looks at them and laughs. They walk over to them speaking in Portuguese. One of the females raises Jr.'s hand to her lips taking a slow pull from his blunt. Her friend does the same to Jr.'s friend. They speak in Portuguese again, laugh and walk away.

"Goddamn...these bitches is easy as shit and they fine as fuck," Jr. says. He turns back around and looks at the female dancers on the street. "Man this shit is wild. Look at what them bitches wearing," he says pointing to one dancers whose body is completely painted with a face of President Obama.

"That bitch ain't got no drawers on and she got Obama's face painted on her body," his friend says.

"Come on let's walk around," Jr. says mashing his blunt out on the rail and sticking it in his Newport box.

"Come on nigga let's roll," his friend responds plucking his blunt over the rail.

Jr. waves goodbye to the females and walks down the steps.

"It's a Kodak moment but hold that thought
Hurricane wrist game
Turn that junk off
Hot as piggly wiggly
Can't Kermit the frog dog"

Jr. begins to rap "Hold that Thought" by Gucci Mane. His friend imitates holding a camera and taking pictures. Jr. holds his hand out showing off his gold and diamond studded watch.

"Hold that thought," his friend says pulling a real camera out of his Louis Vuitton bag. He also reaches in the back-pack and pulls out two cups passing one to Jr. He fills them both halfway with Grey Goose and mixes it with pineapple juice.

"Goddamn…let's go," Jr. yells taking a sip and jumping the last few steps.

"All Eyes on me," his friend yells out referring to Tupac's song.

Jr.'s friend snaps a picture of the woman with gold paint painted on her entire body. He zooms on the picture and shows it to Jr.

"Now that's a good picture…you can see that bitches eye shadow," Jr. says laughing.

"Yea…this camera I got is fucking amazing…I'm go draw this when I get back home," his friend responds.

Jr. feels someone rub a hand on his back. He turns around and sees the females that were at the top balcony looking him up and down. "How you doing?" Jr. asks.

"Good and you," she says in her best English.

Jr. relights his blunt and passes it to her. "Y'all trying to chill?" he asks hand signing.

She turns to her friend speaking Portuguese and they both shake their head yes and laugh.

"Come on nigga…let's get out of here," Jr. tells his friend.

"Nigga…I already know," his friend responds relighting his blunt.

The girls grab their hands and make way through the crowd towards their car. Jr. get in the front seat and she turns on the car turning up the radio.

"Do you think you're better off alone

Do you think you're better off alone
Do you think you're better off alone
Do you think you're better off alone
Talk to me
Oooh
Talk to me
Oooh
Talk to me"
Oooh talk to me
Do you think you're better off alone" Alice Deejay's "Better off Alone" plays.

The girl turns on the light and passes Jr. a dutch and a bag of weed. Jr. locates an insurance book out of the glove box to break up the weed. He throws the dutch filling fillings out of the window and begins to roll up. He looks in the back seat and sees his friend drinking and jamming to the song.

"I told you this was going to be a great trip my nigga," Jr. says reaching back to give him a high five.

"Niggas go be jealous once we show off these pictures," his friend says passing Jr. a lighter.

"A Cidade Maravilhusa…Marvelous city," Jr. says lighting the blunt and inhaling deeply.

"Cidade Maravilhusa," his friend repeats.

The female pulls into the apartment complex and tries to explain that she is not from Brazil.

"I'm not from here either…I'm from Virginia," Jr. says holding his hands representing the two up two down sign.

They park and follow the girls into the apartment. She opens the door and turns on the lights inviting them both to have a seat. She turns on the radio.

"There's a natural mystic blowing through the air

If you listen carefully now you will hear
This could be the first trumpet
Might as well be the last
Many more will have to suffer
Many more will have to die
Don't ask me why
You see things are not the way they used to be
I won't tell no lie
One and all have to face reality now
Though I tried to find the answer
To all the questions they ask
Though I know it's impossible
To go living through the past," Bob Marley's "Natural Mystic"
plays.

Jr. passes the blunt to his friend who looks for an ashtray and decides to use the plastic cup on the table. The girls disappear in the back and re-emerge with a small plastic bag.

One of the females sit beside Jr. and the other sit on the floor in front of the table. She drinks from her cup and empties the white powder out of the baggie on the table. She rolls a ten dollar bill between her fingers and makes two thick lines utilizing a credit card. She leans over and sniffs half the line, wrinkles her nose, snorts and sniffs the second line in her other nostril. She passes the ten to her friend who does the same and passes the bill to Jr.

"We from America...we don't usually do this but since we here...you know what they say...When in Rome," he says laughing and bending over to take a sniff of the cocaine.

He passes the ten to his friend and sits back taking a drink from his cup. The female stands up and holds her hand out beckoning for Jr. to follow her. He throws the deuces sign to his friend and follows her to the bedroom.

She puts her hand on his chest grazing his body and unbuckling his belt buckle. She drops his pants and begins to jerk him off. She looks at him and he leans over kissing her. She pushes him on the bed spilling the contents of his cup on the comforter. She pulls a vial out of her pocket and pours a line of cocaine from his belly button down to his pubic hairs. He puts a pillow behind his head and hits the blunt blowing the smoke in the air watching the ceiling fan suck it up. She inhales the powder off his stomach and licks the residue off putting his dick in her mouth. He thinks of his favorite song "Feelin It" by Jay-z.

"Look I don't need that now
It's just once in a blue when there's nothing to do
And the tension gets too thick for my sober mind to cut through
I get to zoning
Me and the chick on the L and then we're boning
I free my mind sometimes I hear myself moanin
Take one more toke
Then I leave that weed alone man
It got me going"

Jr. wakes up before everyone and grabs his laptop out of his friend's bag. He grabs the half of blunt that's in the ashtray and steps out on the deck, *'this shit is sweet'* he thinks to himself positioning himself in the lawn chair. He lights the blunt and stares at the ocean as the waves overlap each other. He sees a little kid kicking a soccer ball on the beach.

'Now this shit is heaven' he thinks to himself.

He opens his computer and sees two missed calls from his girlfriend and un-mutes the window media player.

"I know you wasn't around when I was leaving myself
Yet you seat back and relax and took all the wealth
Is it material things you're running after
Or is it praises that you're giving on to rest

I really wanna know right now

I gave a hand onto the wicked
But I give him it with caution
Well, I was giving love
He was seeking for reaction, tell me
Is it material things you're running after
Or is it praises that you're giving on to rest
I really wanna know right now
Oh mister wicked" Gregory Isaacs "Material Man" plays.

He calls his girlfriend on voice chat and reaches behind him to close the deck's door.

"Hey baby...I called you twice last night...how is everything?" she asks.

"Good morning baby; Rio De Janerio was off the chain," he tells her.

"Was the parade off the chain or the bitches?" she asks

"Come on man, don't be stressing me out with that shit," he says rubbing his head.

"I'm just saying, I know you...anyway you had a good time? Where's your partner in crime?" she asks referring to his friend.

"That nigga still sleep. Look this weekend put a lot in perspective for me. It made me wake up to a lot of things and I realize that chasing these bitches ain't some shit that I want to do my whole life. I need something more stable and true. I want to take vacations like this with you. I guess what I'm trying to say is...I want to make this official...just me and you. No bullshitting, no cheating, no lying, none of that shit. I'll always keep it real with you as long as you keep it real with me; and that's my word," he says looking at her.

"Is that your word because I want the same thing...I love you but I want to make sure this is what you want to do? I want to make you a good wife...so is that your word?" she asks.

"Baby; that's my word," he says softening his voice.

"Then yes baby, yes…that's my word," she replies giggling and leaning over to kiss the computer.

Chapter Seventeen

"To Love someone means to see them as God Intended"

"Keith"

Keith stands looking out of the window of the Trump Plaza. He puts his hands in his boxers moving his dick around. "Wow…this place is fucking hot," he says to himself.

"Ohh baby, be my sweet lady
Ohh, I want you to be my lady
Lady, oh baby
Sweet lady, would you be my
Sweet love for a lifetime
I'll be there when you need me
Just call and receive me" Tyrese's "Sweet Lady" plays from the speakers that his girlfriend has brought along.

"What you say baby?" she yells from the bathroom.
"Nothing…I'm just saying that it's beautiful out here. You have to see this shit," he yells back.

She walks out the bathroom towards the window drying her hair. She stops momentarily turning up the music. They both look out the window in silence. He lights his Black and Mild inhaling slowly. He waits until the song plays off and laughs to himself.

"We have to change the mood," he says walking over and grabbing her Droid that's connected to the speakers.

"I got ice in my veins
Blood in my eyes
Hate in my heart
Love in my mind
I seen nights full of pain
Days of the same
You keep the sunshine
Save me the rain
I search but never find
Hurt but never cry
I work and forever try
But I'm cursed
So never mind" Lil Wayne's "Drop the World" fills the room.

Keith bobs his head walking to the bathroom turning on the shower. He gets in and reaches for the soap singing along with Eminem's verse. He gets out the shower and uses the hotel's lotion and toothpaste. *'I'm taking this shit with me'* he thinks to himself. He walks out the bathroom and opens the closet door. He picks out his khaki shorts and white high top Nike's.

"I only fuck with those, who only fuck with me
A sucka play for games, a man play for keeps
I keeps me a nine millimeter just in case
A cowards in my face
These bullets he go taste
A waste of your life, stepping wrong, I'm on trees
Best to leave me alone, best to go make some cheese
Enemies come in all shapes, forms, sizes, colors
Could be your best friend, cousin, or brothers" Project Pat's "Don't Turn Around" begins to play.

Keith pulls a plastic bag out of his Coogi suitcase. He pulls out one of his Percocet pills and swallows it dry. He watches her getting dressed and looks in his bag settling on an all white v-neck tee shirt. He stares in the mirror in approval and she passes him a blunt that she's just rolled. He takes off his doo-rag and puts another coat of grease on his head brushing it forward.

"Let's go…I'm ready to hit the streets. I'm starting to feel these percs kicking in," he says as they walk out the room.

They walk out the hotel and she snaps a picture of the building with the sign blinking "Trump Plaza". They walk down the strip and he eyes the Bada Bing's Gentleman club. He remembers the name from the show "The Soprano's".

"Let's go in there," Keith says paying the bouncers and walking in. "Yooo these bitches is fucking naked in here…they don't even get naked in Va.," he says to himself.

"You like that (I like that)
You want that (I want that)
Apple bottom booty, nice rack with a fat cat
Dance like you dancing on a pole (how you like that)
How you like that
Now dance like you dancing on a pole," Three Six Mafia's "Dancing on a Pole" blares from the speakers.

Keith goes to the bar and starts rocking back and forth to the song. A stripper dressed in a yellow and white diamond studded brassiere walks over and ask them for their order. He orders two vodka's and pineapples. She walks away and Keith stares as the stage while a female is pussy popping on the pole. He looks at his girlfriend and sees that she is enjoying herself. He takes the drinks from the waitress and gives her a twenty. He walks to the middle of the club and starts dancing. He looks and sees his girlfriend sitting on the couch talking to two females.

"Bia Bia
Why you acting like a punk
Push em off
Why you frontin like a punk
Push em off
Pour out that hen and coke
And fire up that dro
It's Ludacris
Off Old National and Godby road
The block is sold, "CLEAR!
Then I shocked the globe
I clock the hoes, lock doo's
And drop bows" Lil Jon's "Bia Bia" blares out of the speakers.

Keith walks to the table and sits at the far end. She looks at him and gives both the strippers twenty dollars apiece. The strippers begin grinding their breast on Keith. She looks at him and start laughing. The waitress places two more drinks on the table. She downs hers quickly and beckons for him to drink his while she orders two more.

He slides his hands between the both of their legs and feels on their pussy. The strippers pull the pasties off of their breasts and start kissing each other. Keith laughs and leans over picking up his drink. One of the strippers reaches down and grabs his dick. He glances over at his girl and she is sitting back watching them.

"Fuck this shit…if this is what she wants to see," he says to himself leaning back. He lets them both grind their breasts on his face. The Asian stripper continues to jerk him off and grinds back and forth on his lap. He starts to smile and they stop and reach their hands out for more money.

"Nawwww…y'all did good enough," Keith's girlfriend tells the strippers.

He laughs while the stripper's walk away and she falls in his lap. "You a crazy ass bitch but that's why I fuck with you," he jokes with her.

"Come on let's go. I ain't gon keep letting these bitches dance on you," she says pulling his arm.

"Go on slip me 2 Xanax bars,
I'm ready to get full
5th of Crown to wash it down
I'm downtown snapping rolls
Ain't no shame in my game,
In fact I'm mentally deranged
Oxycotton in my system
Man I'm feeling kinda strange
Watch me choke about this dope
Blueberry from Texas" Lil Whyte's "Oxycotton plays as they walk out the club. Keith reaches in his pocket grabbing another Percocet swallowing it dry. He walks out the club holding his hand in the air jamming from side to side.

"I know that ain't fair but
I don't care
I'm still a muthafucking millionare," Lil Wayne's "I'm Me" is blaring from the OPM club down the street. A guy walks past blowing a cloud of weed smoke.

"Ay yo, ay shawty…let me hit that," he asks the guy.

The guy stops and passes the blunt to Keith. He inhales twice and gives it back to him. His girlfriend passes him a drink and he remembers that they can walk down the strip with open containers. Three different women place their business cards in his hands.

"Damn…even the hoes out here got business cards," he says.

He glances up and sees the "Chapel of Love" church.

"Let's get married," he says in a slurred voice.

"Fuck it…why not," she says jokingly.

"Naw I'm serious. You been a down ass shawty for a long time…this is what I want," he says to her.

"Okay nigga…let's do it," she tells him.

They run across the street and enter the chapel. He talks to the host for forty minutes and thrusts one hundred and fifty dollars in his hand. They walk to the altar and he starts to feel the effects of the Percocet's and vodka. He begins to feel a sense of enlightenment…he tastes air that he's never breathed before. His body is tingling…he sees her laughing but feels as though he is experiencing an out of body experience. The reverend is speaking but all he hears is *'I know pronounce you man and wife'*.

He turns and faces her. She kisses him hard and he feels as though a weight has been let off his shoulders. A tear rolls down his cheek.

Chapter Eighteen

"You know you're in love when you can't fall asleep because reality is finally better than your dreams"

"Kimberly"

"It's been awhile
Since I could hold my head up high

And it's been awhile
Since I first saw you

And it's been awhile
Since I could stand on my own two feet again

And it's been awhile
Since I could call you
And everything I can't remember
As fucked up as it all may seem
The consequences that are rendered
I've stretched myself beyond my means" Kimberly turns down the radio that's playing Staind's "It's Been Awhile".

Kimberly eats the last bite of her macaroni and cheese mixed with tuna placing the Tupperware back in her environmentally friendly carry bag. She reclines her chair and text's her boyfriend. *'I just made it to the Thunder and Rumble bike show...where you at?'* she presses send. Immediately her phone rings.

"I thought if I texted you then you was supposed to text back not call back," she says picking up the phone.

"Hello to you too…I didn't feel like texting and driving. You said you are at a bike show?" he asks.

"Yes; I saw this off the highway and since you are going to be a while getting here…" she says with her voice trailing off.

"Yea that cool…do you have directions to the place?" he asks.

"Yep…I'll let you know when I leave," she reassures him.

"Don't get too fucked up," he says jokingly hanging up the phone. She turns the music back up.

"Why must I feel this way
Just make this go away
Just one more peaceful day

And it's been awhile
Look at myself straight
Since I could
Since I said sorry
And it's been awhile
Since I've seen the way
The candles lights your face," she sings along with the song before turning down the music and getting out the car.

Kimberly reaches into the console retrieving her perfume bottle of Happy by Clinique. She sprays it on herself and throws it back in the console slamming the car door shut. She checks her pink wife-beater making sure she hasn't spilled any food on herself. She brushes her black pants and stomps her black boots on the ground ensuring no crumbs are on them.

"Let's go," she says to herself entering the Thunder and Rumble bike show. She walks to the Budweiser beer truck and orders a tall Pabst Blue Ribbon. She hands the vendor the money.

"No ma'am…just seeing you is worth enough," the server tells her.

"Thank you…you are sooo cute," she says and walks away. Kimberly hears the loud revving of motorcycle engines pumping each other up.

"Hey baby," she hears someone talking to her. She ignores and continues to walk.

"Dammit didn't you hear me?' the biker asks getting louder.

"Yes I heard you," she replies not turning in his direction.

She reads the patches on the back of the motorcycle jackets that she is passing. Iron Horsemen, Death before Dishonour, Hell's Angel, Mongols…Kimberly sips on her beer continuing to walk…Gypsy Jokers, Pagans, Outlaws, Sons of Silence, Free Souls, Brother Speed, Outsiders, Vagos.

"Hey…hello how are you doing?" she hears a much smoother voice and turn to face the biker who was following her the first time.

"I didn't mean to disrespect you but I wanted to know your name," he says.

"My name is Kimberly…now that was a much better introduction," she replies reaching out her hand.

"Richard…Richard Merla," he says proudly shaking hers.

"All those Saturdays, when kids go out and play
Yo I was up in my room
I let the stereo blaze
Wasn't faded, not jaded, just a kid with a pad and a pen
And a big imagination
All this I seek, I find, push
The envelope to the line
Make it, break it
Take it, until I'm overrated!

Click click boom
I comin down on the stereo, hear me on the radio
Click click boom
I'm coming down with the new style and you know its buck wild
Click click boom
I'm on the radio station tour around the nation
Leave the scene in devastation" Saliva's "Click Click Boom"
plays through the loudspeakers. Richard turns around showing
off his Bandido's vest.

"Bandido's sweetheart," he tells her.

"What is a Bandido?" she asks.

"We are the people our parents warned us about," Richard
belts out laughing. "An outlaw gang that's ONLY wanted by the
F.B.I and C.I.S," he yells out proudly revving his engine. "Let
me refill that for you sweetheart," he says reaching in his satchel
for a beer and refilling her glass.

"So you are a gentleman now," she laughs. Now let me
see…this is a Willie G 1983 Harley Davidson…rare…there were
only a handful of these made that year," she says strumming her
hands over the handlebars. "Skull fuel cap, skull hand grips, skull
rider footboards," she says bending down. "I also see you got the
screaming eagle heavy breather…what does this puppy do about
210…220?" she asks.

"Try 250 sweetheart…I see you know your hogs," he says
smiling.

"Richard…Richard Merla…hey look boys it's the famous
Richard Merla," they hear a voice behind them say and turn to
see a pack of riders on their motorcycles. "Richard Merla ladies
and gentleman…you're something of a superstar I hear," the guy
with the tattoo reading Hell's Angels yells out laughing. "We
hear that they are going to denounce you as a Bandido for that
boy you killed…damn shame they go turn their back on you like
that…tsk tsk," he says taunting him.

"I killed that muthafucker…I don't regret it. I don't have any remorse…I don't feel sorry for him or his family…I just don't give a fuck and I don't have any problems laying anybody else down beside him," Richard says stepping off his bike.

The Hell's Angels bikers get off their choppers. "Well let's see what you got sweetheart," the guy says as Richard rushes in the crowd swinging.

Kimberly turns and quickly walks away dropping her cup on the ground. She walks past the group of Bandido's who are rushing to get to the fight. She makes it back to the car, fumbles with her keys and hears gunshots rang out. She gets in the car; starting it at the same time. She puts the car in reverse; squealing the tires and almost hitting another car in the parking lot.

"Let me slow down," Kimberly says to herself reaching in her bag pulling out a small pouch of cocaine. She brings the bag to her nose and swerves out the way of another vehicle pulling out. She turns the radio up.

"Sing with me
Sing for the year
Sing for the laughter
Sing for the tear
Sing with me, if it's just
For today, maybe tomorrow
The Good Lord will take you away" Kimberly sings along with Aerosmith's "Dream on". She grabs her phone and texts her boyfriend *On my way…can't wait to tell you what happened* she presses send. *Cool almost there…see you soon* he texts back. She reaches over for the joint in the ashtray and presses play on the c.d. player.

"Here come old flattop
He come grooving up slowly
He got joo-joo eyeball

He one holy roller
He got hair down to his knees
Got to be a joker he just do what he please

He wear no shoeshine
He got toejam football
He got monkey finger…he shoot coca cola
He say "I know you, you know me"
One thing I can tell you is you got to be free
Come together right now over me

He bag production
He got walrus gumboot
He got ono sideboard he one spinal cracker
He got hair down below his knew
Hold you in his armchair
So you can feel his disease
Come together right now over me

He roller coaster
He got early warning
He got muddy water
He one mojo filter
He "One and one and one is three'
Got to be good looking cause he's so hard to see
Come together
Right now
Over me" The Beatles "Come Together" plays.

Kimberly lights the joint and gets on the highway heading towards Cape Elizabeth. She reads the sign displaying *'Lobster Shack at Two lights'* next exit. She opens her window throwing the joint away and leaving it cracked allowing the smoke to exit the car. She gets off the exit and pulls into the Lobster Shack.

'Where you at?' she texts her boyfriend. *'bout to pull in'* he texts back. She reclines her seat and reflects on her day.

"Richard Merla...I'm going to look him up," she says Googling his name on her IPHONE.

'Richard Steven Merla, otherwise known as Scarface to his Bandido gang; accused of a fatal attack on world champion boxer Robert Quiroga. Quiroga was stabbed fifteen times. The wounds were so deep that it couldn't be told if he was stabbed through the front or the back' she reads off her phone.

She hears a car horn blowing in front of her. She turns off the engine, gets out and snaps the phone back in its case. "Hey baby," she says hugging and kissing him.

"Lobster and blueberry pie huh" he says pointing to the sign on the restaurant.

"You know I love to eat...let's get married," she says kissing him.

"What?" he asks.

"Let's just do it...no big wedding...no family...just you, me and my dog...she would be the bridesmaid or bridesdog or whatever...let's just do it," she says again.

"What do you want?" he asks.

You and only you," she says hugging him tightly.

"I don't know what happened today, but my answer is yes...I don't care what happened today...my answer is yes," he says hugging her back tightly.

Chapter Nineteen

"Better to have Loved and Lost than
To never have Loved at all"

"Lynette"

Lynette gets out the cab fanning the sand; that is blowing, out her face. Her friend pulls her Duster out of the trunk and wraps it around her.

"Thank you," she says pulling the coat tightly around her to block the wind.

"You're welcome," he says as the cab driver sets their luggage on the ground.

"I'm sorry I didn't want to go to the hotel first, but I really wanted to see this place," she tells him.

"That's cool because I don't mind seeing this place as well," he responds. He picks up their bags and they walk to the stone marker plastered on the building.

"It's in Arabic; it reads Heikhal Hasefer, Shrine of the Book," Lynette reads out-loud.

She stares at the white dome building surrounded by a moat of water. He points the black basalt walls.

"The walls represent the Sons of Darkness and the sun represents the Sons of Light," he reads pointing at the building.

"You know…this place kinda looks like a really big piece of Hershey Kisses," she says

"You know…your kinda right," he responds as they both laugh.

He walks behind her and wraps his arms around her waist. "I hope that the plane ride didn't scare you too bad?' he asks rubbing his hands back and forth on her arms.

She leans back and crosses her arms up to meet his. "You're a do right man," she tells him.

"And you're a do right woman," he responds as they both laugh reminiscing over Aretha Franklin's "Do Right Woman, Do Right Man" song.

"Did you know that this is the House of Dead Sea Scrolls and different artifacts where discovered at eh Siege of Masada," she continues to read "They also have the oldest known surviving copies of the bible from the Second Temple of Judaism," she finishes reading.

"Jerusalem is the only place I wanted to visit in the world and when the Bishop suggested that he wanted me to make this passage before being ordained...," she says being interrupted.

"I know baby...you told me a thousand times," he says joking with her. "Well we waited this long; we might as well not prolong the big moment," he says lifting the handle on the carry luggage.

They enter the shrine and listen to the tour guide talking. She quickly takes picture of his yellow striped robe and Taqiyah. They listen as the guide explains the events of the weekend.

"The exhibit of Earth, Wind, Fire, and Water will be shown by Yanka Shonibare all weekend" the tour guide explains to the crowd.

"Can we come back and go there?" she asks her friend.

"Yes baby; this is your weekend, so whatever you want to do is fine by me," he responds. "It looks like it would be interesting," he says pointing to a sculptor of a multicolored suit with the head of a faucet pouring water into a glass.

"No babe...that just looks weird," she replies slipping her hand into his.

"So tell me again…what will you be able to do once you are ordained?" he ask her.

"Well I'll be able to preside over funerals and weddings," she tells him.

"And what will your title change to then?" he continues.

"Well…I'll still be called an Evangelist but they will be able to call me Elder as well," she explains to him.

"That's real cool. I respect a woman who is head strong and motivated... and being cute is a bonus," he says squeezing her hand.

Lynette smiles and says nothing beginning to hum.

"The only one who could ever reach me
Was the son of a preacher man
The only one who could ever teach me
Was the son of a preacher man" she continues to hum.

"Ooooh I know this song, that's ummm…," he continues to ponder while tapping his leg. "Dusty Springfield," he responds. He begins to hum his own tune.

She leans in to hear him better and he lowers his voice. He continues to lean back and quickly snaps his head forward giving her a kiss.

"Oh, mercy, mercy, me," he says pulling back from her lips.

"Oh you think you funny Mr. Marvin Gaye," she says interlocking her hands with his. They walk down the long corridor in silence and enter a room with thick glass.

"This is it…these are the Dead Sea Scrolls that were recovered from the caves at Qumran," she says pulling out her camera to take a picture. "That's right…I can't take pictures in here," she says pointing at the No Pictures sign.

"Hurry up and take the picture. There isn't any security here," he says looking around.

125

"We can't do that. You are going to get us kicked out of here," she replies fumbling with the camera.

"Awww, come on babe, it's just a quick one. Plus no one's going to see us," continues to prompt her.

She looks around quickly and takes a picture.

"I see now…you go get us kicked out of here," he jokes grabbing their luggage and walking away.

'Ooooh I'm go fix this negro' she thinks to herself walking behind him laughing.

"We don't have to see the entire place today since we gon' come back tomorrow and see the exhibit," she begins to say as he cuts her off.

"Baby please don't be so insecure. There is no place I would rather be than right here with you," he says turning to face her. "I am not you're last husband. I don't want you to do things that I want to do but I want to do things that you want to do. The first time I saw you singing I thought wow…she has a voice from heaven and she looks like an angel in every way. I even remember the song you were singing. It was Precious Yahweh. You had the most beautiful voice I had ever heard. I hinted around to the Bishop about you and he told me that you had some hardships with your late husband. I thought, how could an angel lie you be treated anyway differently from exactly what you are? An angel…I don't want to tell you what type of man I am but I want to show you want kind of woman you really are. Don't worry; I'm not asking for your hand in marriage…well at least not yet," he says chuckling. "I know you still focusing on yourself and you need companion…someone who would read the bible with you every morning and pray with you every night. Just continue on your journey and give me the blessing of watching you mature," he finishes. He hugs her tightly and feels her tear fall on his collar. She begins to sing "At Last" by Etta James in his ear.

"At last
My move has come along
My lonely days are over
And life is like a song
Oh yea...at last
The skies above are blue
My heart was wrapped up in clovers
The night I looked at you
I found a dream that I could speak to
A dream that I can call my own
I found a thrill to press my cheek to
A thrill that I have never known
Oh yea
When you smile
You smile
On and then the spell
Was cast
And here we are in heaven
For you are mine
At last"

Chapter Twenty

"Where There is Love;
There is Life"

"Marcus"

Marcus stands in front the mirror checking out his outfit. Hr brushes lint of the collar of his purple collared French cuffed Stacy Adams shirt. He rubs his purple and navy blue Delray shoes on the back of his pants, laughs and thinks of the movie about Frankie Lyman.

"Anybody asked
If anybody asks you
Where I'm going
Where I'm going
Where I'm going
Soon
If you wanna know
I bet you you wanna know
Where I'm going" Marcus begins to sing Rueben Studdard's "Going up Yonder" along with the mix c.d. that one of the sisters from the church has made for him.

He presses his diamond studded purple cuff links on his sleeve and fixes the mirror to get a full view of himself.
"Purple…the color of royalty," he says out-loud walking to the night stand to grab his bible.

"Lord give me the strength and courage to exceed my wildest expectations…through you I know that all things are possible," he prays.

"You already know my feelings
Do I have to tell you again
And I ain't going nowhere
I need you to know they can," Marcus begins to sing and dance around the room to Dietrick's Haddon's "Right There".

"Call my name
Whenever you need me
I'll be there if you
Just believe in me

Wanna be your bread
When you're hungry
Wanna be your water
When you're thirsty"

"Let's go Marcus," he says laughing to himself. He retrieves the c.d. player off the portable speakers and places it in his bag. He exits the Holiday Inn, walks down the street eyeing the El Ladrillo Restaurant. He picks up his phone and dials home.

"Hey baby…how is Puerto Rico?" the female voice asks.

"Absolutely beautiful…everything I imagined…I mean the water is beautiful and the view from the hotel is off the chain. I'm so sorry you couldn't be here with me," he responds.

"That's cool…are you wearing the shirt I got you?" she asks.

"Yes baby…and the shoes…and the cufflinks," he responds.

"Well, you see…I am right there…closer than you think," she replies laughing.

"Well smarty-pants; the reason I called you was to find out what El Ladrillo means?" he asks.

"The brick…I think," she says.

"Ohhh…is that why the entire place is covered in bricks," he says smiling.

"You know; to have all that talent and still be so slow. Enjoy yourself and call me later," she says jokingly.

"I love you," he tells her.

"I love you more than you will ever know…bye baby," she replies hanging up the phone.

Marcus closes his phone and enters the restaurant. The host escorts him to a booth and he orders a bud light. *'I can't read this thing anyway; I'm just going to get some wings,'* he thinks to himself tossing the menu on the table. He gets up, looks at the artwork on the wall and reads the inscription to himself. *'Retracto De Carlos Raquel Rivera'.* Below the portrait is a newspaper clipping stating that he had recently died of lung cancer (1922-2008). There are also hand painted portraits of Wichie Torres, Alexander Rosado, Eddie Soto, Taly Riviera and Olga Lan. *'Cool'* he thinks to himself returning to the table and taking a sip of beer the waitress has bought over. *'No weapons formed against me shall prosper'* he thinks to himself listening to the radio station commercial playing

"Hola y bienvenidos a la explosion del evangelio en Puerto Rico. Usetedes saben unas personas llaman este isla, Tierra del Rios valeroso. Este es quien estamos aqui elogiar hoy. Quisieramos dar la beinvenida a Echen, PaKa, Cristo Rey, El Evangelico Hercules, Flora Cruz, Puchi Colon, Y Diacono Marcus hasta el final de Fayetteville, Carolina del Norte. Ahora empezamos con los festividades! Dar ls bienvenida al dia que il senor ha hecho!"

"That's my name," Marcus says hearing the announcer on the radio. He picks up his phone and texts his girlfriend. *'They just said my name over the radio,'* he sends. *'I say your name over and over and you never get this excited...on second thought...yes you do,'* she responds. *'I'm going to pray for you girl...you got me wishing I was there right now making you say my name over and over,'* he texts back. *'Focus dear...focus,'* she responds. He laughs and places the phone back in its case.

The waitress brings his food to the table. "Ma'am; I'm not even hungry anymore can you just put this in a to-go box?" he asks her as she takes the basket away.

He drinks half his beer. "Lord knows I hope she sees that all this is for her," he says out-loud referring to his girlfriend. The waitress returns and he pays the bill leaving a healthy tip.

"Gracias Senor," she says smiling and nodding her head in approval.

Marcus walks outside and eyes little kids dribbling a basketball. He waves his hands motioning to them to throw him the ball. He begins to dribble through his legs as the kids attempt to get the ball away from him. One of them slaps the ball out his hands.

"I used to be better back in the day," he jokes with them and flags down a taxi.

"Something bout that name Jesus," he begins to sing fixing the tone of his voice.

"I know...I know Jesus...give me the strength to carry out your will," he says to himself as he gets in the cab and passes the driver a flyer with the directions to the Coast Guard base.

"Some people say I'm crazy
But I can't explain
The power that I feel
When I call your name (When I call you name)

131

Said it's just like fire
Shut up in my bones
The Holy Ghost is moving
And it just won't leave me alone
Something about that name Jesus" Marcus turns on his c.d.
player and The Rance Allen Group's "Something about that
Name Jesus" begins to play. The song mixes into the Kirk
Franklin's version.

"Now that sister can make a c.d." he says to himself.
"Thank you Jesus," he whispers looking towards the sky.

They make the short trip to the base where they are
stopped at the guard gate my M.P.'s who asks for their
identification cards.

The cab driver pushes the button opening the trunk. The
M.P. inspects the car with his police dog. *Thank God I left that
blunt back in the room'* he thinks to himself laughing out loud.
The cab driver drives around the base towards the hangar where
a stage is built for this special occasion. Marcus takes his
headphones off and looks at the rows or people standing and
worshipping. *'Baby...this is huge...I'm a SUPERSTAR,'* he texts
his girl. *'Humble sir...humble...but I'm proud of you...knock em
dead'* she texts back.

The driver lets Marcus out at the back of the hangar and he
is met by M.P.'s Marcus shows them him I.D. badge displaying
that he is one of the performers for tonight. He looks on as the
first artist finishes his performance. The d.j. begins playing music
by Yolanda Adams.

"Alone in a room
It's just me and you
I feel so lost, cause
I don't know what to do

Now what if I choose
The wrong thing to do
I'm so afraid
Afraid of disappointing you
So I need to talk to you
And ask you for your guidance
Especially today
When my world is so cloudy
Guide me till I'm sure
I'll open up my heart" Marcus quietly sings the lyrics to the song "Open My Heart".

Marcus picks up his phone and calls his girlfriend. "Okay baby…I need you on this one,' he says.
What do you want me to do?" she asks.
"Just stay on the phone while I perform," he replies.
"Okay baby, I'm right here," she responds

He puts the phone back in its case and cradles his head with both hands.
"Give me strength oh Lord, give me strength," he prays. He pulls out his phone placing it to his ear. He hears her singing the Yolanda Adams song and quietly lowers his phone back in its case. He hears the M.C. announce his name and he runs on stage.

"Is Jesus in the house tonight?" Marcus yells in the microphone. "I said is Jesus in the house tonight…the Everlasting Father, His Holiness, His Greatness, The Beginning and the End, Alpha and Omega?" he asks and the crowd erupts in a frenzy.
"Give him praise if you've been through something and came out on the other end. Give him praise if you know that he is a living God…Clap your hands…Stomp your feet…slap your wheelchair…make some noise if Jesus is in your heart tonight," he yells in the microphone as the band begins revving up the

drums, piano and guitars. "Now that's the blessing we need in here…I come all the way from Fayetteville North Carolina. We call it Fayetnam because of all the disabled vets in the area. I've ministered to everyone that I have laid my hands upon. I've cried with so many people and to see the resilience in so many people eyes and the love that they have for the Lord gives me the strength to carry on. This is the song that I dedicate to them and to everyone here on this Coast Guard Base in Borinquen Puerto Rico," he yells as the choir erupts in a loud roar.

"I found out that even this island means Land of the Valiant Lord…is that amazing or what," he says as the crowd get louder.

"Never would have made it
Never could have made it
Without you
I would have lost it all
But now I see
How you where there for me
And I can say

Never would have made it
Never could have made it
Without you
I would have lost it all
But know I see
How you were there for me
And I can say
I'm stronger
I'm wiser
I'm better
So better
When I look back over all you brought me through
I can see you were the one
I held on to

And I never
Never would have made it" he begins to sing Marvin Sapp's
"Never would have made it".

"Hold on…hold on," Marcus says quieting the singers and
music down. 'There is a very special person in the crowd
tonight…she came all the way from back home with me," he
says taking the phone out of its holster. "Hello" he says.

"Hello what are you doing?" she answers with her voice
echoing through the speakers.

"I am on stage holding the phone to the microphone…the
whole world can hear you," he says.

"OH…MY…GOD," she responds as her voice trails off.

Marcus directs the musicians to stop playing.

"Hey D.J. can you play that Yolanda Adams song one
more time?" he asks as the d.j. as the crowd quiets down and he
gets his breath under control.

"Baby, this day has only been perfect because you've been
here with me the whole time. It was your words, your thoughts
and you're prayers that have kept me grounded and humble. It is
the traces of your perfume that you sprayed on my shirt and the
smell of you in the air all around me…it's simply your presence
why I have made it this far," he says dropping to one knee on
stage.

"Baby…I am literally on one knee on the stage. The bible
says that a man and a woman should join to become one…I am
asking you to be that one…to be my one…will you marry me?'
he asks.

"Yes baby…Yes baby I would marry you a hundred times
over…Yes Deacon Marcus…Yes," she exclaims excitedly as the
crowd bursts out cheering.

135

Marcus removes the microphone and brings the phone to his ear.

"You bring out the best in me," he tells her.

Chapter Twenty-One

"In this life we cannot do great things. We can only do small things with great Love"

"Margaret"

"Please Father give me strength to carry on…I give you all the praise," Margaret says to herself sitting in the truck thirty five minutes after church has began.

"Now when we go in here y'all don't be acting up," she tells her two children. "If your father was here you wouldn't be making all this noise," she says talking to her son as he cries. She unhooks her daughter out of her car seat, grabs her son's hand and walk up the steps leading to the double doors.

"They need an elevator," she says breathlessly entering the church.

The choir director walks up to her.

"Girl; we next…I'll find the kids somewhere to sit and you just go get dressed," the choir director commands taking the kids out of Margaret's hands.

Margaret stops and looks at the Henley singers singing Reverend James Cleveland's "Everything Will Be Alright."

"Everything
Everything will be alright
Everything will be alright"

Margaret walks through the church to the dressing room to change. She takes the plastic bag off her black robe displaying the Powhatan choir emblem and cross engraved in gold with a white stole. She quickly dresses slipping on her black high heels.

"Walk with me," she says zipping up her choir robe and exiting the dressing room. "Hallelujah," she yells out doing a two step.

"Margaret...hurry up," the choir director says.
"Sorry," she replies sheepishly.

Margaret put her finger up and walks to the back of the church while the choir director takes her place in front of the church.

"We've come this far by faith
Leaning on the Lord
Trusting in his Holy Word
He never failed me yet
Can't turn around
We've come this far by faith" the choir starts singing Donnie McClurkin's "We've Come This Far by Faith."

They start moving side to side and marching forward. They reach the front of the church and line up one section behind each other.

"We are so honored to be here in the name of Yahweh Yashuah the Messiah...we are the Powhatan Choir and we came to rock the house," the choir director tells the congregation.

"We just want to let you know that everything will be alright...no matter what you're going through...everything will be alright...put your faith in the Lord and Everything will be Alright...sing it choir,' she says as the choir sings louder.

.

"We are only going to sing one selection because we know that Pastor Hunt has a wide variety of groups for you…Now when we choose singer; we don't always choose the best singer but we aim for the singer with the most emotions…you have to feel life to feel music…she don't even know that she is our honorary singer," the choir director says as the musicians quiet the music down.

'You fool…you bet not call on me' Margaret thinks to herself.

"Sister Margaret" she hears the choir director call her name out.

"I'm go kill this wench," Margaret says quietly to herself smiling and stepping out of the back row. "I'm going to get you," she tells the director taking the microphone.

"Well…as you can tell I wasn't expecting this but God is good right," she says.

"All the time," the congregation responds back as the musicians began to play.

"We need to hear from you
We need a word from you
If we don't hear from you
What will we do
Wanting you more each day
Show us your perfect way," she begins to sing Andrae Crouch's "We Need to Hear From You".

"Amen…Amen…sing it girl," she hears someone from the back of the church say as the congregation begins clapping.

"There is no other way
That we can live"

The choir chants in as the choir director directs the choir. A tear falls from Margaret's eye as she raises her hand to the sky putting her feelings into the song. The choir director directs the rest of the choir to exit giving her a solo. The congregation stands to their feet applauding as Margaret fades out.

"Thank you Yahweh," she says exiting the stage. The choir showers her with approval on her performance. "I'm going to get you," she tells the choir director as they hug.

"The Lord told me that that was your part and I just went with what he said," the choir director responds.

Margaret quickly changes and re-enters the church while a singer is singing "Yesterday" by Mary Mary.

Margaret locates her children who are with one of the members of the church. "Thank you" she says lifting her sleeping daughter and allowing her son to rest his head on her lap. "Thank you Father," she says to herself swaying back and forth.

"Our next selection will be the Sons of Thunder," the mistress of ceremonies says while the lead singer begins to talk.

"One had backslid
And they got into a conversation
And the backslider was complaining because
Everything had gone wrong for him
And the Christian was trying to encourage him
And then the conversation
Went something like this

Say you been sick
Tell me
Where is your faith
Where is your faith in God," the singer begins to sing Reverend James Cleveland's "Where is Your Faith." The singer begins to walk through the aisle speaking to the congregation. "Where is

your faith…where is your faith. I know that sometimes you can't see the light amidst the darkness…but remember the light is soon to come…where is your faith," he continues to sing.

Margaret turns and sees her husband moving through the pew.

"I'm sorry I'm dirty…I just got off of work and came straight here," he says lifting his son into his lap.

"Where is your faith," she singer sings.

"In God," Margaret's husband replies. He leans over and whispers in her ear. "Besides my kids; the day we married has been the greatest day of my life. I will go through hell and high water to be with you and the children you have given me. I thank God for each and every day that I have to wake up and spend with you. I have committed my life to you and God. I will spend each and every day that is possible dedicated to being the best husband I can be. I made a commitment to God to support my wife in any manner possible. I am not the greatest man in the world but to God be the glory; I will be the best that I can be. My faith is in God because my faith is in you," he says reaching over rubbing his hand on her ring finger.

Chapter Twenty-Two

"Stand in Love...Don't Fall"

"Marica"

"Woman get busy, just shake that
Booty nonstop
When the beat drops
Just keep swinging it
Get Jiggy
Get crunked up
Percolate anything you want to call it
Oscillate your hips and don't take pity" Sean Paul's "Get Busy" is
blaring through the speakers at the Amnesia Club in Kingston
Jamaica.

Marica is moving her body from left to right shaking her
ass back and forth. A Jamaican guy walks over and grabs her
thighs pulling her back into him grinding back and forth. Marica
grabs the back of his head and starts grinding on him slowly. Her
boyfriend walks over and stares at her. She looks in his eyes and
starts moving seductively.

"Baby I can't get over you
No matter how I try
No one can love me like you do
And that's the reason why
Baby I can't get over you" Mr. Vegas "Can't Get Over You"
begins to play.

Marica watches as he takes the blunt out of his mouth, knocks the ashes on the floor, and motions for her to come over. She pushes off the Jamaican guy and slowly dances over to him. He cuffs his hands and she reaches her hand to fit his as he blows a hit of marijuana in her face. He laughs as she slowly inhales all the smoke through her nose and mouth. They see the crowd starting to form a circle in the middle of the dance floor.

"Mr. Wakie a di teacher
But a ice a bus da beat ya
Everybody in a di street
Jus a do di gully creepa creepa
People uno see it ya even Senorita
Wat when you hear da beat
Yo what it name gully creepa" Elephant Man's "Gully Creepa" begins to play.

Marica squints her eyes noticing a familiar face moving through the crowd. She shakes her boyfriend's arm and points to the Jamaican guy making his way to the dance floor.
"Who is that?" he asks.
"That's Mr. Attitude from the Youtube video I was showing you," she tells him.
"Oh shit…that is him," he responds looking through the crowd.

Mr. Attitude walks to the middle of the dance floor, bends down and starts rocking his hips and shoulder back and forth.

"That's how you do the Gully Creepa dance," she says standing on her tiptoes to see over the crowd.

She pulls out her cell phone and begins videotaping. Her boyfriend passes her the blunt and sips his Red Stripe at the same time.

"Buck Buck Buck Bwounty Boys," the D.J. blares over the music. Marica looks in the mirror and checks out her outfit; fishnet stockings leading up to her red short shorts. She admires the shape of her body and blows the smoke out slowly. She sees his hand sliding over her ass and starts moving back and forth. The lights flicker on and off symbolizing that the club is ending. He walks to the bar and orders two shots of Patron. He passes one to her and she shakes her head no.

"Come on baby…just one," he says holding the shot-glass out to her.

"Fuck it," she says and grabs the glass, downs it and slams it on the table.

He grabs Marica's hand and they make their way to the exit. He flags down a taxi and tells him to drive to the Christar Villas Suites. They both get in and she leans on her boyfriend and starts kissing on his neck. He leans back looking out the window. She traces her hand down his chest. He adjusts himself and she grabs his dick through his clothes. Marica licks her tongue on his chest as far as his Polo shirt would allow her to go. He rubs on her back and continues to look out the window. They stop in front of the Villa and he pays the cabbie. They walk to the room and she presses him on the wall and starts kissing on him.

"Damn baby…hold on; let me get the key out," he says in his thick accent. He opens the door and she walks over and connects her phone to the docking station.

"T shirt and my panties on
T shirt and my panties onnn
T shirt and my panties onnnnn
T shirt and my panties onnnnn" Adinah Howard's "T-Shirt and Panties" begins to play.

He flops on the bed and lights his blunt. Marica starts moving seductively taking off her top. She takes off her shorts and stands in front of him. He beckons for her to come over. She crawls on the bed and on top of him allowing her body to rub all over his. She kisses on him rising up his shirt pulling it over his head. He taps out the blunt and she pulls off his pants and boxers. She lowers herself on top of him continuing to kiss on his chest. He reaches around and slaps her on the ass. She giggles out-loud and looks in the mirror at the silhouette of her body going up and down on him slowly.

"Gal a shape up back home
And a blow up my phone
Cuz dem waan di Vitamin S
Gal a smoke my cigar
And a run down me car
Cuz dem waan di Vitamin S
Gal a unbutton ar skirt
And a pop off ar shirt
Cuz deem waan di Vitamin S" Baby Cham's "Vitamin S" begins to play.

"Fuck this," he says roughly moving her off of him. He stands up and guides her towards the dresser bending her over. He spreads her legs open and slide inside of her.

"Damn," she grunts out-loud.

Marica places her hands on the wall and pushes herself back meeting his thrusts. She feels his chain slapping back and forth against her ass. He grabs the back of her hair and meets her thrusts with his.

"Oh shit oh shit oh shit," she chants out.

She hears his shave kit and her bottle of Blueberry perfume hit the floor. She hears him grunting and moaning.

"I'm cumming…I'm cumming," he grunts pushing himself inside of her releasing and breathing heavily. He staggers back and falls on the bed.

She lies beside him and starts kissing on his back until they both fall asleep.

"Don't let them fool ya
Or even try to school ya!
Oh no!
We've got a mind of our own
So go to hell if what you're thinking is not right!
Love would never leave us alone
A-yin in the darkness there must come out to light" she hears Bob Marley's "Could You Be Loved" playing and feels him kissing on her neck. She opens her eyes and sees a solitaire ring sitting in a black box.

"Could you be loved
And be loved
Could you be loved
And be loved"

She rolls over and looks at him. She sits up and kisses him long and hard.

Chapter Twenty-Three

*Being deeply Loved by someone gives you strength;
While Loving someone deeply gives you courage"*

"Marisha"

"No matter what I do
All I think about is you
Even when I'm with my boo
Boy you know I'm crazy over you
No matter what I do
All I think about is you
Even when I'm with my boo
Boy you know I'm crazy over you
I met this chick and
She just moved right up the block from me
And she got the hots for me
The finest thang my hood has ever seen" Nelly and Kelly's
"Dilemma" plays through the room of the Sheraton Kauai resort.

Marisha turns off the water and steps out the shower singing to herself. She reaches for her Victoria Secret Love Spell gift bag that she received from her aunt at the wedding reception. She rubs herself down with the lotion and pulls out the spray bottle setting it down on the counter. She opens the bathroom closet pulling out her purple mid thigh sundress. She puts on the dress and fixes her petite breast in the mirror. She twists her wedding ring around adjusting it in the mirror.

Marisha says her new last name twice in the mirror to herself. She reminisces back to the night that he proposed. She recants on how he had tears in his eyes and remembers the guy on the corner singing Musiq Soulchild's "Love".

"Hurry up girl," she hears her husband say as he pounds on the door jolting her out of her daydream.

"I'm hurrying…don't be rushing me," she yells out the door.

"You rushed down that aisle but don't rush out the bathroom," he says laughing and walking away.

She looks in the mirror and repeats her new last name one last time before stepping out.

"Uuh hardly home but always reppin
U hardly on and always second
When I'm awake you always resting
And when they call u the answer you will hardly questioned
I'm doing classic shit in all my sessions
Other niggas situation they are all depressing
And that's why I never follow y'all suggestion
I just always did my own thing" Drake's "Uptown" plays as she walks in the room.

"Awwww…is you mad?" Marisha asks joking with him and jumping on the bed. She presses her body against the wall and grabs both rails. "I know what you looking for big boy," she says playfully in her sexy voice. "Or is this better?" she asks putting a washcloth in her mouth and growling.

"You see…you see…this is why I don't let you smoke cause you start acting all silly," he tells her as she continues to growl.

He walks into the bathroom and Marisha sits on the bed and relights the blunt. She walks out on the balcony, leans on the rail and blows the smoke out. She walks back in the room and switches the IPOD to Pandora radio choosing Aaliyah's station.

"It could all be so simple
But you rather make it hard
Loving you is like a battle
And we both end up with scars
Tell me, who I have to be
To get some reciprocity
See no one loves you more than me
And no one ever will

Is this just a silly game
That forces me to act this way
Forces you to scream my name
Then pretend that you can't stay
Tell me who I have to beee" Lauryn Hill's "Ex-Factor" fills the room. She slides her feet in her purple sandals and pulls the wedding cake topper; of a man and woman holding each other, out of her bag.

"You ready," her husband asks walking over to kiss her.

"Now that's the smell of clean looking boy," she says mocking Hot Stylez's "Looking Boy" song.

"You ready?" he asks again in a softer voice wrapping his arms around her.

"Ready," she replies turning off the radio. "Mr. and Mrs....it feels good to just say that," she says interlocking their hands together as they walk out the room. "Look at this warning sign," she points out to him and begins reading the warning sign on the wall.

"This ocean may be hazardous under any condition and may cause serious bodily injury and sometimes death. At all times use extreme caution when entering or exiting the ocean," she continues to read pointing at the pictures. "Jellyfish, submerged rocks, sudden drop-offs, waves on the ledge...but I don't know what strong urren, high sur, and angerous shore is," Marisha says quizzically.

"That's because some of the letter are missing…that's high surf, strong current, and dangerous shore…God I can't let you smoke anymore," he replies shaking his head.

"Oh" she says putting her hand in his walking beside him out to the beach.

"Are you enjoying Hawaii?" he asks her.

"Very much so," she replies as they step out on Poipu Beach.

"Look over there," she says pointing to the whales swimming in the ocean.

"Those are the humpback whales I read in the brochure…they are beautiful," she says zooming her camera to take a picture.

"This is the late great Israel Kamakawiwo 'Ole; Rest in Peace Bruddha IZ,' the radio announcer announces over the radio and plays "Over the Rainbow".

"Somewhere over the rainbow
Way up high
And the dreams that you dream of
Once in a lullaby
Somewhere over the rainbow
Blue birds fly
And the dreams that you dream of
Dreams really do come true
Someday I'll wish upon a star, wake up where the clouds are
Far behind me

Where trouble melts like lemon drops
High above the chimney tops
That's where you'll find me
Somewhere over the rainbow

Bluebirds fly
And the dream that you dare to,
Why
Oh why can't I" Bruddha Iz croons over the radio.

"OOOOO look at them," Marisha squeals pointing to the Hawaiian man and his son dancing in the sand to the music. "I think it's so manly that they wear flowers," she says referring to the yellow and white flowers they have in their hair and around their necks.

"I think it's kinda gay," he replies laughing and leading her towards the patio furniture. "I'm hungry as hell," he says as they pick up the menus.

"Good evening newlyweds…may I take your orders?" the waitress asks.

He orders a Hawaiian cheeseburger and Corona; she chooses the Volcano shrimp and a Royal Flush.

"You remember this verse," he says beginning to rap.

"What you mean I ain't call you
I hit you when I landed
I'm waiting in my hotel room
Seems like we arguing more and its
Getting less romantic
Yeah I think that she'll be able to tell soon
But I fucked you right I will
I fucked you right I will
I'll fuck you like no one has ever made you feel
I mean its part of our relationship, amazing still
I might just put up with the arguing and stay forreal
You looking mad, girl for goodness sakes" Marisha chimes in.

"You will all those curved and me without no breaks," they both sing Drake's part off of Chris Brown's "Deuces" remix as the waitress sets their drinks on the table.

"Ooooh, let me try that Corona commercial thing," Marisha says reaching over taking the lime out of his bottle. She attempts to squeeze the juice on his face but ends up pinching the entire lime on his face. "Oooops," she says laughing and licking her fingers.

"You see…this is why I don't let you smoke," he says as she laughs and leans over to kiss the juice off of his cheek.

"What about this song," she says beginning to sing TLC's "Diggin on You".

"I was like peace in a groove
On a Sunday afternoon
You were there so was I
In the park 4th of July
I was chilling with my Kool-aid
When Miss Chilli came to relay
That you had a thang for me
Finest thang you ever seen
I must admit to you
I heard them lines a time or two
Although for some apparent reason
Monkey lines are now in season
Lights off, lights on
I guess the groove is on so I am
Digging the scene
Digging on you
Baby baby
It's on like that
It's on like that
I gotta be in love or something like that"

She whispers her new last name in his ear again.

"I'm glad I didn't marry you for the singing but I won't hold that against you…I love you baby" he says leaning over to kiss her.

Chapter Twenty-Four

"When you trip in Love, it is easy to get up. But when you fall in Love, it is impossible to stand again"

"Monica"

"If you want to live my life
Live it all the way and don't you waste it
Every feeling every beat
Can be so sweet you got to taste it
You got to do it you got to do it your way
You got to prove it
You got to mean what you say
Life's a party, make it hot
Dance don't ever stop whatever rhythm
Every minute, every day
Take them all the way you got to listen to them" Jennifer Lopez's
"Let's Get Loud' plays from her rental car.

"Hey baby; I thought I would squeeze in a class before the day started, I Googled the local gym…Hawaii Kay I think is the name of it…get some sleep and I'll call you around lunch time," she tells her boyfriend hanging up the phone.

Monica pulls in the parking lot, turns off the car and reaches in the back seat grabbing her Nike backpack with the Brazilian flag imprinted on it. She picks up her half bottle Voss water taking a sip. She grabs her camera bag and takes a picture of the red, blue and white fitness sign on the front of the gym.

"Aloha," the salesperson at the front desk says greeting Monica.

"Aloha…I'm not a member but I was excited to hear that there was a Zumba class here. How much is the guest pass?" Monica asks.

"Ten dollars Ma'am…and here is a list of our classes going on today,' the host says passing her the group list. "Right now out silver and fit class is in session but feel free to use our other fitness rooms until Zumba begins; Welcome to Kai gym," she says passing Monica receipt.

Monica looks in the playroom and watches the children running and jumping on a rubber deck.

"Awwww," she says as two kids fight over a toy at the table.

A little boy walks to the window and points at her.

"Awwww," she says again before waving at him and walking away.

Monica walks up the steps and chooses a stationary bicycle in front of a class in session. She presses the speed on the bike and puts her headphone.

"When Marimba rhythms start to play
Dance with me, make me sway
Like a lazy ocean hugs the shore
Hold me close, sway me more
Like a flower bending in the breeze
Bend with me, sway with ease
When we dance you have a way with me" Pussycat Dolls "Sway" plays in her ear and she sways back and forth to the song.

She receives a text on her phone *'I'm up…going out…hit me when your done…love u'* it reads.

155

"How nice," she says to herself as the class ends and people file out. She takes another sip from her water bottle and enters the room with the group walking in.

"Zumbaaaa!" the woman on the cordless microphone yells as the crowd finds their place on the floor.

"My name is Dawn and we go jump right into it today," the instructor says pressing the play button on the IPOD filling the room with Ivete Sangalo's "Festa".

"Festa no Gueto Pode vir, pode chegar
Misturando o mundo inteiro, vamos ver no que a que da
Vem gente do toda cor tem raga de toda
Guirtarras de rock and roll batuque candombia via ia"

"Come on ladies…we gonna have some fun today," Dawn says jogging in place warming up the group. "Looks like we got a newcomer," the instructor says pointing to Monica.

"Hello," Monica says waving and placing her bag in the cubbyhole and jogging in place with the rest of the group.

"How you doing? What brings you to Hawaii?" a woman pacing beside her asks.

"Just a romantic getaway," Monica replies.

"Congratulations and welcome to Kai," Dawn yells out quickening her pace.

Dawn abruptly stops in the middle of the dance floor as the song changes.

"It's close to midnight
Something's evil lurking in the dark
Under the moonlight
You see a sight that almost stops your heart
You try to scream
But terror takes the sound before you
Make it

You start to freeze
As horror looks you right between the eyes
You're paralyzed
Cause this is Thriller
Thriller night" Michael Jackson's "Thriller" plays out of the surround speakers in the ceiling.

Monica grabs her thighs and oscillates in a circular motion following the instructor.

"Come on ladies…pump it up," Dawn yells says thrusting her thighs back and forth as the group does the same.
"Y'all feeling good ladies," she yells in the microphone.
"Yeaaah," they all yell in unison.
"I hope y'all don't mind…I was in a thriller mood when I woke up," the instructor says as the crowd rocks their hips with her. "This is our express class so get ready to work ladies," she says as the song remixes into Chalo Eduardo's "Beija Flor Suite." The music fills the room and the group follows the instructor as she shakes, twists and bends them in all sorts of ways.

The instructor begins to prep the class for cool down. "Give yourselves a nice round of applause and let's give our newcomer a mighty Aloha," she yells and the group belts out "Aloha."
They pat Monica on the back congratulating her as she grabs her bags and exit the studio.
"Have a good day," the host calls out as she exits the gym.

Monica finishes the rest of her Voss water and gets in the car. She pulls out her GPS and searches for a restaurant that serves Hawaiian and Brazilian food. It searches and inserts; **Niede Salsa and Samba Restaurant**, address into the system.

'Be there soon…hungry…hurry' she texts to her boyfriend with a smiley face attached to it. She rides the few blocks reaching Niede Salsa and Sambo restaurant. She puts the Hawaiian blue and lavender wrap around her body. Looking across the beach she eyes children playing soccer on the beach.

"Awwww," she says sympathetically as one of the children falls in the sand and begins to cry. She watches as he gets up and run across the beach to kick the ball again. "Awwww," she says again turning to enter the restaurant.

"E pau, e pedra, eo fim caminlto
E um resto de toco, e um pouco sizinte
E um caco de vidro e a vida e-o sol
E a moite e a morte e um laco e o anzul" Elis Regina's "Aquas De Marco" plays in the restaurant.

Monica is greeted by the host who escorts her to a table.
"Can I start you off with a drink?" she asks.
"What kind of wine do you have?" Monica asks picking up the drink list.
"Today's special is our wine from the Tedeschi Vineyard…we have Pineapple Wine and Passion Fruit. Personally; I prefer Passion fruit because it captures all the tropic flavors with a pineapple splash," the waitress recommends.

"Well Passion Fruit it is and I am ready to order; I will take the grilled steak special with Maui onions," she tells the waitress.
"What kind of side Ma'am?" she asks.
"I'll take a fresh garden salad," Monica tells her returning the menu and eyes her boyfriend walking in.
She waves her hand and he makes his way to the table. "Hey baby," she says as he leans over to kiss her. "What's in the bag?" she asks pointing to the bag.

"Well I was buying a few things and saw something that looked like you," he says pulling out a box of Be Delicious by Donna Karen and begins to read the label. 'Modern feast for the senses…served in a sleek metal glass apple bottle. This fragrance combines the scent of apple with a sophisticated blend of exotic flowers and sensual woods…like the city that inspired it…Be Delicious celebrates individuality with a refreshing spirit. It just sounded like you," he says passing her the box.

"Oh my God; this is my favorite perfume," she says reaching for the box.

"I also found something else that matched you," he says pulling out a black and gold Helzberg box.

She puts her hands over her mouth as he gets down on one knee.

"I really didn't know the right words to say but reading that bottle helped me to put a lot of things into perspective…your individuality is amazing. Your spirit is refreshing. When I first saw you the first thing I thought was …she's the one. As hard as I tried to fight that feeling everything just pointed to you. The way you go out of your way to help others is inspiring. Your drive is only one of the things that continuously motivate me. You make me want to Zumba amongst other things when I see you dance," he jokes with her reaching for her hand. "I love you…not because I can tell you; but because my heart shows it. I want you in my life forever…and after forever…forever again," he says placing the ring on her finger.

"Forever and ever," she replies crying and leaning over to kiss him.

Chapter Twenty-Five

"To Love oneself is the beginning of a Life-Long Romance"

"Myles"

"This is where it all began…I've been here for a long time and I've seen a lot of hardship and pain. I saw my first dead body when I was ten years old. I bought my first gun at thirteen. I never used it but I knew that I won't scared to bust it…some old heads let me hit my first blunt when I was walking to school," he says laughing. "I remember those days. I remember when those niggas from Northside tried to run up in George Wythe and try to fuck up one of my niggas. We beat the shit out of those niggas as soon as they walked in. I mean we mullywapped those niggas," he says continuing to laugh. "Yea…yea" he says as his voice trails off.

"I remember they killed my boy Mook…that fucked me up bad. I remember grabbing my gun and ready to kill every one of those niggas out there. But all I could think about was my mom who was always there for me but never there for me…you know…now looking back she was always there for me…but as a little nigga I didn't see that shit. I had my lil boy right here in Virginia. I used to have a lot of ups and downs and I didn't know how to deal with them. It was nothing for me to get a bottle of that Goose, a couple of Percs and just get crazy on these niggas.

Now; I look at my lil man and it just feels like there's going to be a brighter future. When he sees me it has to be like a mirror image reflection. It's like two men looking at each other. Then came the birth of my daughter and even though I have two different baby mama's I don't have any problems out of them. I mean…they know I'm a good man and a great father. Plus they know I'll kill them if they have my kids around another nigga. But I ain't got no child support on my head because I take care of my children. I'm going to court now to get full custody of my daughter.

That club right over there…Have a Nice Day. They used to have this mobile trailer that used to sit in the parking lot. I mean those white boys were doing crazy shit after the club in there. People would go in that mobile trailer and they would have that muthafucker rocking,' he says laughing and holding his hand over his mouth in fist. "I mean they would be playing that white boy music with the disco ball turning and the lights would be coming out the windows. The bitches would be doing everything in there. I mean some people didn't even go in the club. This park right here (referring to Jefferson Park) is where we used to bust our guns every New Year's Eve. Now that shit was wild. Niggas was drinking Steel Reserve's and getting it in. Niggas had like four bottles of that Goose and Henney…I had the forty cal…Mook had the chopper. Ta-Ta had the forty four and the thirty eight automatic. I remember last year when I had popped a couple of Vicodins. It was around eleven fifty nine and niggas just started letting loose. Ratta tat tat…blaka blaka blaka…boom boom boom…is all that you heard around that muthafucker. I mean we were letting those muthafuckers off for like…forever…but even then I was a smart nigga. I won't about to bust my last clip out that muthafucker…what the fuck I look like…empty all of our joints and then we fuck around and get robbed and ain't nobody got no shells," he says laughing and looking into the city.

"My dude asked me a long time ago if I could choose any place in the world where would I want to be. I told him Richmond V.A.. I traveled the whole world through with the military and seen a lot of shit but there is no place like home. This is the place that I learned to how to walk…how to drive a car. This is where I heard my first Jay-Z, Tupac, Outkast, Mad Skillz, Nas, Three Six Mafia. At that time Mobb Deep was on fire. I could never forget them. *'Ain't no thing as halfway crooks; scared to death and scared to look they shook'* Myles begins to rap in his best Prodigy voice.

"I could never forget them. I fell in love with music down here. This is home and I don't think there is no place in the world that I would rather be," he says sliding his hand over his mouth popping a Percocet and chasing it down with his Heineken.

She looks at him surprised that he's talking this much.

"I don't really talk like this but I feel like I'm on cloud nine right now...come on...let's get out of here," he tells her.

They finish walking through Jefferson Park silently looking at the lights that stretch out over the entire city. He presses the lock button and they get in his green Suburban. He raises the cup of Grey Goose to his lips and takes a drink.

"You want to do down to the Ville and see my hood?" he asks her.

"Hell no...not after you told me all that," she says jokingly but being quite serious.

"Well let's go get something to eat," he tells her.

"Cool," she replies as he turns down Hull Street turning up the music.

"You're like a mirror to my soul
but a queen
And finally now I know just what that means
You're like the blessing I never thought I would get
And to the Lord I humbly bow my head
Just remember that
No matter how far I go
And no matter how long it takes
No one and nothing can change

162

Forever yours here I stand" Usher's "Here I Stand" plays out of his speakers.

"What is your favorite color?" she asks him.

He sits back in his chair allowing the question to hover. "I actually have two favorite colors...blue and black...blue because it's the color of the sky. That's beautiful to me...it is serene and peaceful...when I walk outside it's the first thing I always look at...and black because it's the color of my people. I know the dictionary say so much negative things about the color but all I see is my people doing positive stuff," he says responding to her question.

"Ok...Ok...what about your favorite song?" she asks.

"And even as a crack fiend mama
You always was a black queen mama," he rattles off by Tupac.

"Shiiiit...Dear Mama is my shit all day; Dear Mama has got to be my favorite song.

"Now ain't nobody tell us it was fair
No love for my daddy cause the coward wasn't there
He passed away and I didn't cry
Cause my anger
Would let me feel for a stranger" he continues to rap "Dear Mama" by Tupac.

The waitress brings back their drinks and he orders the fish and shrimp combo while she orders a basket of onion rings.

"That song always brings tears to my eyes...I can remember putting my mother through so much stuff and even though we didn't see eye to eye she was a true blessing to me in my life…you sure that's all you want?" he asks.

"Yes; I ate before I got up with you but thank you anyway," she tells him.

"Okay…tell me one thing you love?" she asks him.

"Life…I enjoy life and everything that comes with it. Not knowing what the next level will bring makes me smile everyday. I think that the next level is looking good tho," he says reaching over and putting his hand on top of hers. "It's one of the reasons why I had to see you so bad tonight. I think that you are the next level. You complete me in every way…I mean ways that you don't even know. I know that my kids are my kids but you take care of them like they are yours as well…I love the way my daughter lights up when she sees you walk in a room…this is the first time I ever put my feelings on the table like this. I am confident in all that I do because I like to analyze a thousand times over…but with you I don't need to analyze things at all…it's a no brainer. I know I'm making the right decision because God told me that I was. I prayed every night for the last few months and now I know that I'm making the right decision. I want you to be my partner…not only my wife…but my spiritual partner as well," he says reaching in his coat pulling out a Kay's jewelry box.

"It's not much but it's not the ring that I'm giving you but rather my soul," he says leaning over to kiss her.

"Congratulations," the couple sitting next to them says.

Chapter Twenty-Six

"Have enough Courage to trust Love one more time
and always one more time"

"Najai"

"I'm easily rippin'
Defensively grippin'
My pistol you niggaz play tough
But don't want it
I'm poppin' and cocking and locking the game down
Two zones for da free
So I'm off of da chain
Double o see murder murder I'm urgess
Then kick in yo door wit da muthafuckin pistol
I'm coming to get you
We bustin with no issue
White walls on the rental
Same color as tissue
No kissing me missing me
Yo funeral
Dissing me
Daz a mistake so better not try it
I'm starting a riot too fly like a pilot" Souljah Boy's "What you Know" blares out the speakers in Najai's hotel room.

"You bout ready nigga?" Najai's cousin asks walking in the room passing him a blunt.

"I'm bout to be in five minutes," Najai respondes hitting the blunt and putting on his black Artful Dodger jeans.

"Them shits is hot," his cousin tells him looking at the white label imprinted on the back of Najai's jeans.

"Look at the shit," Najai says lifting up his FU shirt with a logo of a middle finger encrusted in diamonds.

"Fuck the world type shit. Hold on...I'm just about ready nigga," he says passing him back the blunt and pulling out his Indian Musk oil. He rubs it in his hands and wipes his clothes down. He picks up his half eaten cup of applesauce and finishes it off.

"Nigga you gon' turn into applesauce," his cousin jokes while picking up the book bag and slinging it on his back.

"I'm ready," Najai says putting on his Adidas and checking himself out in the mirror.

"Get yo' keys in case we get separated," his cousin says walking out the door.

"Yo...I can't believe that junkie rented a Yukon Denali for you," Najai exclaims.

"Well a forty of that white goes a long way...let's roll nigga," his cousin responds shaking a small bag of cocaine in front of Najai.

"When I holla ay bay bay
I finna get my groove on
It's so hot up in da club
Dat I ain't got no shoes on
I'm holding up a big stack and dem
Girl don't ask me for no cash
Cause I'm not dat other man
Everybody trippin' cause I'm limping'
When I'm walkin' and I'm pimpin' when I'm talking" Hurricane Chris's "A Bay Bay" plays through the speakers. Najai leans the seat back and take the blunt that his cousin is passing.

"Nigga its gon' be some bitches out here," his cousin says turning down the strip.

"Damn shawty," Najai says to the girls beside them in dead stop traffic.

"What y'all smoking?' one of the females asks Najai.

"Why? You want to hit it," he asks her.

"Hell yea," she responds stepping out of her car and walking to their vehicle.

"Damn you fine as fuck," Najai compliments her as she takes the blunt out of his hand taking a hit. The cars behind them start blowing the horn signaling that the traffic is moving.

"Wait the fuck up!" Najai yells out the vehicle to the cars behind them.

"I hope I see y'all around," she says passing the blunt back and getting in her car.

"Show me something," Najai's cousin yells out. She lifts up her bikini top showing off her breast.

"Get the camera," Najai says tapping his cousin on the leg as she pulls off.

"Nigga; we just need to keep the camera on," his cousin responds following traffic.

"Where my hat at?" Najai says reaching in the backseat for his fitted V.A. hat. He opens the visor and bends the hat around his head.

"Hit em up, Peace up A-Town down
Hit em up, Peace up A-Town down
Hit em up, Peace up A-Town down
If you ain't from round here dog
Don't even come around
Twist ya fingers up, bang muthafucker bang
Throw yo hoods up, bang muthafucker bang
Eastside hit em up bang muthafucker bang
Southside hit em up bang muthafucker bang

Do yo thug thang gon get em up
Represent ya side nigga hit em up

167

Disrespect we gon take it there
We thirty deep lil nigga
We ain't fighting fair' Young Jeezy's "Bang" plays out of the system as they drive on the sand following the other cars.

"Look at that shit," Najai says pointing to the hotel filled up with people drinking and dancing on the balconies.

"Penn State Lehigh Valley," Najai reads the banner hanging off the rail.

"Nigga look at all those drunk bitches," his cousine says pointing at the group of white females showing off their breast as guys throw beads at them.

"We should have bought some beads," Najai says.

"Nigga...we got something better than beads," his cousin says reaching in the backseat pulling out a bottle of Bacardi 151 and an ounce of weed. "And if that ain't enough we still got that white girl," his cousin says grinning and pulling out a small bag of cocaine. "These our beads right here," he says they both laugh and park the truck.

Hold up wait one muthafuckin minute
It's the el capatain
I got muthafuckin lieutenants
If I said I'm going in then I mutherfucking meant it
And if I bought it to the club
Them I'mma muthafuckin spend it
Toss a few hundred bands and I'm muthafuckin in it
No need for a room
Yeah you know I'm fuckin in it" Lil Wayne's "I'm going In" plays from the car beside them.

Najai's cousin reaches in the backseat and pulls out two cups filling them both up with Bacardi 151. Najai gets out, steps on the tire and lifts himself on the hood of the truck.

"What you doing nigga?" Najai yells out to his cousin.

"I'm trying to roll up real quick," his cousin replies turning up the music.

"I fucked my money up
Now I can't re-up
Ran off in his spot just to get my stacks back
Now I'm back on deck
So shawty what the fuck you want
Heard he talking shit
But this ain't what the fuck he want" Wocka Flocka Flame's "O Lets Do It" remix begins to play. His cousin gets out the truck and jumps on the hood.

"Hold on…don't light that shit yet…them boys right there," Najai says jumping off the truck to turn down the music

"How y'all fellas doing tonight; I'm going to ask you two this question one time and I hope you're honest with me. How old are you and what are you drinking?" the officer asks.

"We 16 and its liquor sir," Najai's cousin tells the officers.

"I'm going to tell you two to pour it out and if I see y'all drinking again I'm going to lock the both of you two up and impound the vehicle," the officer tells them.

"Yes Sir," they both respond pouring their drinks out in the sand as the police walk away.

"Damn…you told them the truth," Najai says.

"Fuck yeah! If I had lied to them then they would have checked the truck. Fuck that. I ain't catching no felony charge at Daytona Spring Break. The Mexicans crazy as shit in that muthafucka," his cousin says as they both jump off the truck, get in and relocates at another section.

"Look at that shit," Najai says pointing to a lime green Eldorado with a yellow rooftop displaying Mike and Ike's candy symbol printed on the door.

"That shit is fire," his cousin says getting out of the truck.

"Look at them bitches," his cousin says pointing at three females dancing with each other.

"My chain too silly
My wrist too silly
The girls throw me dish cuz my rims big willy
My ride too silly
I ride too silly
We for fantastic
cuz I got a deally
Cuz now I'm worth a milly
Forget a rubber band
Cause you can't put a
Rubber band around a billy" V.I.C.'s "Get Silly" plays out of their car. Najai begins to dance to the music. One of the girls walk to him, bends over and begin shaking her ass on him.

His cousin passes Najai another cup of Bacardi 151.

"Get silly nigga," his cousin says as Najai grabs the female and starts grinding on her.

"Come on…let's sit in the truck," Najai says opening door. She gets in and he begins to kiss on her neck.

"I don't even know you like that," she says as he puts his hand on her breast and she leans back. He rubs his hands down her stomach and begins to unbutton her pants.

"Damn," she whispers as he shoves his hand between her panties rubbing back and forth on her pussy. He hears his cousin turn up the music.

"Soulja Boy up in dis hoe
Watch me lean watch me rock
Superman that hoe
Then watch me crank that Robocop
Super fresh, now watch me jock

Jockin' on them haters man
When I do that soulja boy
I lean to the left and crank that thang
I'm jocking on that bitch ass
And if we get to fightin
Then I'm cockin on your bitch ass" Souljh Boy's "Crank That" blares out the vehicle. Najai begins to pull her pants down.

"I can't. I want to but I really can't. Plus we're outside and my friends are right there. But if you call me later we can get it in," she says writing her number down and pulling her pants up before walking away. Najai walks to the front of the truck.

"Did you smash?" his cousin asks.

"Hell no…that bitch was trippin' but I did get her digits," he tells his cousin showing the telephone number.

"What about that girl you was telling me that you were going to marry?" his cousin jokes with Najai.

"Shiiiit…I'm still gon' marry her…right after I hit this bitch," Najai says laughing as they toss their drinks back.

Chapter Twenty-Seven

"The greatest happiness of life is the conviction that we are loved -- loved for ourselves, or rather, loved in spite of ourselves"

"Neverett"

Neverett sits back in his recliner chair listening to music and flipping through the television channels. He sits up abruptly knocking the remote on the floor. He picks it up and turns down the radio while turning up the television.

"This is Channel Eight News reporting on the demolition of the Eggleston Hotel. The Eggleston Hotel was one of the only three hotels in the 60's that permitted black guests. Neverett A. Eggleston Sr. opened the Eggleston Hotel in the late 1930's as well as Neverett's place which dined guests such as Count Basie, Louis Armstrong, Redd Foxx, Moms Mabley, Joe Louis, Jackie Robinson, Willie Mays, Satchel Paige and many more," the reporter reports.

Neverett gets up, walks to the bar and pours himself a scotch glass of Peach Schnapps mixing it with Iced Tea.

'But they forgot that we housed Malcolm X and Martin Luther King Jr.,' he says to himself. He sits down, changes the music on his radio and turn down the television before leaning his recliner back.

"People get ready
There's a train a-coming
You don't need no baggage
You just get on board
All you need is faith
To hear the diesel's hummin'
You don't need no ticket
You just thank the Lord" Curtis Mayfield and The Impressions "People Get Ready" begins to play as he reclines and reminisces.

"What's up Daddy-O," Neverett says snapping his fingers and pointing to his friend.

"Cool as ice Red, Cool as ice. Just listening to this heavy stuff going down," his friend responds turning up the radio as the correspondent reports on Bruce Boynton; a Howard law student arrested by the police for eating in the white section of the restaurant.

"Well what's the big deal about that?" Neverett asks his friend.

"Well this cat is trying to fight the conviction claiming the interstate commerce act or something like that," his friend responds.

"Shiiiit...the only thing that nigga should have done was slid over one seat...you feel me blood," Neverett says laughing and giving his friend a high five. "Nawww...but you know I wish him the best. How's business going today?" Neverett asks.

"Besides your old man working me to death; business is booming," his friend replies. Neverett grabs his apron and walks behind the stand looking at the expense book.

"Don't worry. My dad is paying you enough slick. You always trying to get another dollar," Neverett says jokingly.

"Well you know what they say...green is the only color that matter to these white folks," his friend says. "Hey Slick; have you heard this?" his friend asks turning up the music.

"Oh…things ain't what they used to be
No, no
Where did all the blue sky go?
Poison is the wind that blows
From the North, East, South and Sea
Oh mercy mercy me
Oh things ain't what they used to db
No, no
Oil wasted on the oceans
And upon our seas
Fish full of mercury
Oh mercy mercy me
Oh things ain't what they used to be" Marvin Gaye's "Mercy Mercy Me" begins to play.

"This that new groove by Marvin Gaye. Now that is one smooth brother right there," his friend says. A car pulls up and three people get out and enter the restaurant.

"Hello fine people; Welcome to Neverett's place. A table for three?" Neverett asks them.

"Yes Sir. We also heard that one of your establishments' house black people?" the gentleman asks while Neverett shows them to their table.

"Yes Sir. The Eggleston Hotel right over there. There is also Brown's and Slaughter's hotel but we are the best in town," Neverett gleams placing the menus in front of them.

I know y'all ain't from 'round here, so where y'all from?" Neverett asks the young man.

"I am Martin King and these are students traveling with me from the student non-violent coordinating committee. This is Horace Bond and Connie Curry. We are traveling to Montgomery Alabama to assist in the Rosa Parks case," Martin answers.

"Well have you heard of the Bruce Boynton case that's going on in D.C.?" Neverett asks.

"As a matter of fact we have heard about it. We've been reading up on it and have written it down to be investigated,' Martin replies.

"Well; y'all look over the menu and I'll be right back," Neverett says walking away to take another customer's order.

"Red...Red...do you know who that is?" his friend asks calling Neverett over.

"Turn that up Slick...who is that?" Neverett asks.

"I was born by the river
In a little tent
Oooh and just like the river
I've been running every since
It's been a long
A long time coming
But I know
A change gon' come
Oh yes it will" Sam Cooke's "A Change Gonna Come" begins to play.

"That's Martin Luther King Jr. in your place. That young blood is the truth right now," he says excitedly.

"As long as his money is green...I don't care who he is," Neverett says jokingly. "Turn that radio up a little louder," Neverett says walking away to cook.

"I feel you man...I feel you," his friend responds.

Neverett feels someone rubbing his head jolting him out of his daydream.

"Awww baby...I see you made yourself a drink and I hear Misty Blue playing. Is everything okay?" his wife asks while rubbing their poodle Mocca's head. Neverett pulls the recliner down and sits up.

"I was watching this segment on my father's hotel about when the building fell. It felt like a legacy had ended. That hotel was a part of history. It was more than a hotel, but it was actually history. The one thing that I've learned is that life is full of challenges. To be able to able to mature; you must face those challenges head on. I know I've failed at many things but I've lived…I've lived. I don't regret one minute of my life. I've lived a good life and bought some of that history to the Croaker Spot and Richmond, Va. That place has so much history and the greatest gift I could give my son is that piece of history. As he takes over operations he will bring history to this great city. I am so proud of him and by the grace of God I know he will do his best. He will make me proud just as I know I have made my father proud," he says sleepily dozing off.

"You're a good man Mr. Eggleston…a good man," she says softly while leaning over to kiss him on the forehead.

Chapter Twenty-Eight

"Limitless undying love; which shines around me like a million suns, calls me on and on across the universe"

"Patricia"

"I wish I knew the stations down here," he says hitting the search button on the radio.

"I keep seeing pictures now of me and her
And those summer nights
My mind fills with her
Oh but it's alright cause I laugh everytime
I start to think about us' Tim Mcgraw's "For a Little While" begins to play out the speakers.

"Now I know we not about to listen to no country," Patricia says.

"Naw baby chill. I hit the search button so I can find the stations around here," he tells her. The radio station switches to 101.9.

"Stop it there…that's my song," she tells him as he turns the radio up.

"I tried to be perfect
But nothing was worth it
I don't believe it makes me real
I thought it be easy

177

But no one…" the radio station shuffles again.

"Go back," she tells him.

"Hold on baby. Let me take the search off," he says switching back to 101.9.

"I'd say all the words that I know
Just to see if it would show
That I'm trying to let you know
That I'm better off on my own" she begins to sing along with Sum 41's "Pieces".

Patricia turns the volume up louder and grabs her food container that she bought from Whole Foods taking out the plastic container.

"Let me try one of those Limpia's" he asks her.

"Lumpia…Lumpia…L-U-M-P-I-A," she spells out to him laughing.

"Whatever, just let me try one," he says as she dips the Lumpia in Soy Sauce and passes it to him on a napkin. He takes a bite.

"Mmmm…not bad," he says reaching over to dip it again.

"I told you that you were going to like it," she says taking bite and turning the radio down. The chime sounds on her phone letting her know that she has a text message. *'Hey…how's the trip going?'* She closes her phone and slides it back in the armrest.

"Who was that?' he asks.

"Just somebody from work. I don't like talking to them when I'm not at work," she tells him. "Oh my God…that's Blink 182. What station is this again?" she asks turning up the radio.

"101.5 or 101.9," he replies looking at the radio station. "101.9," he confirms.

"Late night

Come home
Work sucks
I know
She left me roses by the stairs
Surprises let me know she care
Say it ain't so
I will not go
Turn the lights off
Carry me home" Patricia sings the lyrics to Blink 182's "All the Small Things".

"I like the song but why are they naked in over half of the video…and then one of them starts licking the telescope. They have to be the gayest groups ever," he says.

"Shut the hell up. It's a great song and video. They just having fun," she replies jokingly with him. He turns the radio down and pulls into the parking lot of the National Great Blacks Wax Museum downtown Baltimore Maryland. She dips the last of the Lumpia in the Soy Sauce and holds it out giving him the last bite. They park and Patricia eyes a white woman walking her Pug Nose dog on a leash.

"Awww…look at the wittle doggie," she says as the dog sniffs at the ground and run off.

"Come on girl," he says opening the door to the building allowing her to walk through first.

"Welcome to the National Black Was Museum. We are showing a short informative documentary of the Museum in that room behind you. We also offer headsets that provide you with a verbal tour of the exhibits as you walk around. Would you two like a pair," the man offers holding out a pair of headsets.

"No thank you. I think she can tell me damn near everything in your exhibits," he says slapping her in the arm playfully. She picks up a pamphlet and walks off laughing. They walk into a room and eye a wax figure of Sojourner Truth. Patricia walks over and begins to read the inscription on the wall.

179

He begins to read the quote on the back of Patricia's shirt. *I did not run off, for I thought that wicked, but I walked off, believing that to be right'*. He closely observes the wax figure.

"Hold on…turn around," he tells her as she turns around. "Now I get it. I was wondering who that was on your shirt. Isabella Baumfree…that's Sojourner Truth right?" he asks.

"Yes…didn't you know?" she asks back.

""Well; I see it says 'Ain't I a Woman' but I always thought Sojourner Truth was her real name. I didn't know it was Isabella Baumfree," he explains.

"That's because you don't read," she says joking with him.

"Oh forrrealll…is that how you gon' play me?" he asks.

"I'm just saying," she responds as a matter-of-factly. They walk in another exhibit and he walks toward the figure of Imhotep and begins to read out-loud, *'Imhotep…one who comes in peace. Served as Chancellor to the Pharaoh and High Priest of Sun God-Ra. His aliases were Chancellor of the King of Egypt, Administrator of the Great Palace, hereditary nobleman, builder, sculptor, and maker of vases,"* he reads out loud.

"Does it say that he was raised to the status of a God two thousand years after his death?" she asks him.

"You know…I always wonder how you be remembering some of this stuff," he says quizzically.

"Because I listened in school," she responds.

"You got an answer for everything huh," he says.

"I like to think so," Patricia says sarcastically walking off.

"Hey look baby…remember in the movie when Chaka Zulu was running through the desert barefoot," he says pointing to a wax sculptor of Chaka Zulu.

"Your feet look like you been running barefoot your whole life," she replies jokingly.

"Shut the hell up…I know you ain't talking with your crusty feet," he jokes back with her.

"My feet ain't crusty and if they are at least I keep them covered up," she says smartly.

"Whatever…let me take a picture of you in front of the statute," he says. She walks to the statute and puts her hand on the exhibit displaying Chaka Zulu in his loins, African beads, spear and shield. He takes the picture.

"Damnnn…y'all look like twins," he says jokingly.

"HA-HA," she responds as they walk into another exhibit displaying a wax Henry Box Brown crawling out the crate. *'Top of the day'* she thinks to herself and laugh at the thought of those being the first words Henry Box Brown said when the top of the crate was lifted and the postmen surprisingly looked at him.

"Let me ask you something…why do you always walk around with your head down?" he questions.

"I really don't know. People always ask me that but I guess that's the way I walk," she replies.

"Well; I think you are a very smart and intelligent woman. People can be so judgmental and instantly think that you have low self esteem. I just think that you're always thinking. But I like to see your eyes. It really shows how deep a person you really are. You know your facts about history…black history…and you're comfortable enough with yourself that you listen to Blink 182. I think that's beautiful. You are truly unique in every way. Just your thoughts are on a different level. You are a very intriguing woman and every time I think I have you figured out here comes something new. I love that about you…Will you marry me?" he asks. He places his fingers under her chin raising eyes to match his eyes. "Will you," he says.

"Will I what?' she says meekly.

"Will you marry me?" he asks again.

"Yes," Patricia says with her eyes faltering slightly. She refocuses her eyes to lock with his. "Yes I will marry you," she assures her answer.

Chapter Twenty-Nine

*"Love and compassion are necessities, not luxuries.
Without them, humanity cannot survive"*

"Ronald 1"

"Hey look at that," Ronald says pointing at the two door brown and gold Cadillac with 14 inch Dayton rims.

"Oooohh," he says as the Cadillac goes on two wheels on its hydraulics.

"That shit is hot," Ronald tells his girlfriend. Someone passes them a flyer of the Puerto Rican day parade after party at Pranna's featuring Fat Joe, Enuff, Camilo, C-Lo, Big Ben, Precise, Cipha Sounds, L Boogs, Kast One, Monse, Laura Stylez and many more.

"Damn I wish I could go to that; I can't wait to turn eighteen," Ronald tells his girlfriend looking over the flyer.

"There's Giannini Braschi," they hear someone behind them say as they point to a woman on the float speaking into the microphone...

"I have been a fortune teller. Ages ago I told the small fortune on buffoons and madmen. You remember? I had a small voice like a grain of sand and enormous hands. Madmen walked over my hand. I told them the truth. I could never lie to them and now I am sorry. I have just turned life into a Proverb. I just killed it. On the top floor of the Empire State building a shepherd has stood up to sing and dance. What a wonderful thing. That New York has been invaded by so many shepherds. That work has stopped and there is only singing and dancing and that the newspaper, the New York Times Dispatch, in headlines, and in

the daily news call out New York-New York-New York-New York...listen to it. The buffoons have died and the little lead soldier. Shepherds have invaded New York. They have conquered New York. They have colonized New York. THEY HAVE COLONIZED NEW YORK. The special of the day..." her voice trails off as the float continues to pass.

"That poem is called Empire of Dreams," the person behind them says. Ronald's girlfriend puts her hands in his and they walk through the crowded streets.

"Ooooo that is sooo cute," she says pointing at the Little Miss Puerto Rico float riding past with Yaritza Amaya waving a Puerto Rico banner.

"Look...there's J-Lo and Marc Anthony," Ronald exclaims pointing as they wave to the crowd. Ronald stops behind a group of Spanish females wearing red shorts, white shirts with Puerto Rico airbrushed on the front, and red and white sneakers.

"I knew you would stop and look at those females," she says laughing.

"Look...Daddy Yankee," he says.

"Esa noche contigo la pase bien
Pero you me entere que te debes a alguien
Y tu fallaste Pero Ya es tarde" Daddy Yankee's "Lo Que Paso Paso" plays as she begins to shake her shoulders back and forth allowing her breast to shake.

"Brrrr...get it mami, get it mami," Ronald yells out.

"Puerto Ricooooooo!" Daddy Yankee yells out.

"Hooooo!" the crowd yells back. Puff Daddy stands on the other side of the float waving a Puerto Rican flag.

"Look...that's um...um...that rapper...what's his name," Ronald says snapping his fingers.

"Fabolous," she yells so loud that Fabolous turns around and flashes them the peace sign continuing to walk through the crowd.

"I'm hungry as hell. Let's get something to eat," he says grabbing her hand and walking toward the Puerto Rican family sitting in red, white and blue lawn chairs.

"What do you want to eat?" Ronald asks looking over the menu.

"You order…I'll just get whatever you get," she responds.

"Let me get two Empanadas and Arroz Con Pollo's," he tells the woman.

She reaches in her heater bag and packs two paper plates covering them with aluminum foil.

"Let me also get two cokes," he tells her. He pays and they walk towards the chain fence to eat.

"It's Mr. 305 checking in for the remix
You know that S75 Street Brazil
Well this year's gon' be called Calle Ocho
Ha-ha
Que ola cata, Que ola omega
And this how we gon' do it
One two three four
Uno dos tres cuatro
I know you want me
I know you want me
You know I wantcha," Pitbull raps "I Know You want Me" off the float riding past.

"What time do we have to meet up with your mom?" she asks.

"I think she said around eleven since we leaving early tomorrow," Ronald replies. They finish eating and throw their trash away. They walk through the crowded streets weaving in and out of the people walking past them. They stop, lean against the wall and he pulls out a bag of his magic mushrooms.

"Finally we can take one," she says as he pulls two mushrooms out the bag and passes one to her. They eat the mushrooms and chase it down with their Coca Cola's. They lean against the wall holding hands.

"Look at all the flag colors blending together," he says feeling the effects of the mushrooms.

"Yea that's cool," she replies.

"To all of my Boriquas in the crowd," someone yells out from a float riding past.

"Who is that?" she asks.

"I know that voice," he responds standing up and looking over the crowd.

"This is a day of celebration…so we need to celebrate right…Play that shit D.J.," Fat Joe yells out.

"I don't wanna be a player no more
I'm not a playa I just fuck a lot
But Big Punisher still got what you're looking for
For my thug niggas, for my thug niggas

I don't wanna be a playa no more
I'm not a playa I just fuck a lot
But you know Big Punisher still down by law
Who's down to crush a lot" Big Pun's "I'm still not a Playa" plays from a float passing by.

"If you down to crush tonight say Puerto Rico," Fat Joe yells out.

"Puerto Ricooooo!!!" Ronald yells out with the crowd.

"Hooooo," Fat Joe yells back.

"He gon' be at Pranna's tonight. Damn I want to go bad as shit. Next year we gon' hit it up. Look, there's Ricky Martin," she says pointing to Ricky Martin standing on the *Ricky Martin*

Foundation float. The background of his float is an American flag in gold with the image of an apple in the middle of the traditional red, blue and white colors.

"Who is that?" she asks pointing to a float riding past with Mayor Michael Bloomberg and former Mayor Rudy Giuliani.

"I don't know who they are," she says as they ride past waving. "Isn't that your group right there?" she asks pointing towards the Nu-Life float riding past.

"13 de diciembo del ano 80 a las 3:24
Nacio un nino mucho orgullo
Despues de tanto tiempo
Al fin sonrie de emocion
Lloraba inquietamente
La enfereman pregunta cual es la razon
Pues el padre con solo 6 meses de aquel
Embarazo los abandono
No dejo ni motives ni hueelas ura
Manamita se fue y no volvio
Y la madre no olvida ese dia que
Aquel hombre
Ingrate le fallo" Aventura's "Amore De Madre" plays as Ronald begins to dance with his girl to the music.

"Get it Papi," she says as he twirls her around puller her closer to him.

"Mami…forever me and you. We will marry and travel the world partying everywhere we go," he says.

"You're not Puerto Rican," she responds jokingly.

"Well you know what they say…today everyone Puerto Rican," Ronald says doing the salsa.

"Then yes Papi…forever me and you…and we will see the world as husband and wife," she says crossing her arms to meet his.

Chapter Thirty

*"Love is the strongest force the world possesses
and yet it is the humblest imaginable"*

"Ronald 2"

Ronald focuses his camera on the flag hanging off the flag pole. *'Non Ducor Duc'* he reads to himself.

"What does that mean?" his girlfriend asks.

"If I'm not mistaken it means 'I am not led. I lead.' You know that the nickname for this place is called Terra da Garoa which means Land of Drizzle," he tells her.

"Well ain't that the truth," she says closing her umbrella.

"Awww baby…this is the best weather right here," Ronald says opening the door to the Brazilian Pavilhao Ciccillo Matarazzo Art Museum. He wipes his shoes dry and shakes the rain off of her umbrella placing it in its plastic case.

"Welcome to Sao Paulo Art Biennial. I am Moacior dos Anjos and this is Agnaldo Farias," Moacior says shaking both of their hands. "Today's exhibit is inspired by Jorge De Lima titled 'Ha Sempre Um Copo De Mar Para Um Homende Navegar' or in English 'There is always a cup of sea to sail on ever without ships, even without waves and waves'. We welcome you both to our exhibits and hope you enjoy," he says releasing Ronald's hand.

"Thank you. Can I get a picture with the two of you," Ronald asks passing his girlfriend the camera and standing between them.

187

"Say I love art," she tells them.

"I love art," they reply in unison. Ronald shakes hands with both men again and step on the moving sidewalk ascending to the second floor.

"Ooo baby baby
Ooo baby
Mistakes I know I've made a few
But I'm only human
You've made mistakes too," he begins to sing "Ooo Baby Baby" by Smokie Robinson and the Miracles.

"Come here babe," he says leaning over for a kiss.

"What's that for?" she asks.

"Baby, Baby," he says turning back around looking over the balcony. "Let's walk through the second floor," he says grabbing her hand.

"You will not be led huh?" she replies sarcastically pulling her hand back and continuing to ride to the third floor.

'Funny babe,' he says stepping back on the beltway. He walks quickly behind her as she playfully power-walks. "Ohhhhh you gon' be funny huh? Don't forget that we in a museum," he says quickening his pace.

"I know where we at," she says stepping off the beltway onto the third floor.

"Woooow look at this," she says entering the exhibit of Gil Vincente. "Damn…this exhibit could never be in the states," she says pointing to a portrait of the assassination of George Bush.

"Look at this one…this is nice…different but nice," Ronald says pointing to a portrait of the assassination of Luiz Inacio Lila Da Silva. He steps back to take a picture.

"Sir; no flashes are allowed in the exhibit," the guard says pointing towards the sign on the wall.

"Ooops sorry," Ronald says flipping the flash off and taking the picture. "I'm getting hungry," he says as they continue to walk.

"I'm hungry too. We can always come back and see the other two floors," she says with reservation.

"Cool babe. Let's get out of here," he says slipping his hand into hers as they walk towards the beltway. Os Mutante's "Le Premier Bonheur Du Jour" plays through the museum.

"This music is kind of cool...kind of relaxing," she says snapping a picture as they descend from the beltway. Ronald grabs her around the waist and does a slow two step with her.

"You don't even know how to dance to this music," she says.

"Yeah...but you know the idea...fake it 'til you make it. New York State of mind," he replies laughing.

"Well you definitely faking it," she says as he stops dancing, laughs and wraps her in his arms. "I'm glad the rain has stopped," she says as they walk out and hail down a taxi.

"Hello Sir; where is a good place to eat and shop?" he asks the cab driver as they get in.

"I know the perfect place ...Oscar Freire Street," the cab driver responds in broken English.

"What is a good place to eat at on that street?" Ronald asks.

"Eh...Antiquarius. It is a Mediterranean Portuguese restaurant. That is the traditional place to eat at here. They are famous for their codfish," the cab driver tells them.

"Well I'm in the mood for some chicken," Ronald says.

"Si...you should the spicy chicken. It is delicious," replies the cab driver.

"Well Antiquarius it is," Ronald agrees with the cab driver leaning back in his seat. The cab driver turns up the music. Stan Getz and Joan Gilberto's "The Girl from Ipanema" plays through the cab. Ronald's girlfriend begins to hum to herself.

"Next time you visit; the Tower of Peace will be structured. It is said to cover the entire Pari neighborhood. It has its own power source, will have a rotating restaurant and it rumored to be the world's tallest building. We have proven ourselves to be one of the largest and most important financial countries in Latin America," the cab driver replies proudly.

"You are very proud of your country, Si," Ronald says.

"Si Senor. Shouldn't we all be," the cab driver responds.

"Si…and we definitely are," Ronald says as the cab stops in front of Antiquarius restaurant. Ronald pays the driver and they walk into the restaurant. He sees an elderly woman struggling with her bags.

"Hold on babe," Ronald says and walks over to assist the elderly woman to her table.

"Thank you Senor, God will bless you," she replies.

"He already has; Thank you Ma'am," Ronald says returning to his seat.

"That was nice. I see your taste. You like them a little older I see," she says jokingly.

"Yeah…she would probably pay for my meal," he says laughing and looking over the menu. "I wonder if they have Budweiser's," he says to himself.

"Honey; we're in Brazil. Try something new," she tells him as he picks up the drink list.

"May I help you Senor?" the waiter asks.

"Let me get a cold chopp…that is draft beer correct?" Ronald asks.

"Si Senor and it is pronounced 'Shopp'e," the waiter responds pronouncing the word out.

"Well I'll take that and your spicy chicken," Ronald says.

"And you Ma'am?" the waiter asks turning to her.

"I'll take your Casa Valduga and Codfish A Lagereira," she tells him.

"Very good…very exquisite choice," the waiter says picking up their menus. Ronald starts dancing in his seat to

Marjorie Gil's "Chiclete Com Banana" playing over the restaurant speakers.

"This got a real nice beat," he tells her.

"It's real Caribbean like…excuse me while I find a ladies room," she says excusing herself from the table. He looks around at the middle age and older couples in love at the tables around him. *'This has been more than a perfect day'* he thinks to himself still dancing slightly.

"Sir…Sir," Ronald beckons the waiter over.

"Carlos Pericos; I am the owner. How may I assist you Senor?" the owner asks.

"I want to make this day special…a day to remember. Could you accommodate me? I would like to sing to my lady friend" Ronald asks.

"Si Senor; I know exactly what you mean. Congratulations! I will make it very special Si," he responds.

"Si," Ronald answers as Carlos walks away quickly.

"I saw you talking to him…what's up?" she asks.

"Senor and Senorita…we have a very special couple in the house tonight. If I could possibly interrupt your meals for just a moment I would greatly appreciate it," Carlos tells the patrons in the restaurant as they stop eating and look. "Senor…the restaurant is yours," he says nodding to Ronald.

"Babe…I always wanted to do this," he says standing up. "Thank you for your cooperation and I hope my singing is not too terrible," Ronald tells the patrons.

"What are you doing?" she whispers to him.

"My woman is worried that I will embarrass her and I probably will but here goes nothing.

"You and me girl
Go a long way back
And I'm so proud
I'm so proud

191

You and me girl
Go a long way back
Yeah, we go a long way back

I remember when loving you wasn't easy
It wasn't easy, baby" he begins to sing Bloodstone's "We Go a Long Way Back".

"But I stuck on in there with you and we made it through it all. Baby this moment to me just seems like the right time…the right place…the right lady. We go a long, long way back. I mean since High School and you have stuck by my side the entire time. I know it wasn't easy but you stuck on in there with me and we made it. I can't begin to tell you how much character you have worthy of my praise. I could possibly tell you in words how I feel about you…you already know. You know my heart and it has not always been easy but we made it through it all. I'm asking more than a hand in marriage but I want the whole kit and caboodle," he says laughing. "But I'm ready if you are," he says leaning on the table and bending halfway to the floor. "I can't go all the way down because of my knees but I will go as low as my body will allow me," he says laughing and taking her hand in his. "What about it babe…you and me?" he asks.

"Baby…it's always been you and me. Of course…yes…yes…of course baby…yes!" she says standing up to hug him as the patrons' clap.

"Thank goodness…anymore time down there and I would have been stuck," he whispers in her ear.

"I know baby…I know," she says as a tear rolls off her face onto his collar.

Chapter Thirty-One

"If you enter this world knowing you are Loved and you leave this world knowing the same, then everything that happens in-between can be dealt with"

"Rueben"

Rueben lights his Cuban cigar as he drives around downtown Chicago in his black Mercedes Benz. He allows the smoke to linger before lowering his windows down halfway. He turns the radio up.

"My money, money, money
My bitch is my money
Ooo money my honey
Money is my bitch
Ooh money, money, money
Love her cause she keep a nigga rich
Ohhh money you my honey,
But I think you got me pussy whipped
My money, money, money
My bitch is my money" Nas's "Money is my Bitch" plays through his speakers.

Rueben raises his glass of Grand Marnier to his lips and lean his head back on his Celtics headrest. He rides past the Chicago United Center and glares at the famous Michael Jordan statue. His car slides when he hits the brakes from the light snow that has began. He touches the defrost button and cruise to the Congress Plaza Hotel. He pulls in front and throws his keys to Valet. This is the only hotel he likes to stay at when he comes to the city. He loves walking into the Congress Plaza with their high vaulted ceilings and plush red couches. He makes his way to the bar and chooses a table that sits in the corner of the restaurant. He watches the Bulls versus Celtics game and claps as Rajon Rondo and Kirk Hinrich get in each other's face.

"Sir," is all he hears from the waitress. He looks her up and down noticing that her top button is unbuttoned showing cleavage.

"Double shot of Grand Marnier on the rocks and a Heineken," Rueben orders in his baritone Haitian voice. She walks away and he looks at her ass swinging side to side. He calls his girlfriend on the phone and tells her to meet him in the lobby. He quickly checks his outfit over…brown slacks and a button down shirt with suspenders.

"Do you serve red beans and rice?" he asks the waitress.

"Yes baby," the waitress responds handing him a menu. He feels her eyes on him and smiles. She walks away trying to maintain her composure.

"You still think you smooth huh?" he hears turning around and seeing his girlfriend standing there with a smirk on her face.

"Naw babe…it ain't even like that," he says laughing as he stands to give her a hug.

"You can catch me in the cherry red one fifty
Got the grizzy locked in the stizzy
Pop the clizzy going sixty down a one wizzy
Drunk pissy, trying to cruise through the avenue
While my people's is poppin bottles up in Sue's rendezvous
Fuck that spun the u-ey lost a hubcap
It's back to the shack" Big Pun's "It's so Hard" plays from the hotel's nightclub. The waitress sets his drink in the table and his girlfriend orders a Sex on the Beach.

"Mmmmmhmmmhm," Rueben girlfriend whispers in his ear.

"Niggas want to fuck my wife
Niggas want to take my life
It's sooooo hard"

"Let's go in there," he says pointing to the room playing music. The waitress set his girlfriend's drink on the table. He pays the tab and they enter the Hotel's clubhouse.

"Night Nurse
Only you alone can quench this Jah thirst
My night nurse
Oh gosh
Oh the pain it's getting worse" Gregory Isaac's "Night Nurse plays as they walk in.

"Oh shit…that's my shit," he says as they locate a table near the flat screen television so he can finish watching the game.

"You know I got some weed upstairs," she whispers leaning over to him. *'Damn this a bad bitch'* Rueben thinks to himself. He fixes the ring that he has on his pinky and allows the music to vibrate through his body.

"What's that?" she asks pointing at the ring.

"A pinky ring," he responds.

"Stop playing stupid," she says laughing playfully slapping him on his shoulder. He takes off the ring that is barely fitting on the tip of his finger and places it on the table. She picks it up and tries it on her ring finger. She waves it over the candle's flame that is sitting on the table allowing the diamond to sparkle in her eyes.

"It could have been bigger," she says laughing.

"Yea…it could have been smaller too," he replies jokingly leaning over to kiss her.

"Whatta man whatta man whatta man Whatta mighty good man," she sings in his ear. He beckons for the waitress to send the food and tab to their room. They walk to the elevator and she grabs the drink from his hand finishing it off.

"That's dirty," he says to her as they step in the elevator.

"Oh, Honey you can have me when you want me
If you simply ask me to be there
And you're the only one
Who makes me come running
Cause what you got
Is far beyond compare" Mariah Carey's "Honey" is playing in the elevator.

She stands in front of Rueben and begins to grind on him slowly. He looks at her as she bends over and arches her heels. The elevator stops on their floor and they walk into the room directly in front of the elevator. She connects her phone into the docking station and opens the curtains allowing the city to look in on them. She curls her leg on the window and arches her back as the music begins to play.

"Like a moth to a flame
Burned by the fire
My love is blind
Can't you see my desire?
That's the way love goes

Like a moth to a flame
Burned by the fire
That's the way love goes
My love is blind
Can't you see my desire" Janet Jackson's "That's the Way Love Goes" fill the room.

She starts walking to the bed seductively stripping off her jeans to the beat of the music exposing her dark red panty-bra set. Rueben positions himself on the bed, lights a cigar as she walk over and sit in his lap. She begins kissing on his chest through his clothes while removing his suspenders slowly. He looks at her and crosses his arms behind his head so he can look out into the city. She unbuttons his shirt slowly exposing his chiseled chest. He puffs his cigar and look in her eyes as she lowers herself down unbuckling his pants and pulling them off.

"Make me feel like a King," he tells her blowing cigar smoke in the air. "You never did tell me your answer about being my wife," he tells her. She looks at him.

"I'll tell you when I'm finished," she says going down on him as he closes his eyes and allows his muscles to relax.

Chapter Thirty-Two

"Love is not finding someone to live with.
It's finding someone you can't live without"

"Sonia"

"Hope the ride wasn't too bumpy," the tour guide behind the counter wearing a jacket reading 'Equestrian Safari' says.

"I had a great flight," Sonia says in her thick Italian accent.

"So you think you're ready to tackle the wilderness on horseback huh…have you reviewed the requirements online?" the tour guide asks while pulling up her reservation.

"Well; I have good balance, a positive attitude and I'm in great shape. What do you think?" she says putting both hands on her hips pulling back her coat to show off her figure.

"I see we have a live one here," he says passing her the waiver form highlighted for her to sign.

"If you will follow me to the back; the rest of the group have already picked out their horses," the guide says exiting the side door as she follows.

"What kind of horses do you have?" she asks.

"Criollo's…they are compact and are strong with broad chests, well developed joints and small in stature. They are the native horses of Argentina and are able to withstand the harshest conditions of any rough terrain," the tour guide says pointing to one of the brown horses.

"This one here is called Valentine. We call him that because of the way he easily adapts to women," the guide says as the horse walks over and nudges Sonia's hand. "See…he likes you already," the tour guide says laughing.

"Valentine…a lovely name," she says rubbing the horse.

"A lovely name for a lovely woman," the tour guide responds winking at her.

"Why thank you," she replies.

"Well…I'll leave you two to get acquainted…pack your stuff quickly because it is almost time to go," he says walking away.

"How you doing Valentine?" she asks as the horse neighs and shake its mane.

"A che io canti presto
Le cosec he sei
Fammi fermare il tempo
Che danza tra noi
Lascia che sia respire
Finche tor ci sei
Il mio salute al giorno
Per non lasciarsi
Andare mai
Io vorrie
Che il mio viaggio" she begins to sing Franco's Simone's "Respiro" softly to the horse.

"Ma'am…you have a beautiful voice," she hears the tour guide say as he places a saddlebag on the horse.

"Now you can only carry what you can fit in your bag," he says fastening the saddlebag at the bottom.

"Well Cowboy…I travel light so I'm already ready," she says as he cuffs his hand to help her up. She places her foot in the stirrup and raises her leg over sitting on the horse.

"I don't know what you were expected; but I am a woman. Always light and always ready," she says.

"Well excuse me Ma'am," he says clapping his hands together shaking the dirt off. He grabs the horse's reign and guides her to the rest of the group.

199

"Alright Cowboys and Cowgirls…this is Sonia," the guide says introducing her to the rest of the group. The tour guide steps in front of the group and begins to explain the rules and regulations of the trip.

'Cute' she thinks to herself.

"Now, if you see wild bulls; which there are a great abundance of them with very sharp horns roaming around…don't get afraid…when you see me speed up just click your teeth twice and kick your feet on the horses' side. Don't worry…they will speed up. Now I want you all to give it a try," he says as the group clicks their mouths twice and the horses advance forward. "Good…we will be leaving in five minutes so mingle and be ready for an adventure when I return," he says riding away.

"Howdy…how you doing…where you from?" a white male asks riding towards her.

"Italy," she responds.

"Hello; I'm Mork and this is my wife Mindy," he says as they both reach out her hands to shake hers.

"Like the show," Sonia says laughing hysterically.

"Yes…like the show," he says and they all laugh again.

"Let's roll rangers," the tour guide says trotting past them. They all click their teeth and heels at the same time following the guide.

"Over there is the famous Les Eclaireus. People sometimes confuse it with the 'Lighthouse at the End of the World' which is actually only 200 miles east," he says pointing in the East direction. "That large metal sailor clipping sticking out of the ground once was 'The Duchess of Albany', which is rumored to be part of an insurance scam that started at the dawn of age of the steamships," the tour guide says pointing to fin of a ship sticking out the sand. "If you look over there; those are orcas," he says as they look at the killer whales floating in a perfect triangle. Sonia reaches in her bag pulling out her camera and taking a picture as the whale's surface fully to the top.

"And right over there," the tour guide says pointing to a old abandoned building. "Are the ruins of an old whaling station. For many of you who don't know what a whaling station is; it is a colony of people who hunted and killed whales," he explains as a herd of horses ride past them competing for the lead.

"We are going to pick up the pace because the horses usually run from wild bulls," he says clicking his teeth twice. "The wild bulls are not fast but they can get pretty dangerous," he says as the group pick up their pacing matching his.

"Would you take a picture for us?" Mork asks Sonia passing her the camera while he and his wife dismount and stand beside the metal hull sticking out the ground.

"Saaaaaay Killer Whales," Sonia directs them.

"Killer Whales," they reply in unison as Sonia snaps the picture.

"Tonight we shall camp out at Guacho Pestos; it is that old storm shelter about 100 yards yonder," the tour guide says pointing in the direction.

They stop at the storm shelter and he helps everyone tie their horses to the post.

"How are you enjoying beautiful Tierra Del Fuego?" the guide asks Sonia.

"Living life to the fullest! It is a very beautiful island and the sky is beautiful," she says looking up at the grey and avion colored sky.

"The cormorant birds always seem to give the sky a nice effect," he says as they stare at the black and white birds flying in a flock.

"The cor-cor," she stutters.

"The cormorant's. They are very enormous birds with skin color that ranges from bright blue, orange or red. They are coastal birds that eat fish, eel and even snakes. Their feathers are actually weatherproof which gives them extended time in the water to catch their meals. There is a small stove inside where you can get warm and warm up your clothes," he says pointing towards the cabin.

"Thank you Sir," she says grabbing her bag and following the rest of the group. She quickly changes her clothes and joins the rest of the group sitting outside around the open fire.

"What y'all looking at?" she asks Mork and Mindy who are holding each other.

"Can you see those shadows over there? The guide says those are sea lions," Mindy replies pointing.

"Ohhhhh I see," Sonia says as the sea lions flap their flippers together. She walks to the tour guide cooking on the grill.

"How do you like your meat," he asks flipping over the chicken, ribs and hamburger's.

"Raw," she answers.

"Okay…raw chicken for the lady," he says laughing.

"Yes…exactly," she responds matter-of-factly.

"Seriously?" he asks quizzically.

"Yes…I'm like a vampire. I like the taste of raw meat. It's something about that real meat taste that I love," she says showing her teeth like Dracula.

"Okay my lady…raw chicken it is. A little different but if you like it; I love it," he says jokingly.

Sonia returns to her place by the fire and pulls a small brown package out of her bag.

"What is that?" the guide asks passing her a plate of food and stooping down.

"It is Buddha. I am a Japanese Buddhist," she tells him.

"Interesting…tell me something about it?" he asks nestling down beside her.

"Well; we believe in reincarnation which is when the spirit leaves the body after death and comes into the life of a newborn. I believe that when we dream; or at least the times when we remember our dreams, it is a portal to a previous life," she explains.

"Eccentric…but it makes sense. You are a very interesting individual. Japanese Buddhist…raw meat…and travels alone. Why are you not snatched up yet?" he asks her.

"In my country a woman has to be strong. They have to chew metal and shit nails. The men I meet in the Western world thinks that a woman is supposed to succumb to the man. I love to love but only when true love is truly understood. I pray that a man will appreciate a headstrong woman like me. The Western world idealize that a woman is supposed to follow everything that a man say or do. I believe that love is only in its rarest form when it is truly felt in the soul. I do not need to talk to you all the time or follow a man's orders to feel love. Only when a man can accept me for who I am will I marry and that marriage will last because we will have an understanding that no one else understand but him and I," she says.

"Well·I pray to God or Buddha or whoever that you find that love," he says.

"I will…I will," she says biting in her raw chicken and shaking her head in approval.

Chapter Thirty-Three

*"Don't ever think I fell for you, or fell over you.
I didn't fall in love, I rose in it"*

"Stacey"

"So did you have a good flight?" he asks Stacey as she looks out the passenger window.

"Yea it was cool. Long as shit on those cramped ass seats; plus the dude beside me kept talking so finally I had to put my earphones on to shut him up. How have you been?" she asks him.

"It's been all good down here. I finally made Sergeant after six years so I can't complain. Plus; I start school next semester to finish up my Master's Degree," he tells her.

"UH-OH...doing big things I see," she says.

"Yeah...trying to get it in. I can't be doing this military shit my whole life. I mean it's cool but I got other plans," he says.

"That's real cool. Where are we going anyway?" she asks.

"I thought we hit up the Magic Johnson movie theater. They 'bout to shut it down for good; so I thought we hit that up before it's torn down. That shit is just like Southside Plaza back in Virginia. They be selling all types of shit in the parking lot. You can buy incense, shoes weed...whatever you want from right there,' he says laughing. "Plus you can buy fried chicken right in the movie theater," he says and they both burst out laughing.

"Really? Fried chicken? Now you know that's some hood shit right there," she says turning up the radio.

"My block pumpin' and I'm trying
To keep that hoe pumpin'

If niggas snitchin' then I let
Them niggas hold something
If a nigga owe something
Need a doctor's note from 'em
Or his throat from 'em
These lil niggas thinking they
Fresh, get whipped out ya
Clothes youngin'
I got I all but I'll beat you
Like you stole something
My bitch trippin' say I
Treat her like my old woman
I tell the bitch I'm probably
Better off with no woman
Yea, I get that brand new money
I'm the boss bitch, I'm touching
Every dollar that's comin
Stop playing, I kno' what I'm doing
Let me get 'em
I hope his kids not with 'em
Y'all muthafuckers know me
I'm a rider in the side of the south" Lil Wayne's "Get 'Em" plays
through his car stereo.

    "There it is right there," he says turning the music down.
He eases his car through three lane traffic stopping at the red light.
    "Damn," Stacey says looking at the green bubble Caprice
classic painted with green alligator skin and 24 inch Diablo Spade
rims. The guy leans out and looks in the side mirror fixing his red
and white Houston Texas fitted cap.

'The rover the lambo the rrai the rrai
If I wasn't rapping then I'll be robbin'
Probably pull out my jag tomorri'
The V's 200 g's and they saggin' darling

Shoes by Prada
The shirt Ralph Lauren
Pull up to the park in something foreign
Tangerine Porsche same color a orange
I stay real high like my car insurance" Gucci Mane's "Freaky Gurl" video is playing on the car's thirteen inch fold down television.

"That shit is tight…it looks like an alligator with teeth in the front. That paint job is sweet as shit," Stacey says tapping him on the leg so he can look.

"Yea yea yea…wait till you see what I do to my car," he says.

"What is this…a Camry?" Stacey replies sarcastically.

"Shut the fuck up," he says joking with her. They turn into the Movie Theater and park. They get out and walk towards Magic Johnson Theatre.

"Hey…hey stick of dynamite," they hear a guy behind them calling. "Hey come check me out. I got some shoes for you," he says.

"We good," Stacey's friend tells him.

"Is those Nike's you're wearing? I got the newest Air Max's over here," he says talking to Stacey.

"Let me see what you got," she says walking toward his car.

"Swang swang and I swang to the left
Pop pop my trunk yep, yep, yep, yep
Imma swang I'm a swanger slab lean to the left
Pop my trunk and show what I'm about so
Houston Texas gotta be felt
I'm a vet so it's automatic when I be swangin' my wide frame
44's to 24's I'm subject to glide man
Like a pimp without the numbers still so fly
When I slide man

He gangsta and it ain't too much you can do to stop us
Don't try to knock us cuz these diamond got
Boppas trying us" Trae's "Swang" Chopped and Screwed begins
to play.

"Who is this?" Stacey asks listening to the music.

"Oooooh shiiiit…that's Trae…that's his newest song
Swang…the chopped and screwed version. Younnnn know
nothing 'bout that," he says pulling the Nike Air Max 95's out the
box. "Now see here," he says pointing at the shoe. "You can only
buy these shits overseas. They call these shits Dark Shadow
because of the color of the black suede. The orange is on the heel
and in the bubble," he says turning the shoe over. "It looks like
orange fits you well anyway," he says.

"Orange is my favorite color but you just saying that to get
a sale," she says and they both laugh.

"Naw it matches your American Eagle shirt," he points out
to her as she looks down at her shirt.

"Very observant; I like that. I'll get them," she tells him.

"Cool, 55 dollars," he says passing her the box. Stacey's
friend takes the box and walk back to the car as she pays the guy.

"Thank you," she tells her friend when he returns. They
walk pass a car with a group of guys dressed in all red throwing
up gang signs and BloodWalking to 47 Millers Gang "If you
Blood Throw it up."

"If you Blood throw it up
Bz up cz down, cz upside down, bz up uptown, bz up downtown,
cz down in btown, bz in btown only time I say be wen they be
trying to b down, I rep 1 4 red and I rock btown, rb back streets,
stand up and breathe now, so if blood nigga start throwing them cz
down, fuck that, the whole hood start throwin them cz down, start
throwing them bz up, thro rb up, backstreets till I die, start rollin
dat weed up, if u need sum trees that wut up got re-up, we got no
love for ya ass if u throwin them cz up. See around cz don't rock,

207

fuck going to the bookinz, around here the dz tet knocked, cause we keep them blocks and we pop back cottles, so come to the block an watch a crab git dropped"

Stacey notices one of the guys take a blue bandanna out, throw it on the ground and begin to BloodWalkk over top of it.

"What are they doing with their hands?" she asks.

"They're telling a story with their hands," he tells her.

"Hey Blood...Blood," one of the gangbangers yell out to her friend. "What you reppin' Blood?" he asks.

"H-Town nigga," her friend replies.

"B-Love," the guy responds and turns back to his crew.

"Oh...so you banging now?" she asks him.

"Naw, but you have to know how to get around. As long as you say you repping H-Town it means that you're neutral. Gotta respect the streets,' he says opening the door for her to enter the movie theater. "You want some fried chicken," he says in his best ghetto voice.

"You stupid; I'm good but I will take a Coke," she says laughing as he walks to the concession stand. He returns and they give the usher their tickets to watch the Exorcism of Emily Rose.

"Wow, its jumping outside but it don't look like there's anybody in here," she says.

"I know...that why I like coming here," he says picking seats in the middle of the theater. They sit down and she begins to drink her soda fast.

"Thirst aren't you?" he asks.

"Not really," she says reaching in her army cargo shorts pulling out a small bottle of Hennessy.

"OOOHHH," he says and starts drinking his soda fast as well. She pours half the pint in hers and passes the rest to him.

"Damn, what else you got in those pockets?" he asks touching the side of her shorts.

"My shank for those gangbangers outside," she replies and they both laugh.

"Listen to that," he says cocking his head towards the speakers.

"Don't wanna make a scene
I really don't care if people
Stare at us
Sometimes I think I' dreamin'
I pinch myself just to see
If I'm away or not
Is it real
What I feel could it be
You and me
Till the end of time" Jagged Edge's "Gotta Be" plays through the theatre's speakers.

"That's my jam…We'll take this vow to love one another make this thing a reality," she sings along with the song.

You know…ever since I joined the military all I could ever thing about was you. It didn't matter if I was in Boot Camp, A-School, or Sergeant School…I always seemed to be reminded of you in some way, shape or form. I regret being gone for so long and all the ups and downs that we've been through; But I'm proud of your success. You in college and moving on with your life and me doing my Sergeant thing…but something has always been missing and I know what that is…I want to take this relationship to a whole other level," he says slipping his hand in hers.

"You know a lot has happened since we broke up and I've matured a lot. You know I'm experiencing a lot with my life and you know my situation. I just don't want to say that me being BI-Sexual is just a phase that I'm going through but I do need to know for myself where I stand with myself. You know I love you more than anything else but I have to figure this thing out for myself first. I enjoy every moment that I spend with you and that will never change. I love you but I have to know who I am truly before I can get to know anyone else. I hope that's not being too straightforward," she says.

"No baby…that's just you. I respect your honesty and that is what has always attracted me to you," he says as the song switches.

"Woooow…they playing this in here?" she asks.

"I told you baby…this place is too hood," he responds and they both start singing Michael Jackson's "Dirty Diana".

"You'll never make me stay
So take your weight off of me
I know your every move
So won't you just let me be
I've been here times before
But I was too blind to see
That you seduce every man
This time you won't seduce me".

Chapter Thirty-Four

"The more you are motivated by Love, the more Fearless and Free your action will be"

"Tarez"

Chuck Brown's "Get Your Freak On" plays through the cabin speakers. Tarez stands in the mirror dancing back and forth in his towel. He grabs the baby oil off the dresser and oils himself down.

'This bitch gon' look good tonight' he thinks to himself sifting through his carry-on bag pulling out his pink bottle of Betsey Johnson perfume. He drops his towel and sprays himself all over before sliding on his drawers. He puts the finishing iron touch on his American Eagle dark Indigo Stretch jeans. He puts his pants on an walks to the IPOD changing it to Jill Scott's "Golden".

"I'm taking my freedom
Pulling it off the shelf
Putting it on my chain
Wearing it around my neck

I'm taking my freedom
Putting it in my car
Wherever I choose to go
It will take me far
I'm

Living my life like it's golden

Living my life like it's golden"

Tarez opens the balcony door, steps out, leans over the rail and watches the waves overlap each other.

"This is beautiful," he says out-loud. He feels a few sprinkles of rain fall over his body and shivers. He walks back in, sits at the table and begins to write.

> 'Hey baby,
>
> It is so beautiful out here. I already had two glasses of Moscatto, went shopping on the lower deck and sunbathed. I tried working out but started sweating and you know how much I hate to sweat...unless I'm with you (haha). But I'm living my life like it's golden with Chuck Brown and Jill Scott about to get fucked up...love ya and will write more later.

He looks at the picture of his boyfriend on the table, picks it up and kisses it.

"I love you so much," Tarez says to the picture. He takes his Mizwicki boots out of the Aldo's box and slides his size ten feet inside. He takes his V-neck purple tee off the hanger and puts it on looking in the mirror. He grabs his tailored black blazer out of the closet and puts in on cuffing the sleeves mid way up.

'Almost forgot' he says to himself as he digs in his bag reaching for his Amherst Bamboo ring with the matching color fashion earrings by John Hardy. He slides the purple and blue scarf around his neck tying it into a knot and pulling off the price tag. He grabs his wine glass and finishes off the rest of the Moscatto.

"Damn I look good," Tarez says twirling around in the mirror. He turns off his IPOD and reaches for his phone sticking it in his front pocket.

"Now where is that key?" he says to himself walking around the room tidying up. "Here it goes," he says finding it under his carry bag. He switches off the T.V. and exit the room.

He speaks to a couple walking past as he heads towards the elevator. The couple gives him an odd stare.

"Dirt off my shoulder…I'm used to the stares," he says to himself. He takes the elevator up to the restaurant and hears music playing as he reaches the floor. *'I shoulda smoked before I left'* he thinks to himself stepping off the elevator entering Portfolio's restaurant.

"How many for this evening," the host asks in his Swahili voice.

"Just one," he says as the host shows him to a table. *'Damn he's cute and has a great butt'* Tarez thinks to himself as he sits down. The band is playing Calypso music.

"Can I start you off with a drink?" the waiter asks.

"Oh yes please…can I get a White Russian…more Russian than white," he says laughing.

"I got you. A lil' stronger than normal huh? I think we got just the thing you need. Just look over the menu and I'll be right back with your drink,' the waiter says walking away. *'I an dying for some pasta'* Tarez thinks to himself looking through the pasta selection.

"I'm coming home to you
Wear something see through
So I can see your heart
For night can never come
Soon enough for me
I watch the sky all day
Night is where I find
You and peace of mind
My days are filled with glee
That's why I truly g
Gve you what you need
Because you love me for me" Raphael Saadiq's "Stillray" plays over the speakers. Tarez sits back in his seat and closes his eyes.

"Here you go Sir and the guy at the counter wants to know if you are dining alone?" the waiter asks pointing towards the bar. The guy raises his drink and nods. Tarez nods back in approval.

"Tell him that I decline his offer but thank you," he tells the waiter.

"Are you ready to order or do you need a couple more minutes?" the waiter asks.

"Yes, I am ready. I will have the Chicken Alfredo with a salad and I'll take another drink when the meals come," he tells the waiter.

"Very good selection," he says walking away. Tarez sips his drink and bobs his head to the music.

"You didn't really turn down my offer did you? I just saw a pretty face and wouldn't mid holding a chat before I head back to my room," the guy from the bar says indicating that he would like to sit down.

"I guess I wouldn't mind some company while I eat. Have a seat," Tarez responds.

"Thank you; how are you doing?" he says reaching out to meet Tarez's hand gracing it with a kiss.

"My name is Tarez and yours Mr. Gentleman?" Tarez asks.

"Francisco…what brings you on the great Royal Caribbean alone?" Francisco asks.

"I just had to get away…away from everything. No boyfriend, no friends, no nothing…just me," Tarez responds.

"I know how you feel. When you live this lifestyle sometimes you just get tired of all the heckling and stares that come with it but out here no one cares. I love to clear my mind before I go back into the hectic world," Francisco replies.

"I know that's right," Tarez says in agreement laughing and checking out Francisco's Hollister shirt with his bulging muscles.

"So what brings you out alone? You seem like the player type," Tarez says. Francisco burst out laughing and grabs a napkin to catch the beer that he spit out.

"No it's nothing like that. I'm single and I like to have fun but it's nothing like that. Look around…see how beautiful and peaceful it is out here. Being alone just gives me a chance to clear my mine and since I get a chance to talk to someone as pretty as you are it makes this trip so much more worthwhile," Francisco says. Tarez feels himself blushing as the waiter sets down the Chicken Alfredo, salad and White Russian.

"Getting it in I see," Francisco says.

"This ain't my first and it sure as hell won't be my last," Tarez says finishing the rest of his beverage and transferring his straw to the next drink. He says a quick prayer and digs into his food.

"I don't usually like to eat around people but I am starving. Would you like to taste it?" Tarez asks holding the fork so Francisco can take a bite.

"Mmmmm…that is good," Francisco says taking a bite.

"Oh
Ay baby welt you ah deal with
We come tru' a lot a tings you kno'
So wahamum to you
Me make one little mistake you wan dun us

If I had you back in my world
I would prove that I could be a better girl
Oh oh oh
If you let back in my world
I would sho nuff never never let you go again
Oh baby
I was so foolish to ever leave your side
Searching for was right before my eyes
It was me who didn't realize

215

Till it was gone
But now I need you in my life" Jazmine Sullivan's "Need U Bad"
begins to play.

"That's my shit," Tarez says and begins to dance along
with the music.,

"I'm about to go insane….I feel so good right now," Tarez
says bobbing his head back and forth to the music. "Let's make a
toast…to the things that matter," Tarez says as Francisco raises his
beer toasting it with him.

"The things that matter," he repeats and the both take a sip.

"I'm full now. I don't think I can eat anymore," Tarez says
pushing his plate back.

"Why don't you let me show you my cabin?" Francisco
asks.

"Sure; I hope it's better than my cramped up little space,"
Tarez says.

"Probably not but I'll give you the grand tour," Francisco
says reaching for Tarez's hand assisting him to stand up.

They exit the restaurant and enter the elevator. Francisco
slides his car key in and pushes the button to the lower deck.

"Well I guess it's a good thing I got the private code,"
Francisco replies pushing the code in as they ride down.
"Welcome to the Deluxe," Francisco says turning on the light.

"Damn…you don't have a room you have an apartment,"
Tarez says looking over the loft at the first floor of the room and
walking down the steps.

"What is this?" Tarez asks looking at the fish swimming
back   and   forth   on   the   Plasma
Television.

"Well; fish help me to relax so when I saw my niece's
Finding Nemo DVD I saw this special feature with just fish
swimming back and forth. I thought what the hell? It sure is a lot
cheaper than actually feeding them," Francisco replies.

"You are really funny," Tarez says laughing hysterically. Francisco walks over and switches on the radio filling the cabin with music.

"I hope you're a Drake fan?" Francisco asks.

"Yea I love Drake…that's my real boyfriend right there," Tarez yells out.

"Well tell him he got some competition," Francisco says turning up the music. "Do you smoke?" he says lighting a blunt.

"Thing have been so crazy and hectic
I should've gotten back by now
But you know how much I wanted to make it
It's probably better anyhow
So if you gotta go
Is there's anything I should know
If the spotlight makes you nervous
If you're looking for a purpose" Drake's "Karaoke" fills the cabin.

Francisco turns the lights down, walks behind Tarez, puts his arms around him and presses the blunt to his lips. Tarez hits the blunt slowly exhaling deeply. He turns around meeting Francisco's lips. Francisco places his hands under Tarez's shirt and begins to rub on his back to the beat taking off Tarez's coat.

"I can't," Tarez says.

"Just relax," Francisco says feeling on Tarez's ass. Francisco moves him to the couch continuing to kiss on his neck.

"I can't,' Tarez says again tapping him on his shoulder. "I can't," he says pleadingly.

"I only want this if you want this," Francisco says sitting up.

"I want this…trust me. I came here to clear my head but if I go through with this; as tempting as you are, it would only clog up my head even more," Tarez says.

"I understand," Francisco replies as Tarez picks up his jacket off the floor.

"I'm sorry...I didn't mean to lead you on. I think it would be best if I left," Tarez says. "I   understand...I   respect   that," Francisco replies.

"Good night Francisco," Tarez says walking up the steps.

"Good night Tarez," Francisco replies as Tarez shuts the door behind him. Tarez takes the elevator to his floor and enters the room. He walks onto the patio and looks out into the sea before returning in to place his IPOD on the speakers.

"Everything
In you
I found my everything
And I trust in you

I found my
Can't you see look at my face it's glowing
And it's all because of you
Everything about you
You see I need
And I thank God for sending you through" Mary J. Blige's "I Found My Everything" begins to play.

Tarez pulls out the letter he was writing earlier. He taps his pen on the desk thinking. He kicks off his boots and looks at the moon shining in.

'Hey boo...the trip is going great. I've had a lot of time to clear my mind and really focus on the important things in life. I used to worry about what everyone would think when I actually came out the "CLOSET". I didn't want people looking at me differently. I didn't want people thinking of me in...in "that way". But this trip has taught me that I have found my everything and I mean completely everything in you. I see it in your smile, the way you laugh, the way you talk...everything about you makes me absolutely comfortable with myself. I am ready to tell my family,

218

friends and the entire world that I found my everything. I have seen your strength and I will match it. I will be your all and everything that you want me to be. Thank you for helping me find me. I love you forever and ever…Love…Yours Truly…Tarez…P.S…my answer is yes.

Chapter Thirty-Five

*"Loving someone is giving them the power to
break your heart, but trusting them not to"*

"Taryn"

"Okay…right this way ladies and gentleman. Remember we walk in front of the helicopter so the pilot can make eye contact with each and every one of you. Why should we walk in front of the helicopter?" the groundsman asks the little boy.

"Because the rotors are turning," the little boy responds.

"Good job…you have been paying attention to the instructor in the class," he tells him. They all walk out the hangar holding their ears shut blocking out the loud whirring of the helicopter. They walk to the front of the helicopter and the groundsman looks at the pilot and gives a thumb up. He shoots back a thumbs up.

"Okay ladies and gentleman you are now free to walk," he tells them. They walk towards the helicopter keeping their eyes fixed on the pilot as they climb in the open helicopter door.

"Welcome aboard the Island Express," the pilot says turning around to help fasten everyone's safety belt. The pilot points towards the headsets and watches as everyone secures their chin strap.

"Now that's a lot better," the pilot says pressing the chin strap button. "Good morning and welcome aboard the Air Express. The headset that you are listening on is the Telex and is the best brand for canceling out loud noises. The two levers on the side," he says reaching to touch his. "One is to let as much noise in that you want so if you want to hear the choppers you can adjust the noise level. The other level is so we can talk amongst

220

each other. I will be able to hear you but you won't hear me. If you want to talk to me just say hey or pilot or whatever," the pilot says jokingly. "Now, I will tell you when you can take your safety belts but you have to remember to remain in your seats and welcome to Catalina Island," he says turning around.

Taryn grabs her son's hand and her friend does the same with her other son. The helicopter shakes back and forth as they ascend into the air. Taryn reaches out and grabs her boyfriends' hand while shutting her eyes.

"Mommy...mommy look," her oldest son says into the headset.

"Baby your knuckles are turning white," her friend says jokingly.

"Please God...let me survive this trip," Taryn says and everyone laughs.

"Alright...we are hovering around 15,000 feet and you are free to take off your safety belts. We are about 32 kilometers off the coast of Southern California. The Indians used to call this island Pemu'nga until it was first discovered by Rodrigues Cabrillo in 1542 who renamed it San Salvador. In 1602 Sebastian Vizcaino renamed it Santa Catalina for Saint Catherine of Alexander. The town of Avalon is also known as the Island of Romance," the pilot says switching off his microphone.

"This is amazing," Taryn says grabbing her youngest son's hand to ensure that he does not get out of his seat.

"I told you not to worry about anything...and look...your knuckles are changing back to their right color again," her friend says jokingly.

"Shut up," she tells him.

"Mommy...mommy look; Are we in heaven?" her oldest son asks pointing out the window at the clouds.

"No but we can't get any closer than this," she tells him.

"Oh…if this helicopter goes down we can meet the maker face to face…ohhh yeah…we can get a lot closer," her boyfriend says laughing.

"You see…you see…that's why I didn't want to come 'cause I knew you were going to act like this," she tells him.

"I'm just joking baby," he says reaching over rubbing her knees. The pilot chimes in.

"Over to your right is the Casino; Catalina's most famous and prominent landmark. It has never had a slot machine, roulette table or dice game since gambling is illegal in California but it is used for social gatherings and entertainment. Inside the Casino holds a movie theater on the bottom floor and the top is a ballroom where greats such as Glen Miller and Benny Goodman have both performed," he says before clicking back off.

"I've been here before but I never been on a helicopter tour," Taryn tells him.

"This is my first time on one as well but when I saw online I thought the kids would enjoy this experience. You know with that headset on, you kinda look like Amelia Earhart," he says pulling out his camera. She leans down, grabs both of her kids in her arms tapping them and pointing towards the camera. He snaps a picture and moves beside them to take a picture of everyone together.

"Now that's going in the archives," he says looking at the photos.

"Look at my son," Taryn says laughing as her son holds a peace sign in the air. "He is sooo cute," she says grabbing the camera and zooming in on her boyfriend.

"I thought you was talking 'bout your son?" he asks.

"Well, you're cute too," she says leaning over to kiss him.

"Our last sight of the evening is the Wrigley Memorial. It honors William Wrigley Jr. the manufacture of Wrigley's chewing gum. He was also the owner of the Chicago Cubs baseball team which holds its annual spring training right here in the Catalina Island," the pilot says before chiming off once again. Taryn picks up oldest son and her boyfriend lifts her youngest son in his lap. She places her hands in his and squeezes tightly.

"Thank you," she says.

"You're welcome," he responds. They gaze out the window for another fifteen minutes as the pilot brings the place back to the hangar.

"I hope you all have enjoyed your ride on the Air Express and remember to walk in front of the helicopter as you exit," the pilot says landing and reaching out to shake everyone's hands. "And you two boys have been the most well behaved kids I've ever flown with," he says reaching in his pocket giving them both a sucker. The pilot reaches over and opens the door. "Just set your headsets down and thank you again," the pilot says as they all exit the helicopter and jog towards the hangar. They all say goodbye and shake the instructor's hand. They get into the rental car and drive towards their Villa. He opens the console and takes out the C.D. case putting in Music Soulchild's album.

"You're my baby
My lover, my lady
All night you make me
Want you it drives me crazy
I feel like you
Were made just for me, babe
Tell me if you
Feel the same way
Cuz it just feels so right
I don't wanna waste no time
If I had to choose I know
I'm gon always choose to be with you
Cuz girl

Girl don't you know
You're so beautiful
I wanna be always

223

Here by your side
Girl don't you know
You're so beautiful
I wanna give all my love to you girl
Not just tonight
But the rest of your life
I wanna be always there
By your side," her boyfriend sings along with Musiq Soulchild's "So Beautiful". She leans her head on the window and looks at the silhouette of the trees over the car. He turns up the radio and slides his hand in hers.

"Cuz it just feels so right
I don't wanna waste no time
Girl if I had to choose I know
I'm gon' always choose to be with you" he continues to sing squeezing her hand with each high note. He pulls into the Villa and turns off the car allowing the song to keep playing. She turns around and looks at her kids.

"They are so precious when they are sleeping, monsters when they're awake but angels when they're asleep," Taryn says looking at them.

"Come on let's go," he says turning the car off. They get out and each grab one of the kids while they sleep in their arms. They walk into the Villa, enter the room with double beds and lay the children down.

"I'm going to take a quick shower," he says and kisses her on the forehead.

"Okay babe," Taryn responds walking into the kitchen to make herself a mixed drink. She grabs her speakers, walk out on the deck and looks through the window at her children sleeping.

"Thank you God," she says to herself. She leans on the rail and admires how the red sun lights up the sky. *This is truly God's creation'* she thinks to herself. She scrolls through the playlist on her IPOD finding the song that she wants and connects it to the speakers. She sits in the lounge chair and takes a sip of her drink.

"Don't wanna make a scene
I really don't care if
People stare at us
Sometimes I think I'm dreaming
I pinch myself
Just to see if I'm awake or not

Is it real
What I feel
Could it be
You and me
Till the end of time
Never part
Take my heart
Hold it tight
Its true love
You know I gotta be" Jagged Edge's "I Gotta Be" plays.

"Whoa…I see we had the same idea," he says clinking the ice around in his glass. Taryn scoots forward in the lounge chair allowing him to sit behind her. She leans against him and curl her legs up in the chair.

"I have to tell you something," she says. "You scare me. After my first marriage I lost apart of myself. It took me a very long time for me to get that part back and I'm just fully really getting it back. My kids had a lot to do with that. They are my inspiration. They inspire me to do better…they give me the strength to go through my day with my head held high even when I'm down. I wasn't expecting you to come along but you did. I'm messed up on the inside and at the same time I feel so happy when I'm with you. I'm not ready to give that part of myself up again…no…I'm afraid to give that part of myself up again. I only ask for you to go slow and be patient with me. I care for you deeply and what's more my children absolutely adore you," she says looking at him. "I'm not looking for a response. I just felt like that's something that I needed to say," she says and leans her face against his chest as he strokes her hair.

"Okay baby; I hear you, I will always love you so take all the time you need.

"I gotta be the one you need
I'm just telling you that I gotta be

I picture you and me
Starting a life together
We could be
We'll take this vow to love one another
Make this thing a reality" Jagged Edge continues to play.

Chapter Thirty-Six

"The desire to love someone always exceeds the desire to be loved by someone & that's exactly why we end up loving the person who doesn't deserve that LOVE"

"Tasha"

Tasha sits back in the cab and lifts up her Versace shades to look at the billboard of Paris's Prime Minister Francois Fi'hon.

"My president is black
My Lambo's blue and I'll be goddamn
If my rims ain't too
My money's light green
And my Jordan's light grey
And they love to see the white
Now how much you tryna pay" she begins to rap Young Jeezy's verse from "My President is Black.

"You are so immature," he says laughing.

"I'm just saying…my President is black. What hotel did you decide on?" Tasha asks.

"Don't worry…I got this whole weekend planned out; so just sit back and chill," he replies. The cab driver stops in front of Hotel George V.

"I knew you were going to choose this place," Tasha says.

"How did you know?" he asks.

"When we were looking online I knew you were going to choose the best. I know you so well," she replies laughing at him.

They get out the cab and the driver pops the trunk and grabs their bags.

"Merci," the cab driver says as he pays the fare.

"De Rien," he responds.

"Been touching up on your French I see," Tasha says to him.

"Shiiit...just the basic words," he says laughing.

"I don't remember a lot but I like to think I can move around a little bit," he tells her grabbing his bag. "Well I got my bags. I don't know yours are going to get in," he says walking away. Tasha shakes her head up and down in amazement.

"Okay...okay...I'll take that," she says picking up her suitcase and following him through the revolving doors. He sets his luggage down by the couches.

""I'm going to get the key...I'll be right back," he tells her.

"Wow this is nice," she says to herself removing her shades and walking to the tall glass vases with the pink and purple flowers leaning slightly over. She walks to the statute of a woman holding a bouquet of flowers; pulls out her camera and takes a picture of the statute. *'This place is beautiful'* she thinks to herself as she walks across the lobby to take another picture of the light green flowers in the marble vase.

"I know these are tulips," she says touching one to ensure that it is real.

"Come on baby...let's go," Tasha turns around and sees her boyfriend holding her luggage beckoning for her to come.

"So now you want to be a gentleman...I don't need your help now," she says taking her bag off his shoulder.

"Ooooh...so it's like that now?" he asks.

"Yep...just like that," she says smiling. Tasha places her shades back on her face and follow him into the elevator.

"I got my billions up

Fucking with them white folks
Now I don't give a fuck
Cause I'm richer
Than them white folks
Lamborghini trucks
Y'all ain't seen it yet
Bought me Teterboro
Just to diddy-bop
And land my jet" he begins to rap Puff Daddy's part.

"I fucked my money up damn
Now I can't re-up
Ran off in his spot
Just to get my stacks up
Now I'm back on deck
So shawty what the fuck you want
Heard he talking shit
But this ain't what the fuck he want" she interrupts him and raps Wocka Flocka Flame's verse from "Oh Let's Do It" remix.

"You can never let me have a song to myself huh," he says.

"Now when you rap wack ass Puff Daddy's part," Tasha answers sarcastically. They walk out the elevator heading towards their room. He opens the door allowing her to walk in first.

"Goddamn…did you get the Presidential Suite?" she asks.

"Something like that," he responds.

"You're it," she says punching him in the arm and running off.

""Here we go," he says throwing the bags down chasing after her.

"Damn…how many rooms up in this place?" he yells out.

"This shit is too big…come out," he says getting quiet listening for any movement. He turns toward the bathroom pushes the door open. "I hear you breathing…getting closer," he whispers putting his hand on the shower curtain yanking it back.

"Raaa," he yells and she jumps in his arms.

"You found me," she says kissing him.

"I'll always find you; Come on let's check out the rest of this place," he tells Tasha taking her hand and walking through the hotel room. She rubs her hand across the yellow covered wall entering into the most beautiful room she's ever seen. She pulls back the curtains and allows the sun of Paris to illuminate the room. She releases his hand and begins to jump on the bed.

"Parissss!!!" she yells at the top of her lungs.

"Baby go take a shower so we can get out of here," he says.

"Party pooper," Tasha responds jumping off the bed. She enters the bathroom and look at her silky black body in the window.

"Paris," she mouths in the mirror as she hears him turn on XM Radio.

"Ride till I die
Lord knows I stay high
And I love it
And I love it

Let's go
We count hundreds on the table
Twenty's on the floor
Fresh outta work and on the way with some more
And I love it
And I love it
I got gangsta's in the crowd
Bad bitches at my show
Parked outside
And sitting on Fo's
And I love it

And I love it" Young Jeezy's "I Love It" plays from the other room. She turns the shower on and undresses slowly while staring in the mirror. *'Damn I'm one bad bitch'* she thinks to herself. She pulls out her body wash, steps in the shower and bounces back and forth to the song.

"And I love it
And I love it" Tasha continues to sing as she steps out the shower and dries off. She puts on her red Victoria Secret bra and panty set and stares in the mirror at herself. She puts on her Mother of Pearl True Religion jeans, Bebe's red tank top and her Christian Louboutin sandals. She loves the way that all of Louboutin shoes have red on the sole of the shoe as well as the heel. She stops out the bathroom and sees him sitting in the chair looking out the window smoking a blunt. He gets up, passes her the blunt and enters the shower. Tasha hits the blunt twice and sets it in the ashtray. She sits in the chair and watch the weed smoke float in the ceiling fan.

"I got a feelin nigga grilling and my
Money be the root
Look up at the stars
She like
Honey where the roof
Pull up, hear the dogs,
Canaries dey go on the roof
Even once had a job pouring tar up on the roof" Rick Ross's "Mafia Music" plays as she dozes off to sleep and is awoken by him tapping her on the shoulder.

"Let's roll," he says undocking his IPHONE and placing it in its case.
"You look good baby," Tasha says walking past him.
"Three-sixty huh," he says taking a whiff of her perfume.

"Only the best," she says grabbing her Versace shades and looking in the mirror.

"Come on," he says

"Be Easy," she quotes T.I.'s song "Be Easy".

They leave the room and ride the elevator to the first floor entering the restaurant. The waiter shows them to their table on the deck facing the Eiffel Tower. Tasha's boyfriend pulls out her chair.

"Thank you," she says lowering herself down. He reaches over and caresses her right hand.

"You hear that?" he asks listening to the music.

"That's um...um..."Breaking My Heart" by Mint Condition...the jazz version of course," she says closing her eyes and adding lyrics to the song.

"You keep telling me
That your time is always taken
But I keep seeing you out alone
Listen to love
Your heart is pounding with desire
Waiting to be unleashed" she stops singing and opens her eyes. He's holding a Zale's box in his left hand.

"I think you are the most beautiful female I have ever laid eyes on. But I see so much more to you than that. You are so strong and straightforward but you are still so sensitive on the inside. I love to see that part about you because I know that side is only reserved for me and only me. That's the side of you that I see that gives me inner joy every time it's revealed. That is the unbreakable bond you hold with me at all times. That is the side that I would like to hold on to for the rest of my life," he says and she feels a tear roll down her cheek and wipes it away with her hand. He grabs her hand and kisses it. "I'm sorry I took so long for this moment to happen but as I told you earlier…I will always find you…I love you Tasha," he says placing the ring on her finger.

"I love you so much," Tasha says leaning over to hug him.

Chapter Thirty-Seven

"The eye through which I see God is the same eye through which God sees me; my eye and God's eye are one eye, one seeing, one knowing, one love"

"Towanta"

Towanta leans over her boyfriend and stares out the window as they fly over the beautiful city of San Tropez, Europe.

"San Tropez," she says to herself leaning over to kiss him on the cheek.

"Are we there yet?" he asks turning over on his pillow. She allows him to finish sleeping as the plane descends.

"Thank you God for carrying us safely over these dangerous waters,' she says in a quick and silent prayer. The plane lands and he steps over top of her to retrieve their luggage from the top compartment. She is so excited that she can barely contain herself waiting for the slow line that's taking its time to exit the plane. They retrieve their luggage and exit the airport hailing down a cab requesting him to drive to the Santa Marie Villas.

"This city is beautiful," Towanta says getting out of the cab and entering the hotel. He goes to retrieve the key and she stands by their bags and pulls out her camera.

"San Tropez…Inkadoo," Towanta chants her favorite word that she made up to use when she is excited about something.

"Let's go," her boyfriend says returning and slipping his hand in hers. They walk until he stops at Villa Two. They have their own Villa separate from everyone on the beach. She walks onto the patio and stands observing the scene. She allows a tear to fall from her eye. He comes behind her and wraps his arms tightly around her waist.

"You like?" he asks. She cannot speak but nods her head in approval. *'Heaven'* Towanta whispers to herself as she notices children running and playing on the beach. She watches the waves as they overlap each other and hears him breathing softly in her ear.

"Go take a shower baby and then we can walk out on the beach,' he tells her.

"Okay baby," Towanta replies turning around to kiss him. She hurriedly jumps into the shower and hears him playing one of her favorite songs.

"I couldn't seem to fall asleep
There was so much on my mind
Searching for that peace
But the peace I could not find
So then I kneeled down to pray
Praying help me please
But then he said
You don't have to cry
Cause I'll supply all your needs

As soon as I stop worrying (soon as I stop worrying)
Worrying how the story ends (When I let go)
I let go (and I let)
And I let God (let God have his way)
(That's when things) that's when things start happening
I'll stop looking at back then
I let go and I'll let God have his way" Dewayne Woods "Let Go and Let God" plays.

"Please God; I have to remember that he's a preacher. If your will be don...if he is the one...please show me a sign. I don't want to be fooled again," Towanta says turning off the shower and beginning to lotion herself up. "Please God let him be the one," she say to herself tying her brown sundress tightly around her waist because she wants him to slightly see her butt. She puts on her sandals with the straps leading up to her ankles. She walks out the bathroom and does a half-turn for him.

"Dang baby…you are going to make me break my vows tonight," he tells her.

"Let's go punk," she says grabbing a pillow off the couch and flinging it at him. He deflects the pillow and laughs as he opens the patio door. She walks onto the patio and gasps. They sky's color is blending yellow and white fading into a dark blue.

"Baby…you're not crying again are you?" he asks as they walk through the sand hand in hand. Towanta playfully punches him in the arm and he turns and faces her.

"Baby; I want to start this weekend right. I know that God has bought you in my life for a reason. I was lost and I prayed to God to send me a woman…A strong woman…an intelligent woman, a God Fearing woman. An Angel fell from heaven and here you are standing right in front of me. I praise God for sending me one of his Angels and he bet not want you back because he would truly have a fight on his hand. You're apart of my soul now," he says bending to one knee and pulling out a Helzberg box out of his pocket. She starts to tremble as he opens the box showing off the half carat solitaire diamond ring.

"This is the purest state of mind that I've been in …in well a long time. I feel closer to God because I feel closer to you. Will you marry me Towanta?" he asks.

"Yes," she says looking towards the heaven and allowing a tear to fall from her cheek onto his fingers.

Chapter Thirty-Eight

"The Love of Money is the Root of All Evil"

"Tayshone"

Tayshone looks in his rearview mirror at the earrings that he has just purchased from Jacob's Jewelry store.

"See me on the ave
Chain with no shirt
Blocks with no socks
I'm so dirty" Brisco's "Why you Hatin" blares through his speakers.

He hears a car horn behind him blowing indication that the light has turned green. He sits peering through his rearview mirror waiting another minute before pulling his black on black 2010 Mustang away from the light.

"Niggas act like they've never seen money before," he says to himself.

"You better get your mind right
If you hatin' on me
Why you hatin on my
If you think a nigga soft
One day you go see
Why you hatin on me" Tayshone continues to rap along with the song. He pulls into the Palais Omnisports De Paris, Bercy (POPB) Paris, Italy. He drives into the lower level lowering his window to show the security guard his identification badge. The security

guard checks his I.D. and passes it back to him with a pad and pen that he has pulled out of his shirt pocket.

'I'm gon' kick their ass tonight and they still want my autograph' Tayshone thinks to himself. The guard waves him through and he locates a parking spot. He gets out the car, opens the trunk and takes out his Miami Heat basketball bag. He removes his Varsity Core Coogi jacket and throws it in the trunk.

"Excuse me...Excuse me," he hears and looks down noticing two white boys asking for his autograph. Tayshone signs the paper and hands it back to them. He momentarily flashes back to when he and his younger brother used to play basketball back home in Powhatan, Virginia. Tayshone walks in the locker room and gives his famous cheer by putting his finger over his lips and shhhhhshing everyone. He puts his hand in the air and abruptly brings it to the ground signifying a plane crashing and the city burning. He whistles and when his hand gets close to the ground everyone yells out "BOOM". He hears "Hustler's Music" by Lil Wayne playing off someone's radio. He opens his locker and starts unpacking his bag. He pulls out the flat basketball that he and his stepfather used to play with; the only man he could never beat. He reaches back in the bag pulling out the note that his mother put in his lunch box in the seventh grade which reads *'Life is short...play hard...I'm your first agent'*. He laughs and sets the note down. He pulls out a black box and looks at the receipt. His teammate snatches the box out of his hand.

"Give me that back," Tayshone says reaching for the box.

"Damnnnn nigga this shit is hot...you think you ready for this?" his teammate asks opening the box and staring at the ring.

"Yeah man...I know...but she's been the realest thing that I've ever had in my life. Fucking these bitches in every city ain't cool. I don't think...I know I'm ready," Tayshone replies as his friend passes back the box.

"Damn man...as a kid would you have ever believed that all this shit would be possible?" his teammate ask glancing over the locker room.

"Hell yea…I was a superstar the day I was born. But this is a dream come true," Tayshone replies laughing.

"Alright pansies…it's game time so let's go out there and do exactly what we do in practice…it's game time fellas…GAMETIME let's go!" the coach yells and they all charge out the locker room and into the arena.

"I got ice in my veins
Blood in my eyes
Hate in my heart
Love in my mind" Lil Wayne's "Drop the World" starts blaring through the loudspeakers.

Tayshone hears his name called on the sound system and runs onto the floor giving his teammates high fives. He looks in the first row and sees his girl wearing white stretch pants with a black shirt with red letters displaying *'Drop the World Baby'*. He puts his arms up and flexes his muscles at her. Tayshone plays the game of his life scoring and assisting a double-double for the night. The team rushes back in the locker room and Tayshone takes off his Heat jersey and waves it in the air like a helicopter. He grabs his little bottle of Black Label Gin out of his locker and drinks it all down.

"If you want to
We can supply you
Got enough work to feed the whole town
They don't shoot you
Unless you try to
Come around and stomp on our ground
Cause we taking over
One city at a time
Say we taking over

One city at a time" D.J. Khaled's "We Taking Over" is playing from one of his teammate's radio. His teammates move out the way as his girlfriend makes her way into the locker room and stands in front of him. He walks over and tries to hug her.

"Naw nigga…not before you shower," she says.

"Drop the world huh," Tayshone says pointing to her shirt.

"Baby you dropped that shit tonight. You didn't show them no mercy," she says while laughing and falling into his arms.

"Hold on," he says fumbling in his locker. He grabs the box and hears one of his teammates start to play Jagged Edge's "I Promise".

"Y'all ain't gon' put me on blast like this is y'all?" Tayshone asks as the locker room gets quiet with his teammates laughing at him.

"Nothing is promised to me and you
So why will we let this thing go
Baby I promise I'll stay true" Jagged Edge's "I Promise" continues to play as they edge Tayshone on.

"Come on Dawg" and "Get it nigga" his teammates chant as his girlfriend smiles in bewilderment.

"This game, this life, this world means nothing to me if you're not there. You have held me down since day one and been one of my biggest supporters. You know how I hold my breath on every shot. I though basketball was my one and only true love; but I've realized that there is a love stronger than what is out there…it's the love that I have for you inside that keeps me alive," Tayshone says dropping to one knee. His teammates yell out woohoo's and yeaaaaahh's in excitement.

"Will you be on the next Miami Heat's championship team," he says opening the box. "I love you so much," he says feeling a tear drop on his arm.

"Yes baby…I would love that so very much," she says as he stands up to kiss her and his teammates cheer him on.

Chapter Thirty-Nine

"It matters not who you love, where you love, why you love, when you love or how you love, it matters only that you love"

"Tealaza"

Tealaza walks around Deep Six Surf and Shop.

"Hey boo; you like these shorts right here?" she asks holding a pair of shorts in the air.

"Yea those are nice but I like these better," he says pointing to a red bikini set.

"Boy you stupid. Come on…seriously…do you like these shorts?" she whines.

"Yea babe; you know I'm just messing with you," he responds.

"Oh snap," she says listening to the music playing through the store.

"Pop lock and drop it
Pop lock and drop it
Pop lock and drop it
Pop lock and drop it" Baby Huey's "Pop Lock and Drop It" plays throughout the shop.

"Tonight it's going to be some changes
No acting sadity
St stop acting and get it clapping
Cause I'm knowing you feeling me

Yea you cute
But don't let that shit go to your head
Cause what this cutie won't do pimpin'
Another one will"

"That's my jam right there," Tealaza says moving back and forth with the music.

"You know you a lil' freak," he tells her slapping her on the ass.

"Yea but only your freak. Let's get that one and get out of here," he says pointing to the shorts she's holding in her hand.

"Oh shit…you hear that," he says and starts bobbing his head to Lil Wayne's "Go D.J.".

"Now that's my joint right there; if they jamming like this we might just need to stay in here," he says walking to look at the display posters of Miley Cyrus, Justin Bieber, Bob Marley, Jackson Five and Nas that they have on sale.

"Hey look at least they got Nas in here," he tells her as she walk past him towards the door.

"What did you think…that they would have some reeeeal artist in here? Let's go," Tealaza says pushing the door open. They walk down the strip looking at the various shops.

"Forget this. Let's get a bike. It's too hot out here to be walking," he suggests.

"Cool…I'm going to get a smoothie from that stand," she says.

"I know…I know…I'll get the bike," he responds walking towards HighGear Cycling shop. She pushes him in the direction of the store and walks towards the smoothie stand sliding on a thin layer of her favorite Avon Cherry Blossom lip gloss. *'My lip gloss is popping'* she thinks to herself and burst out laughing when she sees her boyfriend returning with a stupid grin on his face and a two-seater bicycle.

"I thought this was cool 'cause it's like we can take turns pedaling," he says laughing with her.

"You are soooo stupid," she says continuing to laugh. He kicks the kickstand down and sits beside her.

"Where's my iceee at?" he asks. Tealaza leans over and holds the icee out allowing him to take a bite.

"You know...your mom is super cool to let me come on this trip with y'all," he tells her.

"Yea...I was scared to ask her but she was like you needed to see some other places besides the ghetto," she says mocking her mother.

"Unh uhhh...she didn't say the ghetto did she? You know I gets money out there," he replies.

"Yea babe...I know...and you look soooo cute doing it," Tealaza say and they both laugh.

"Come on let's go," he tells her.

"I got the back," she says.

"Of course you would," he says and they both laugh again. She throws the rest of her icee and they ride away.

"You know this is wack right," she tells him.

"Yea but you like this wack stuff," he replies. They begin to ride and she takes her feet off the pedal.

"I knew you were going to do that. You better start pumping or we won't be going anywhere far," he threatens and she laughs beginning to pedal.

""Come on, let's go in there," he says slamming on the brakes and pointing at the Video Kiosk. They lock the bike in the bike rack and walk over to the kiosk. She starts flipping through the songs.

"Well...what song do you want to do?" she asks pushing the button flipping through the songs. "They got Jamie Foxx and Ne-Yo "She Got Her Own" Tealaza suggests.

"How does that go again?" he asks. She wraps her arms around his neck and begins to sing.

"I love her cause she got her own...she don't need mine; she leave mine alone...there ain't nothing in this world more sexy than a girl that want but don't need me…I love her cause she got her own," she finishes and he begins to laugh.

I always thought that he was saying I love her 'cause she got a room," he says.

"That's because you're stupid," she replies jokingly as he pushes her away.

"Keep looking crazy," he says.

"They got Rihanna's "We Ride", Cassie's "Me and You", Mario's "Crying out for Me", Trey Songz's "Lol Smiley Face", Justin Timberlake's "Until the End of Time", Bow Wow's "Outta My System" she continues to read.

"I'm sitting looking out the window like damn tryna fix this situation that's at hand. You're still running through my mind when I knowing that you shouldn't be me all on yo mind and I'm knowing that it couldn't be," he begins to rap Bow Wow's part from the song "Outta My System".

"I knew you was a sensitive thug; you want to do that song?" she asks him.

"That's dead…I don't want niggas seeing me doing that soft shit. Who would you do? T-Pain's part? You may sound like him but that ain't sexy," he says laughing and pushes the search button.

"On snap; I can't believe they have Lil Flip's "Sunshine" she yells out.

"I can call you my baby boy
You can call me you baby girl
Maybe we can spend some time
I can be your sunshine
I can call you my baby boy
You can call me your baby girl
Maybe we can spend some time
I can be your sunshine"

"Yea that's my joint too but let's see what else they got," he says pressing the button. "Look what they got," he says pointing at the screen that's displaying Vistoso Bosses "Delirious". "I know that's your jam and I fucks with Soulja Boy's part…let's do this one," he says.

"Yaaa…you know this is the best song in the world," she tells him as he inserts money and they enter the booth. The green background fades into a swirl of blue, red and yellow lights. He steps in front of the camera.

"Yoooo this dope boy fresh all the way from the hoods of Virginia…holdin' it down in South Beach for my niggaz…you heard…and I got the baddest girl from the Southside getting it in with me…so respect that and we won't have any problems…you heard…Lil' T drop that shit," he says into the camera.

"Man this ridiculous
I got you so delirious
Kiss me through the phone
While I lick you just like licorice
I'm Hov back in 96
And you can be my Sasha Fierce
Baby you so sexy
I love the way them jeans fit
Put you on my team list
Call you Ms. Beazy
I'm Soulja Boy tell 'em
I can make your life so easy
And if you don't believe me
Please don't tease me
Delirious for my love better yet
I got you feenin…let's do it" he finishes Soulja Boy's verse and she steps in front of him into the camera.

"Hey over there what's your name
Are you forreal

Is this a game
And I do the same
I look away
But you remain
Your eyes staring back at me
My heart starts to skip a beat
I pray that you'll never know
I've fallen and you look in my eyes
You make me delirious
That's when I start to fall
Something serious
When you look in my eyes
You make me delirious
That's when I start to fall
Something serious"

He walks over and swings his silver V.A. chain over her shoulder. She grabs the chain and makes her cute face and slides his chain over her head.

"Your eyes staring back at me
My heart starts to skip a beat
I pray that you'll never know
I've fallen and you look in my eyes" Tealaza sings and begins to grind her hips on him slowly.

They finish the song and walk out laughing. They wait for the DVD to finish burning.

"Baby I can't wait for the future. I know we still young but as soon as you turn 18; I'll be 20, then we can get married," he tells her.

"Well as soon as I turn 18 I will marry you," Tealaza replies as he leans over and kisses her. The DVD ejects and she grabs it and taps it on his chest.

"You make me Delirious," she says.

Chapter Forty

"If, in thirst, you drink water from a cup, you see God in it. Those who are not in love with God will see only their own faces in it"

"Tera"

"I can't wait to hit the beach," Tera says as she and her boyfriend walk through the shops of Bal Habour, Florida on Collins Avenue.

"Look at this" he says pointing and walking toward The Art of Shaving shop. "I heard this place was like a spa for men," he says rubbing his beard. "Traditional shave, facial massage, pre-shave, fave towel…yea…I thing I'm going to check this place out. I hope they got some hot young female doing this instead of some old white man," he says and they both laugh.

"Well I hope in this case they got a really old man for you," she replies jokingly.

"If you're going to hit this up then I'm going to walk to the Dolce and Gabbanna store right there," Tera says pointing a few shops down.

"Don't spend too much money," he warns leaning over to kiss her.

"Is there such a thing?" she responds returning his kiss. She walks down South Beach strip and enter the D&G store.

"See I don't need no alcohol
Your love makes me feel ten feet tall
Without it I'd go through withdrawal

Cause nothing even matters at all" Lauryn Hill's "Nothing Even Matters" featuring D'Angelo is playing as she walks through the shop.

"These buildings could drift out to sea
Some natural castastrophe
Still there's no place I rather be
Cause nothing even matters to me" Tera begins to sing to herself as she walks towards the wall of shoes.

"These are cute" she says to herself picking up a pair of burnt orange sneakers with D&G imprinted on the side.

"280...not bad," she says turning over the shoe and looking at the price.

"May I help you Ma'am?" the salesperson asks. She gives him her shoe size and he quickly rushes off to the back. She places the display shoe back on the rack and walk towards the wall of high heels.

"Very nice taste," the salesperson says returning with the shoebox as Tera admires a pair of Leotard Print high heels.

Would you like to see those in the same size?" he asks.

"Yes please; bring them out," she replies thinking of what she has in her closet back at home to match it with. She sits down and uses the shoe horn to slide the shoe on. She stands up and walks in front of the mirror admiring the shoes.

"Here you go Ma'am," the salesman says returning and setting down her high heels. She sits down and tries the high heels on.

"I know he's going to say something smart if I get both pairs," Tera says looking in the mirror. "Yes...I'll get both pairs," she says switching shoes and walking to the cash register.

"$585 Ma'am," the salesperson tells her as she pulls out her Visa Card.

"Everyone who spends $500 receives a coupon for over forty percent off their next purchase," he tells her handing over a gift card.

"Can I use it on this purchase?" she asks laughing.

"No Ma'am…sorry…the sale is only on these particular days," he replies chuckling and pointing to the dates on the card.

"Thank you anyway," she says signing the receipt.

"Thank you and make sure you visit us on those dates," he tells her as she walks out the store returning to the Art of Shaving shop. Tera stops at the Armani Exchange store and begins to sift through the outside rack picking up a pair of burnt swim trunks with Emporio Armani written in a white strip from one side to the other.

(Get on X) Anything is took, it's gonna be a breakdown
Come thru like 'Hmmm..what I'm go take now
Whatever the fuck I want, trust me dog
It gets ugly even when it comes to the hunt" Busta Rhymes "Touch It" remix plays on the outside speakers.

"Those are hot," she hears her boyfriend voice behind her and turns around looking at his fresh face.

"They did a good job. Do you like these shorts," she says rubbing his face and holding out the shorts.

"Yea I'm feeling those," he responds.

"Well let's get them," she says walking in the store pulling out her credit card.

"Remember when Eminem came on stage at the BET awards show?" he asks listening to the music.

"Yea but DMX part was hot. If he had came on stage instead of via cam then I would have went crazy," she responds signing the receipt. "But Em did his thing…I'm getting hungry," she say as they walk toward the beach.

"Let's stop in one of the shops…how about here?" he says pointing at the D'vine Hookah Lounge.

"You know I don't like all that smoke," she replies.

"Come onnnnnn…we can get a drink in there. We can get it to go…this is South Beach" he suggests grabbing her hand and pulling her towards the restaurant.

"Sold," she responds following him in the restaurant.

"How may I help you Sir?" the cashier asks.

"Ummmm…I'll take a Hummus and a Pita…what do you want baby?" he asks.

"I would like some fries and a Margarita Mojito," she orders.

"This is kinda cool. If I was a smoker then I would like my smoke to smell like this," Tera says as a customer purchases an Apple Hookah.

"Want to get one?" he asks as their order comes up.

"I said I like the smell…not kill myself with it," she replies laughing as they exit the restaurant towards the beach.

"Let's change first," he says guiding her towards the beach's changing rooms. They both change and she steps out wearing her Fuschia and Olive Green Victoria Secret's two piece bikini set.

"Damn," he says looking her up and down.

"Boy you silly," she chuckles as she picks up her D&G bag and food. "Those shorts are nice," she says following him to the lawn chair and umbrella area.

"I'm going to jump in the water first and work up an appetite," he says as Tera wraps her towel around her chair.

"Well, I'm going to eat my fries before they get soggy," she says sitting back.

"I'll be right back," he says taking a sip from her drink and turning to walk away.

"Watch out for Jaws," she yells out nestling back to eat her fries. She reaches in her bag and pulls out her Christian Dior sunshades and IPOD. Tera places her earbuds in her ear and presses play.

"I never knew such a day would come
And I never knew such a love could be inside of one
And I never knew what my life was for
But now that you're here I know for sure

I never knew until I looked in your eyes
I was incomplete til the day you walked into my life
And I never knew that my heart could feel so
Precious and pure
One love so real" Eric Benet and Tamia's "Spend my life with You" begins to play.

Tera closes her eyes and begins to snap her fingers rocking back and forth. She feels drops of water splashing on her face, opens her eyes and eyes her boyfriend wiping himself down with a towel.

"Damn," she says to herself as he wipes the towel across his washboard abs. He leans over to hug her *Wow that Degree stays on* she thinks to herself reminded of her favorite scent.

"Is it weird that I love the way your deodorant smells?" she says as he laughs and grabs a handful of her fries.

"A little…but nothing surprises me about you anymore; what are you listening to?" he asks as the song on her IPOD switches to the Isley Brothers "For the Love of You". She removes one of the earbuds and passes it to him.

"Driftin' on a memory
Ain't no place I rather be
Than with you
Yeah
Loving you (well, well, well)

Day will make a way for night
All we'll need is candlelight
And a song

Yeah
Soft and long
Well, Oooh"

He reaches over and grabs Tera's hand. "I've been meaning to do this for a long time but I could never think of the right words to say...you have truly been an inspiration in my life and I thank God everyday for sending someone so special like you to me. It's the power you give off that draws a lot of energy no matter where you're at or what you're doing. I know I don't have a lot; but the one thing I do have is love that's 100% genuine. I'm not one of those insecure brothers that worry about a woman making more money than me. I worry more about what I'm going to make you for dinner. You bring out the best in me and I want to continue to grow with you as we travel through this journey of life. I love you more than I love myself and that kind of love is a very powerful aphrodisiac. It's just your presence that gives me the inspiration that I need to do this," he says bending down to one knee.

"Will you give me the honor of being my wife," he says opening a Zale's box.

"It's nothing fancy. It's only a...," he begins to say as she reaches over and kisses him in mid sentence.

"It's perfect," she says kissing him again.

Chapter Forty-One

"The truth is, everyone is going to hurt you. You just got to find the ones worth suffering for"

"Terrell"

"I knew we should have fucking flew. Now we lost as a bitch," Terrell tells his girlfriend as he eats the last bite of his steak.

"We are not lost. The sign said that we are 150 miles outside of Las Vegas," she tells him.

"But if we had flown we would have been there in two hours," he says lighting a cigarette and throwing the empty container out of the window.

"Well we almost there so stop tripping," she tells him.

"I'm not tripping…I'm just saying we would have been there a long time ago," Terrell replies.

"Okay okay Terrell. Just stop fussing," she tells him as she turns up the music.

"Ex-girlfriend; How you been?
I see you still trying to fuck with other women men
Remember when
I first met you in my cousin's house; a week later
We was fucking on your momma's couch
Now it's been said that big girls don't cry
But they damn sure lie
Look you in your eye, saying you they only
You and I till the day we die
Said you never
Leave me lonely, fly tenderoni but you phony

Should've listened when my momma told me
Soon as I turn my back you try to fuck my homies
That was then this is now
I got a new friend, ever since
I cut them loose ends you wanna bone me
Add strife to my life; pussy that'll make me think twice
About leaving the wife even, picture that
You ain't want me when you had me
Now you on your third baby daddy and you hate to see a nigga happy
So you trying mad ways to trap me
Looking at my girl nasty
Trying to throw the pussy at me" Method Man and D'Angelo's "Break up 2 Make up" plays through the speakers.

'What up nigga...you made it yet' Terrell reads the text from his brother. *'Nah not yet but it's cool seeing the sights...nothing but desert hahaha'* he texts back. *'I got the supervisor position and a new school closer to my house...I'm bout to be on my nigga'* his brother text back.

"Hey my brother got the supervisor position," Terrell tells his girlfriend while turning the music down.

"Tell him I sad congrats," she says.

'Good ups nigga you deserve that shit...how my kids doing?' Terrell texts back. *'It's all love nigga they sleeping now...just get at me when you touchdown'* his brother responds. Terrell takes the blunt out of the ashtray and lights it up while passing the cigarette to his girlfriend.

"I'm getting tired of driving. Let's switch for a little while," she tells him.

"That's cool. Just pull over wherever," he responds blowing circle rings of his weed in the air. She sees the sign stating 132 miles to Las Vegas and pulls over.

"Where the fuck we at?" Terrell asks.

"The GPS say that we are in the Mojave Desert," she replies turning the headlights off and getting out.

"It's quiet as a bitch out here," he says stepping out the truck and looking across the desert.

"Hit me
All the chronic in the world couldn't even mess with you
You are the ultimate high
You know what I'm saying baby?
Now check this out

Take my money
My house and my cars
For one hit of you
You can have it all baby
Cause making love
Everytime we do
Girls its worse than drugs
Cause I'm addicted over you
And you know that I
Can't leave you alone
You got me feenin
Girl I'm feenin for you" Jodeci's "Feenin" plays from out the SUV.

"My brother said that the kids are straight and don't worry," he Terrell tells her.

"I knew your brother would take care of them; but thank you for telling me," she says reaching for the blunt. Terrell walks towards the cactus and grabs it.

"Goddamn that bitch sharp as shit," he says looking at the blood on his finger.

"Well you not supposed to be grabbing things...let me take a picture of you in front of it" she says lightly touching the cactus. Terrell carefully places his hand on the cactus and throws up a peace sign. He takes her digital camera out of her pocket and aims it towards him.

"Say ouch," she jokes with him.

"Ouch," Terrell responds sarcastically as a vehicle's headlights blinds his eyes. They notice a car slowing down as it approaches them.

"Hey brother…do y'all know where the rave party is at tonight?" a white guy yells out leaning out of the side of his car.

"I don't know…there's a club out here?" Terrell asks peering into the wilderness.

"Naw brother; you don't know what a rave is? I mean a real rave…well this ain't no bullshit club shit…you get a phone call probably about thirty minutes prior with the directions and then you just show up. We just be getting fucked up man. I got some Percs if y'all want one?" the white guy asks.

"Fuck yea," Terrell answers walking to their truck.

"If y'all want to stop by…just stop by…you should see it right off the road," he says passing Terrell a Percocet.

"Thanks man," Terrell says as the white guy pulls off. He walks to the back of the Hummer and retrieves a pint of Hennessy. "Now those where some cool white boys," Terrell says popping the pill in his mouth and chasing it down with the Hennessey. He passes her the bottle and they both stare into the sky.

"Uh-Oh…let's go," he says moving quickly after hearing a coyote howl. He walks to the driver side and settles in the seat putting his seatbelt on. She does the same and presses fast forward on the C.D. player.

"I remember when
I remember when
I remember when
I lost my mind

There was something so pleasant
About that place

Even your emotions had an echo
In so much space" Gnarls Barkley's "Crazy" begins to play. She attempts to change the song. "Don't do that…I like this song," Terrell says playfully slapping her hand and singing along.

And when you're out there
Without care
Yeah I was out of touch

But it wasn't because I didn't know enough
I just knew too much

Does that make me crazy
Does that make me crazy" she sings along with the song.

"Hey look; is that the rave party that white boy was talking about? Let's stop for a minute," he says.

"I ain't going to no crazy ass party with some crazy ass white people in a place that we don't know Terrell…what is wrong with you? That's how black people get killed," she says.

"We just gon' stop by for a minute. I mean we don't even have to get out but we can at least look at it," he says turning off the highway onto the unpaved road.

"You know this is absolutely crazy," she says.

"What happens in Vegas stays in Vegas," he says slowing down and turning off the headlights.

"As long as it's not our bodies staying in Vegas," she says half seriously.

"Baby you're all I want
When you're lying here in my arms
I'm finding it hard to believe
We're in heaven

We're in heaven

Oh thinking about all our younger years
There was only you and me
We were young and wild and free
Now nothing can take you away from me
We've been down that road before
But that's over now
You keep coming back for more"

"HOW MANY OF Y'ALL BELIEVE Y'ALL IN HEAVEN? SAMMY...TELL THEM ALL ABOUT IT," the D.J. yells in the microphone turning up D.J. Sammy's "Heaven". The crowd of people begins dancing in a circle while hoisting green, yellow, and red glow sticks in the air.

"Look...look," she says pointing at the white boy sitting on a rock staring intently at a glow stick.

"They look fucked up," Terrell says laughing. He opens the vehicle's door and she grabs his arm.

"Hold on baby...where you going?" she asks alarmingly.

"I'm not going anywhere. I'm just going to sit on the hood," he replies taking the rest of the blunt out of the ashtray. She opens the truck door and gets out as well. He hoists her on the hood, and climbs on accidentally knocking off one of his Nike sandals.

"Shit," he says and she laughs.

"What's so funny? Remember it's a long way to the ground," Terrell jokes with her indicating that he would push her off the truck.

"I guess driving won't so bad after all," she says hitting her shoulder with his. "Baby listen," she says and he leans back hearing the music playing faintly from inside the truck.

"That's your song isn't it?" she asks.

"Last night
We had an argument
You told me you love me

All the things I said I never meant
No baby
I didn't mean to make you cry," Terrell starts singing Silk's "Lose Control" and snapping his fingers at the same time. He sits up and she leans against him.

"Have you given any thought to what we talked about?" she asks.

"You mean about us getting married?" he questions.

"Yes, about us getting married," she replies tightening her grip around his arm.

"Yea…I thought about it. I want to say yes but I'm not ready. I have to be fully sure that this is the life that I'm ready for. We came here with all of our bills paid and only three hundred dollars in our pockets and I am having the time of my life. I love you and that's the honest truth. I want to say that I will always be here but shit happens. You just have to give me time to grow. I'm growing with you and this is a first for me. I promise you…if you are the one for me then I will marry you…I promise," Terrell responds.

"You know as much as it hurts to hear you say no…or at least no for now…I totally respect the reasoning. As long as you're real with me I will promise to always be here," she says.

"I love you baby," Terrell says stroking her hair.

"I love you soooo much Terrell," she replies squeezing him tightly.

Chapter Forty-Two

"L'amor che move il sole e l'altre stele"
(The love that moves the sun and the other stars)

"Thomas"

Thomas sits in his SUV waving his hand like a conductor as "1812 Overture" by Peter Tschaikowsky plays through the speakers. He turns the radio up allowing the music to full his 1997 Honda Pilot.

"This is one of the greatest composure's ever," he tells his girlfriend while turning the radio down. They exit the vehicle and he walks to the rear of the vehicle and unsnaps their bikes off the bike rack. She reaches in the back seat and grabs his laptop bag.

"Hey…don't forget my sunshades," Thomas yells out and she reaches over and picks his pair of Oakley Jawbone green cycling glasses and their lunch bags.

"You did want your computer right? So you can download some of the songs that you were talking about," she asks.

"Yea that's cool," he replies walking both bikes to the front of the vehicle.

"Yellowstone National Park," she reads as she points at the sign made of wood from one of their fallen trees. "Take a picture," she tells him as he walks in front of the sign holding both of their bicycles. She snaps the picture.

"There is a picnic table right there," he says pointing to the tables. Thomas sets the bikes on the kickstand and wipes the table with a napkin. She places the food on the table; two roast beef sandwiches and a bag of low fat Lays potato chips.

"Here's your Sushi. I can't see how you eat that stuff," she says disgustedly.

"Like this," he says picking one up and placing it in his mouth.

"Smart ass," she responds. He pulls the laptop out of the bag and inserts a blank C.D.

"Just burn me whatever you're burning for yourself," she tells him. He sifts through the playlist choosing "Jumper" by Third Eye, Train's "Soul Sister", Violent Femmes "Blister in the Sun", Smash Mouth's "Moondance", and Barenaked Ladies' "Pinch Me". She passes Thomas a fork and he mixes the soy sauce and wasabi together before dipping the Sushi.

That is so disgusting," she says wrinkling her nose in the air. "OOOOOOH get me Van Morrison's Redwood Tree," she exclaims.

"Now that sounds like a very fitting song for this setting," he replies looking through the playlist adding the song to the library.

"Play something while we eat," she requests.

"I have the perfect song in mind," he answers.

"I wish you would step back from that ledge
My friend
You could cut ties with the past
With all the lies
That you've been living in
And if you do not want to see me again
I would understand
I would understand

The angry by, a bit too insane
Icing over a secret pain
You know you don't belong
You're the first to fight
Your way too loud

You're the flash of light
On a burial shroud
I know something's wrong
Well everyone I know has got a reason
To say
Put the past away
I wish you would step back from that ledge my friend" Third
Eye's "Jumper" plays from his laptop.

"What do we have to drink?" he asks her.

"Ginger Ale of course...I also thought we could mix a
little of this in your water bottles," she says pulling out a small
bottle of Crown Royal.

"You mean while we are riding? That is fine by me. Are
you ready to go?" he asks grabbing a handful of potato chips.

"Don't forget to change your shoes," she reminds him.

"Thank you...how did I almost forget," he replies getting
up from the table and jogging back to the vehicle. The turns the
laptop around and scrolls through the songs that he's picked out.

"Hey Hey Hey
Your lipstick stains
On the front lobe of my
Left side brains
I knew I wouldn't forget you
And so I went and let you blow my mind
Your sweet moon beam
The smell of you in every
Single dream I dream
I knew when we collided
You're the one I have decided
Who's one of my kind

Hey Soul Sister, ain't that Mister Mister
On the radio, stereo

The way you move ain't fair
You know" she begins to sing Train's "Soul Sister" as Thomas
returns to the table wearing a pair of white and green Sidi Genius
6.6 Carbon Lite sneakers.

"You ready?" she asks as he gathers the trash.
"Yes...I'm just trying to be environmentally friendly
before we ride," he tells her throwing the trash away. She adjusts
her bike helmet strap fastening it under her chin. He fixes his
chinstrap as she walks the laptop back to the SUV. He places the
C.D. in his disc player and slides it in his pouch.
"Where mine at?" she asks and he points towards the C.D.
on the table.
"What song are you listening to first?" she asks.
"I was just going to let the C.D. play through," he tells her.
"Okay...let's start at the same time,' she says.
"On the count of three.....1....2...3," they both chant and
press play.

"It's the perfect time of the year
Somewhat far away from here
I feel fine enough I guess
Considering everything's a mess
There's a restaurant down the street
Where hungry people like to eat
I could walk but I'll just drive
It's colder than it looks outside" Barenaked Ladies' "Pinch Me"
plays.

"Let's roll," she says as they mount their bikes. They ride
in silence until they see a group of tourists standing around a
geyser. "I always wondered how those things worked," she says.
"Well, a geyser is formed when three ingredients come
together in one place. Subterranean water, usually water pressure,

it's sorta like a plumbing structure. It brings hot water and steam to the surface and blasts it in the air," Thomas explains to her.

"How do you like so much stuff?" she asks.

"I like to think I'm sort of an historian," he replies. "I also like to think I'm a connoisseur of modern art, music and a good drink," Thomas says laughing and picks up his water bottle of Crown Royal and Ginger Ale that's she's mixed.

"Well Mr. Historian...how hot do they get?" she asks.

"I don't know how hot "Old Faithful" here gets buts they generally range anywhere between 120-400 degrees and it shoots up approximately between 110-185 feet and is well known because of its frequent and predictable eruptions," he explains.

"Okay Mr. Smartie Pants...how many times does "Old Faithful" erupts?" she asks.

"Wow; your really testing me huh?" he asks her.

"I know you like talking about this stuff," she says to him.

"You're right...it erupts roughly every 45-90 minutes and usually has the duration of four minutes. Here's the tricky part though; if the eruption is less than four minutes the next eruption will be approximately 40-60 minutes later and if it's..." Thomas continues and is interrupted by the ground rumbling. "I'll tell you more later," he says as he pulls out his small video camera and begins recording the thick white steam shooting through the air.

"I can feel the heat all the way over here," she says quietly.

"Well...that lasted about two and a half minutes so the next one will be in about an hour. If it had lasted longer than four minutes then the next one would have been in about two hours," Thomas says looking at his watch as the geyser dies down. "You know what else I'm a connoisseur of...rocks," he says.

"What do you know about rocks?" she asks him. Thomas digs in his carry bag and pulls out a Helzberg ring and bends down to one knee.

"What are you doing?" she asks looking around nervously as the small crowds of tourists face them and begins to snap pictures.

"I thought that this would be the perfect setting. Being here with you reminds of Eric Clapton's song "Tears in Heaven". It took me so long to find the perfect person because I had to find myself. I am a connoisseur of many things but love is new to me. I know that this ring is not a lot…it's merely a symbol of how I feel about you. I love you truly. That is one of the things that I do know. I want to take a tour of Europe with you. I want to go to a classical musical with you. I want you to want to do all those things with me. Will you marry me so we can do all those things together?" Thomas asks. She bends down on her knees allowing her eyes to meet his.

"I want to do all those things with you…yes…yes…I will marry you," she replies collapsing in his arms as the onlookers begin taking pictures and clapping.

Chapter Forty-Three

"Does your Wedding make you Cry?
Or does He?"

"Tiffani"

Tiffani stands front of the mirror reading the stationary card that she has clutches in her hand. *Today is our special day. First United Methodist Church 77 West Washington Street Chicago Illinois 60602'*. She picks up a napkin and quickly dabs her eyes trying not to smear her make-up. She hears a knock at the door.

"Yes," she answers meekly clearing her throat. "Yes," she says again louder.

"Pastor Ma'am...just wanted to check and see if you're okay. I want to pray for you before the ceremonies proceed," the associate Pastor Claude King speaks through the door.

"Yes Pastor; I'm ready," she yells out. "As ready as I'll ever be,' she says quietly to herself.

"Ooooooh...you are absolutely stunning," he says walking over and grabbing both of her hands.

"I just prayed for your husband and he was shaking like a fig tree. By the feel of things you're not doing much better yourself," he tells her.

"I'm so nervous," Tiffani replies using the napkin to wipe her hands dry.

"That's quite okay...I want to do something before I pray...I want you to close your eyes," he tells her.

"This is the air I breathe
This is the air I breathe

Your holy presence
Living in me
This is my daily bread
This is my daily bread
You're very word spoken to me
And I desperate for you" he begins to sing Byron Cage's
"Breathe".

"Dear Father; bless this child and this Holy Matrimony that is about to take place on this snowy January day. Today, her soul will join another to form one. Bless their love that is everlasting just like yours...Thank you God. Amen. Look at you...beautiful as the God given day. If y'all both shaking like this at the altar then we are going to have to build new floors," he says and they both laugh. "I think there's about five minutes left so I'm going to give you time to get yourself together," he says.

"Pastor...how does he look?" she asks.

"Like the perfect fit," he replies turning to walk out. Tiffani's girlfriend enters the room.

"Girl you are absolutely stunning. That man better know what he's getting and if he don't I got the switchblade to remind him," she says and they both laugh. I'm just joking but you do look good and you do know I got that switchblade," she says tapping her right breast. "Let's do this. Your husband is already walking down the aisle and that fine best man of his is looking better by the minute," her friend says.

"Stop cursing...we still in a church," Tiffani responds.

"I'm just saying don't be surprised if I snatch him up but first things first...let's get you married,' she says.

"Let's...before I have to hose you down," Tiffani replies grabbing a hold of her girlfriend's hand. The usher escorts them through the hallway facing the double doors.

"I'm going to find a seat," she says walking away to enter the chapel.

"Dear God…if you let me fall in front of all these people I will never forgive you," Tiffani jokes to herself as the song begins to play.

"I'm so ready to love, I'm so ready to promise my all
I'm so ready to give till the day that my life is no more
I'll be everything that this woman can possibly be
Cause I'm ready to be like the olden days when commitment was golden

Be the man of my dreams and get down on one knee, love
Say you'll be all I need and then ask me to marry you, my love
Let's take two golden bands and let's walk
Down the aisle, love
I'll say I do and you'll say I do, make a commitment" Chrisette Michele's "Golden" plays.

'Don't fall, don't fall, don't fall…damn he is fine stand there in his white tuxedo…Thank you God' she thinks to herself as she walks down the aisle beside her father. She looks at the Fuchsia and White flowers that her niece and her fiancé's youngest son has thrown on the aisle runner.

Tiffani laughs to herself as she eyes her girlfriend mouthing *'Best man…Best man'*.

"Who gives this bride away?" the Pastor asks.

"I Do," her father replies kissing Tiffani on the cheek and walking away to take his seat.

"You may all be seated," the Pastor tells the congregation. "Before I begin with marrying these two I want to give you all a history lesson. After WWI; times were so bad that people believed that the church should shut its doors and move to the suburbs. But it was a Chicago Architect by the name of Daniel Burnham who said *'Make no little plans. They have no magic to stir the people's blood and probably themselves will not be realized. Make big plans. Aim high in hope and work,'* it is the vision of these two people standing before us whom he was talking about making those big plans for," the Pastor tells the congregation.

As he begins the ceremonies Tiffani feels her fiancé's grip tighten around hers. She hears her mother crying softly in the background and begins to cry herself. One of her bridesmaids passes her a napkin.

"Now we will have the pouring of the sand. The brown sand is a representation of God. God is the foundation of all that we do," the Pastor says as he begins to pour the brown sand in a heart shaped jar. "And this is the combination of the two coming together as one. You hear me church? You see they will not survive if God is not the foundation," the Pastor says as they both step to pour their individual bags of sand into the jar.

"Amen," someone yells from the back of the church.

"Amen," Tiffani says to herself.

"Turn and face the crowd...Ladies and Gentleman...if anyone should come in-between the bond of this new relationship then woe to that person. Welcome these new souls into your heart and minds," he says as the church begins to clap. "You may now kiss the bride," he tells the groom. Tiffani wraps her arms around him and kisses him hard.

"Thank you God," he whispers in her ear.

"Hold on my brother don't give up
Hold on sister just look up
There is a master plan in store for you
If you just make it through

God's gonna really blow your mind
He's gonna make it worth your time
For all of the troubles you been through
The blessings double just for you
Today is the first day of the best days of your lives" Donald Lawrence's "The Best is yet to Come" begins to play. They walk down the aisle and she begins dancing and singing to the song.

"Yea girl...get it," Tiffani hears her friend yell out. Her husband stops and does a two step with her. They two step their way out of the church with their bridesmaids and groomsmen following. They head to the waiting area while people file downstairs for the reception. Tiffani and her husband stand by the mirror talking while the groomsmen and bridesmaid congratulate them.

"This is our moment...our day," her husband tells her.

"I know but we have to eat sometime today," she says laughing.

"Well...what does my future wedding planner have in store for us? I know you couldn't resist putting your touch in this," he says laughing.

"Well you knooow...what can I say," she replies doing her best J.J. Evan Good Times impression.

"Everyone is downstairs and seated when y'all are ready," the usher announces. The newlyweds follow the groomsmen and bridesmaids as their names are being called to enter the reception area.

"And now Ladies and Gentleman...the best that was yet to come is finally here. Please stand and give a round of applause for the Newlyweds," the D.J. announces as everyone stand and claps.

"Girl close your eyes
Let that rhythm get into you
Don't try to fight it
There ain't nothing that you can do
Relax your mind
Lay back and groove with mine
You got to feel that beat
And we can ride the boogie
Share that beat of love
I wanna rock with you (all night)
Dance you into the day (sunlight)

I wanna rock with you (all night)
We're gonna rock the night away" the D.J. begins to play Michael
Jackson's "Rock with You".

"This is beautiful," he says looking at the Clear and
Fuchsia glass candlesticks reflecting off of the mirrored paneled
tables.

"The flowers were my idea," she says pointing at the
Purple Roses and White Peonies in the crystal vases. They enter
the reception hall as the crowd stands and applause.

"Ladies and Gentleman we are going to have our first
dance by our newest couple," the D.J. says as "Rock with You"
fades away.

"Father can you hear me
We need your love today
I know that you are listening
You hear me everyday
Father please hear us
And we will be okay
Father we need you
To heal families today" the D.J. begins to play "Father Can You
Hear Me" from Tyler Perry's 'Diary of a Mad Black Woman'.

"Thank you God...Thank you God...Thank you God,"
Tiffani says clutching him tightly.

Chapter Forty-Four

"You know you're in love when you can't fall asleep because reality is finally better than your dreams"

"Toeka"

Toeka rides through the city with the windshield wipers flickering back and forth. She rolls the window down slightly allowing the smell of fresh rain to hit her nose. *'God knows I love how it smells when it's raining'* she thinks to herself. Her phone vibrates and she reads the text message. *'Next week we are going to Blackfeet's Indian reservation'.* Toeka responds with a *'Hell yea'* and a smiling face. She turns up the music.

"I wanna be a billionaire
So freekin bad
Buy all the things I never had
I wanna be on the cover of
Forbes magazine
Smiling next to Oprah and the Queen" Toeka sings along with Travie McCoy and Bruno Mars's "Billionaire" song.

"Oh shit…this is my song," she yells in between the hook. Her phone rings and a picture of her boyfriend flashes on the screen.

"What's up baby?" she asks turning the radio down.

"I just wanted to check on you and make sure you're wearing your seatbelt," he tells her.

"Babyyyy…I'm good," she replies laughing.

"Take care of my baby," he tells her and she begins to rub her stomach.

"Okay baby…I'm putting it on right now," she tells him reaching up to secure her seatbelt.

"If you came here by yourself tonight
Cause he wouldn't pick up the phone
He was supposed to" the song changes and she begins singing New Kids on the Block song "Single".

"Baby baby baby…I don't want to hear all that shit in my ear," he says.

"Bring you here tonight
Couldn't find him
So you came alone"

"Shut up," Toeka tells him continuing to sing. "I'll be there in a few," she tells him and hangs up the phone. She turns the radio to 102 JamZ.

"I just want to get your attention
I really want to be all up in your head
Cause what I got you gon' want to get some
But girl that's only if you ain't scared" Usher's "Daddy's Home" comes on.

Toeka turns into Monticello court in downtown Greenville, North Carolina. She grabs a Harris Teeter shopping bag to cover her freshly done hair-do and walks up the flight of stairs to the second floor.

'Damn I can't wait till this baby come' she thinks to herself entering the apartment. "Hold on…I'll get dinner started in minute," she yells out.

"Baby just chill…come in here real quick," he yells from the bathroom. Toeka enters the bathroom and sees that he has run a bathtub of water for her. She notices a green lily with a pink rose floating on top of the bubbles. She turns around and he kisses her quickly.

"Don't say nothing just get in…how's my baby doing?" he asks rubbing her stomach.

"Absolutely beautiful…now," she responds.

"Get in the tub baby," he says lightly slapping Toeka on the ass as he exit the bathroom. She begins to strip down and notices a pink and white box sitting on top of the hamper. *'Don't open until your done'* the note reads. She looks in the mirror and starts to do her made-up happy dance.

"Baby I just don't get it
Do you enjoy being hurt
I know you smelt the perfume
The make-up on his shirt
You don't believe his story
You know that their all lies
Bad as you are
You stick around
And I just don't know why" Mario's "Let me Love You" plays from the stereo in the living room.

Toeka imagines her boyfriend stripping in front of her; rubs her stomach and closes her eyes. *'Damn I love this man'* she thinks to herself rising out of the tub. She quickly dries off and looks in the box pulling out a Victoria Secret Pink bra and panty set. She looks in the small bag and shake out a bottle of Japanese Cherry Blossom spay. She sprays the scent in the air and all over her body before putting on the set. She looks in the mirror and does her happy dance again.

"It's calling my body

It's calling my soul
It's calling my mind
Girl I gotta go
Baby it's the grind
Yes I had a good time
You was sooo good
And I really wish I could
Stay a little bit longer
Love you a little bit stronger" the music switches to Trey Songz "Gotta Go".

Toeka walks out the bathroom and notices read rose petals and pink candles illuminating the entire apartment. She tiptoes in the living room and eyes her boyfriend sitting on the floor beckoning her to sit between his legs. He holds his hands out assisting her to the ground. She starts to rub his arms and he rubs her stomach.

"Baby you are so sexy," he tells her kissing on the back of her neck. She allows her body to settle into his.

"I was wondering maybe
Could I make you my baby
If we do the unthinkable
Would it make us look crazy
Or would it be so beautiful
Either way I'm saying
If you ask me I'm ready" Alicia Key's "Unthinkable" begins to play. Toeka suddenly sits up and turns to face him.

"Can I marry you? I will be the perfect wife. I will cook, clean and take care of you. I know it's not right for a woman to ask a man but…please say yes,' she pleads with him.

"Baby you beat me to it. I didn't want you to ask me," he says pulling out a small box. "I was already planning on making this official. You are carrying a part of me inside of you. I don't want to marry you because I need you to marry me. You are the air I breathe and I suffocate when you're not around. I worry about you all the time and not only because you are carrying my child but because you are carrying my heart. Yes I will marry you but only if you will marry me. I love you baby," he says opening the box and placing the ring on her finger.

"I love you so much," she says hugging him as he rubs her stomach.

Chapter Forty-Five

"Trust is not an obsession; it's an extension of love. When we truly love someone, we give them our heart to hold in their hands. And when that love is returned, that very trust is balm to our souls"

"Tyrell"

'*Kanilai*' Tyrell reads to off the sign hanging on the bow of the ferry.

"Hey watch this," he says tapping his girlfriend on the shoulder as she turns around. She observes a young African male talking to a white tourist. Another African guy walks behinds the tourist and slices the back of his pocket with a razor blade. The white tourist walks away and his wallet falls out the back of his pocket.

"Oh my God," she says watching as they quickly pick up the wallet and walk away.

"That's why I hide my shit whenever I come home," Tyrell tells her. The ferry docks and the lip of the ferry lower so everyone can exit.

"You know you look like a Mexican," she says referring to his shirt that he's wearing with the two top buttons buttoned and the rest unbuttoned showing off his white undershirt.

"It goes with the belt buckle," he replies adjusting his gold Liberian belt buckle.

"It looks good on you," she says rubbing her hands across his beard. They exit the ferry and he stretches his arms out.

"Welcome to Juffure Gambia. Right over there is Senegal. This is where Kunta Kinte is from," he tells her. They walk towards the pillars the read *'Roots Heritage Trail''*. She approaches the pillar and rubs her hands over the imprint of shackles going around the sign.

"Take a picture," she says running back to Tyrell passing him the camera. She runs back to the sign and places her foot on the shackles pretending to climb up.

"You look good in chains," he tells her jokingly. She sticks her middle finger up at him and he snaps the picture.

"You know Kunta is from an Islamic tribe; The Mandinka Tribe. He was bought as a slave in Annapolis, Maryland. His name was changed to Toby. He tried to run so many times that they cut off his foot so he could not run anymore. Did you know he could read and write?" he asks her.

"How do you know all this stuff?" she asks.

"Jeopardy," Tyrell replies nonchalantly but looking at her seriously. "Naw...I read a lot but I do watch a lot of Jeopardy," he says as they both laugh. They enter into Serekunda Market and he hears music playing softly.

"Gal we wanna fi just squeeze
You put me ting right around ya
Gal you give me the tightest
Hold me seen inna my life, ohhh
Me eye dem dry and me nuh care
Mi tek anytime and anywhere
Inna de spare so we nuh care
And as a woman I will be dere" Tyrell walks over to the tall African guy wearing a blue dragon button down shirt and red Nike cap selling Dashikis.

"What album is that on?" Tyrell ask. The man reaches in a box and pulls out Soca Reggae God 2010. "What song is this?" Tyrell asks.

"Song number 12...Gyptian "Hold Yuh" the vendor replies.

"This shit is hot," he says dapping up the vendor. Tyrell walks around the stand looking at the Dashiki's on the wall. He picks up a green Dashiki with a strip of god imprinted on the front. He stops at the table and picks up a matching set of pants.

"That's a good look on you," the African guy says passing him a Kofi. Tyrell tries on the Kofi and holds the Dashiki in front of the mirror swaying back and forth to the music.

"You look good in that," she tells him. He nods his head up and down in approval.

"Cool…I'll take this and the C.D.,' Tyrell says paying the mane and they continue to walk through the market.

"Watch this," he says. He walks over to a tree, picks up a stick and knocks down a Mango by hitting the tree. "Come here," he says and she walks over as he cracks the Mango over a rock. He passes it to her.

"Mmmmm," she moans biting in the fruit.

"See…that's fresh fruit right there…see how sweet it is," he says biting in his own piece. "Look," Tyrell says pointing to an African woman wearing her traditional red scarf over her head that stretches all over her body.

"That's picturesque," she says taking a picture of the woman as she walks past them balancing a basket on her head. They continue to walk through the market and approach an African stand of women cutting cabbage and selling cucumbers, tomatoes and various sorts of vegetables and fruit.

"Let me get a piece of Jakfruit," he tells one of the women. She picks up her machete and chops the fruit down the middle, sideways and crossways. She cuts the top part out containing the seeds. The woman cuts pieces of the fruit out and places it in a plastic bag.

"Let me get a little more," Tyrell requests. The woman cuts deeper in the fruit placing more in the bag.

"Yea…that's good," he says as she twists the bag in a circle passing it to him. He pays the lady and they walk away.

"To all the ladies in the dance
I lose all control when I see you
Standing there in front of me
Your style, your clothes, your hair
You fair woman, you look so sexy
The way you wine and
The way you dance
And the way you
You twist and turn your waist
Leaves me wanting, leaves me yearning
Leaves me feeling for a taste" Rupee's "Tempted to Touch"
plays from someone's stand.

Tyrell eyes two young African females walking past him. He eyes the dark-skinned girl wearing a two piece red and white bikini set. The female makes eye contact with him and bats her blue eye shadowed eyes at him. He looks out the corner of his eye as she walks past.

"I see now I'm gon' have to fuck you up before this trip is over with,: Tyrell girlfriend says. He claps his hands together and laughing at the same time.

"No baby...it's not like that," he replies placing his hand around her hips pulling her closely.

"You're living dangerously," she says joking with him referring to Bounty Hunter's song.

"Come on...let's get to the campfire," she tells him. They hear Soca music playing from the beach as they make their way to it. He takes his Newport's out of his pocket and shakes out the half of blunt that tucked away. "Muchachito" by Bombo Infierno play by the band. He stops momentarily lighting his blunt. She takes the bag of fruit out of his hand and puts a piece in her mouth.

"Mmmmm this is really good," she says biting into it. He inhales and blows the smoke out as they walk towards the fire. They sit in the sand and he passes her the blunt. She takes the blunt and places the half eaten fruit in his mouth. He catches the fruit before it falls on his shirt, takes off his sandals and taps his feet in the sand as "Arrow's Bills" plays by the man on the congoes. He eats the rest of the fruit and light up a cigarette. She plucks the blunt in the sand and leans beside him swaying back and forth to the music.

"Let's go get something to eat," he says helping her to her feet. They walk to the table set up with food. He picks up a plastic plate and looks over the buffet selection: Chin-chin, tortoise, squash, sweet potatoes, biltrong, potjiekos, hake, frikkadel, and shrimp. They both load their plates and he places an extra helping of shrimp on his plate.

"You love that shrimp I see," she says to him. He looks at her and puts an extra helping on her plate.

"Just in case this ain't enough," he jokes with her. They walk towards the ocean leaving the music behind as they eat off their plates.

"Hold on," Tyrell says passing her his plate. He walks back and returns with two ice follies. He takes his plate back passing her the drink and a napkin. They locate a tree and he sits down Indian style in the sand. He reaches up, grabs her drink and assists her to the ground.

"This place is beautiful," she says peeling a piece of shrimp. He sets his plate down, stands up and begins to dance to the band's version of "Whoa Donkey" by the United Sisters.

"This is how I want to live when I get old," Tyrell says stretching his hand out to help her onto her feet.

"You can if you pick the right person," she says dancing with him.

"What if I decide to pick you?" he asks suggestively.

"Then I guess I would have to say yes because I would want to live like this forever too," she tells him.

"You know...we could have the wedding right here," he says twirling her around.

"Would your mom come?" she asks.

"Of course…that's the only person I would want here," he tells her.

"They yes…that's the only person I would want here as well," she says as Tyrell pulls her closer to him dancing under the moonlight.

Chapter Forty-Six

"There comes that mysterious meeting in life when someone acknowledges who we are and what we can be, igniting the circuits of our highest potential"

"Wandrell"

They sit inside Shanghai Park restaurant downtown Princeton, New Jersey. Wandrell sips on his Heineken and watches the exotic fish swimming in the fish tank.

"How's your beer?" she asks him.

"Good; how's your drink?" he asks in his thick Haitian accent pointing towards her glass of Moscatto.

"Fine…you know this is my drink," she responds. The waitress set down his plate of orange crispy beef over a bed of white rice and places her jumbo shrimp in front of her. She instantly leans over and plucks a piece of beef off of his plate.

"Hey," he says as she laughs and pops the meat in her mouth. They both begin to devour their food in silence only looking up to take sips of their drinks.

"How's your meal?" he asks breaking the silence. She nods her head in approval and plucks another piece of shrimp in her mouth. He lifts his empty Heineken bottle in the air signaling to the waiter for another drink. The waiter quickly moves at his beckoning.

"I wonder if those fish can be ordered to eat?" he says pointing towards the fish tank.

"You would eat one of those?" she asks.

"Hell yea; If they cook it right," he responds in a joking manner that she is not sure if he's serious or not.

"Oh shit," he says and grabs a napkin to lift the food that has fallen on his clothes. He knew he shouldn't have worn his white Polo linen shirt to a restaurant. He dips his napkin in the glass of water and rubs the spots ferociously.

"No stain," he says looking up smiling. She loves the way his dreads fall just below his shoulders.

"What are we going to do today?" she asks.

"I thought we just ride around and explore the city since this is your first time in New Jersey," he says asking the waiter for a to-go container. They exit the restaurant and he presses the alarm on his black 1980 Maserati car. They both get in and he turns on the oldies but goodies station.

"I come home in the morning light
My mother says when you gonna live your life right
Oh mother dear we're not
The fortunate ones
And girls just want to have fun
Oh girls just want to have fun" she begins to sing Cindy Lauper's "Girls Just Want To Have Fun".

'She doesn't know I love this song' Wandrell thinks to himself turning up the music.

"You like this song?" she asks him.

"Yep; this is my jam…after the girls dance to it in the club they all run to me 'cause they want to have fun," he replies laughing as they pass a sign that read *'Asbury Park'*. He turns down the music noticing a crowd gathered and they hear live instruments coming from the platform.

"Let's check this out," he tells her.

"Cool," she responds as he finds a place to park and pulls out a spare blanket that he keeps in the trunk.

"If I have to beg and plead

For your sympathy
I don't mind
Cause you mean that much to me" Temptations "Ain't Too Proud to Beg"

Wandrell walks over and asks the white couple next to them about the concert. They tell him that the Temptations are giving a free concert to raise money for Katrina victims. He walks back to his girlfriend who is rocking back and forth and singing along with the Temptations. He lies the cover blanket down so they can sit. He slips off his open toe sandals and gets comfortable on the ground. She sits beside him and lean her body on his.

Oooh-ooo-ooo-ooh
Soon we'll be married
And raise a family
In a cozy, little home out in the country
With two children, maybe three
I tell you, I can visualize it all
This couldn't be a dream for too real it all seems
But it was just my imagination
Once again
Running away with me
I tell you it was just my imagination
Running away with me" The Temptations sing "Just My Imagination".

Wandrell watches the sun setting and notices the sky is a bright orange. He allows his imagination to run wild. He imagines a house with his Mercedes Benz in the driveway. He imagines himself laying in the front yard on his hammock and her bringing him an ice cold Heineken. He doesn't notice that he has his eyes closed.

"What are you thinking about?" she asks. Her voice snaps him back to reality and he sees her faces as soon as he opens his eyes. She looks at him inquisitively waiting on a response.

"You...you are what I'm thinking about. I just imagined a lifetime with you and I know it was only my imagination but I want it to be true," she replies. She looks at him not quite knowing what to say.

"I've been wild my whole life; but you are the only one who's caught my heart and attention. You know what I'm trying to say?" he asks her.

"Yes I do but I need to hear you say it," she says as he begins to laugh nervously.

"Ok...will you marry me?" he asks her.

"Huh...I can't hear you...speak up. Will I what...carry you," she jokes with him. Wandrell places his hand on top of hers.

"Will you marry me?" he asks again.

"I thought you never ask," she says leaning over to kiss him.

Chapter Forty-Seven

"A man is lucky if he is the first love of a woman. A woman is lucky if she is the last love of a man"

"Yvonne"

"I don't like you
But I love you
Seems that I'm always
Thinking of you
You treat me badly
I love you madly
You've really got a hold on me
You've really got a hold on me" Smokie Robinson and The Miracles' "You Really Got a Hold on Me" plays through the house radio.

"Mmm Mphmm," Yvonne moans to herself clutching a wooden spoon in her hand dancing back and forth. "YOU REALLY GOT A HOLD ON ME," she sings using the spoon as a microphone. She walks to the counter, picks up the knife and continues to chop the bread crumbs. She scoops them up in her hands and spreads it evenly over the macaroni and cheese. She takes the top off the pot, stirs the greens and fatback allowing the smell to penetrate her nose. Yvonne reaches for her cup and takes a sip of Hennessey while pulling a cigarette from her pouch. She walks in the living room, turns on the light and looks at her grandchild sleeping. She walks over, pulls the cover over top of him and kisses him on the cheek. She walks back in the kitchen listening to the radio personality; Mitch Malone from 105.7 fm talking.

"Hey hey hey...this is Mitch Malone on the midnight tip just wanting you to have a happy and safe thanksgiving evening. I just want you to know that I'm still in love with you," Mitch says spinning the record.

"Spending my day
Thinkin' bout you girl
Being here with you
Being near you
I can't explain myself
Why I feel like I do
Though it hurts me so
To let you know that I
Look in your eyes
Let me know
How you feel
Let me know that love is really real
And it seems to me
That I'm wrapped up in your love" Al Green's "I'm still in love with you" plays.

"That's my jam right there," she says and begins to sing along with the song. She opens the pot of chitterlings stirring them to allow the bay leaves to mix deep within.

"Mmmmmm now this is good," Yvonne says pulling a strand off of the slotted spoon and tasting it before placing the lid back on the pot. "Thank you God," she says to herself sitting in the chair thinking of the beautiful life she has while taking a sip from her cup. She checks to make sure the oven is on low, turns off the lights and enters the bedroom. She lies down beside her husband falling asleep.

Yvonne is awoken by her dog barking and biting at the comforter.

"Shut up," she says waving her arm aimlessly and tiredly.

"Grammie grammie wake up," her grandchild says throwing his rubber hammer at her.

"Good morning darling; come here and give grandma a kiss," she says and reaches over to kiss him on the cheek.

"Good morning grammie," he says in a funny manner because of his missing front teeth.

"Grandma's getting up...I'll be there in a second," she says as he runs out the room.

"Murph...you know your friend is on the way to cut your hair," she tells her husband.

"Happy thanksgiving," he tells her.

"Unh-uh; Happy thanksgiving," Yvonne mutters. She slides her slippers on and walks out into the kitchen.

"Boy get out of that," she yells at her oldest son who is peeking in the oven.

"I washed my hands,' he says shutting the oven door. She takes the macaroni and cheese out lightly tapping it with the spatula.

"Happy thanksgiving mom," her oldest son says walking behind her kissing her on the cheek.

"Happy thanksgiving son," Yvonne replies.

"Murph...hurry up; your friend is here to cut your hair," she yells out pulling the curtains back and tapping on the window waving hello.

"Happy thanksgiving," the guy says waving back and enters the garage to set up his barber equipment.

"Make sure you tell him not to take too much off the top. I want you perfect for today," she tells her husband as he emerges from the back bedroom and exits the door. She watches him enter the garage.

"I
Need you baby
I need you right now
Say can you understand you're my man
And my one desire is keeping you satisfied

Baby when we
When we're together say
I'm alright
And you're alright
It's like paradise
I just want you to know how I feel
How I feel" Patti Labelle's "Love, Need and Want You" filters through the house speakers.

Yvonne turns the oven up to 350 degrees and places the homemade biscuits inside.

"Give that boy a bath we gon' be eating soon," she tells her oldest son and begins to set the table.

"Okay mom," he responds picking up his son and walking to the bathroom. Yvonne sets a rack on the table and begins to lift the turkey.

"Hey mom how are you…whoa whoa whoa…let me get that," her youngest son says walking in and rushing to grab the turkey.

"Thank you. I'm so tired. I was up 'til about four this morning but the macaroni and cheese is ready. The turkey is ready. I got pigsfeet and chitterlings too. Once the biscuits are done and Murphy finishes getting his haircut we can eat 'cause I'm getting hungry," she says.

"Where my stupid brother at?" her youngest son asks.

"He in there giving your nephew a bath…don't be starting no mess today," she says playfully.

"Awwww mom happy thanksgiving," he says leaning over to kiss her and walks away.

"What you think dear?" Murphy asks re-entering the kitchen from outside.

"It looks good. I like it when he leaves a little on top. You are so handsome," she replies leaning over to kiss him.

"Turn off the light
And light a candle
Tonight I'm in
A romantic mood
Yeah
Let's take a shower
Shower together
I'll wash your body
And you'll wash mine
Yeah
Rub me down in some hot oils baby
Yeah
And I'll do the same thing to you," Teddy Pendergrass's "Turn off the lights" is playing on 105.7 fm.

"Murphy twirls his wife around in a circle and brings her close into his arms kissing her.

"Hurry up...I'm ready to eat," she tells him as he walks to the back bedroom.

"Hey mom sorry I'm late," he daughter says walking in the back door and assisting with setting the table with the orange plates and cups.

"That's okay because we were just about to eat," Yvonne tells her. Yvonne's oldest son enters and places his son in the high chair.

"'Took you long enough. We were gon' eat without you," the youngest brother jokes with his sister.

"No you won't and this is your first year getting here before me," she responds to him.

"I told you to behave boy…don't be starting no trouble," Yvonne warns him.

"Awww mom…I'm just joking with her," he says taking a seat.

"Mmmmm mphmm…something sure does smell good," Murphy says entering the kitchen and taking a seat.

"Mom this turkey sure looks good. You really outdid yourself this year," her oldest son tells her.

"Well let's pray so we can dig," Yvonne say as everyone hold each other's hands.

"Alright let's bow our heads…I thank the Lord for this blessed day. Thank you for all the things that he has prepared and blessed the ones whom are less fortunate than us. Amen," Murphy prays.

"I would also like to thank God for having my entire family home. I know each and every one of my kids have had their hardships and struggles but through it all we have remained a family. There are so many things to be thankful for but the only one that really matter is family. I love each and everyone one of you with all my heart," Yvonne says beginning g to get teary eyed.

"Happy thanksgiving," she tells everyone.

"I love you mom," says her oldest son.

"I love you mom," says her youngest son.

"I love you mom," says her daughter.

"I love you baby. You have really outdone yourself this year. Thank you for being the perfect wife and mother in each and every way," her husband says.

"Happy thanksgiving grammie," her grandchild says whistling through his missing front teeth. Everyone laughs.

Chapter Forty-Eight

"I love you not only for what you are, but for what I am when I am with you. I love you not only for what you have made of yourself, but for what you are making of me. I love you for the part of me that you bring out"

"Zenobia"

"Wow this place looks interesting," Zenobia tells her girlfriend as they stand outside of Borrowed Bucks Roadhouse Pub.

"What are all those logos on the building?" she asks pointing to the logos plastered on the front of the Pub. Mobil, DX, Shamrock, and a picture of a Pegasus displayed over top of the Borrowed Bucks sign. "What is Lube Sinclair...or what was it?" Zenobia ask her girlfriend.

"This place used to be a service station and then they turned it into a Pub. Come on let's go in...I love the band that's playing tonight," her girlfriend says as they walk across the street.

"I don't know why I always wanted to visit this place but so far I'm really digging North Dakota," Zenobia says.

"Well; I think you just like the all natural thing that they have here," her girlfriend jokes referring to the weed that they smoked in the car ride over.

"Well shit...that was some good weed though," Zenobia tells her girlfriend as she holds the door open for her to enter. They are blasted by the sounds of the live band playing on the center stage. Zenobia passes the bouncer her identification card and picks up a flier. *Trick Grenade tonight...tomorrow's feature...Kamilla*. They receive their identification cards back and make way through the crowd of white people who are looking at them curiously. Zenobia's girlfriend finds her friend standing at a table in the middle of the pub.

"Hey girl...I would like for you to meet Zenobia," the girlfriend says to the white girl at the table. The white girl extends her hand offering her name.

"I heard so much about you. It is a pleasure to finally meet you. Welcome to Bismark," she says letting go of Zenobia's hand.

"I told my girlfriend that I always wanted to visit here and ironically she ends up at a school down here. I don't know if I wanted to make multiple trips though," Zenobia says laughing while brushing back the dreadlocks that have fallen in her face.

"So what's going on tonight?" Zenobia ask.

"Thursday night is ladies night so the house beer is a dollar and all the mixed drinks are two fifty," the white girls answers raising a paper sack to her mouth.

"Why is she drinking out of a sack?" Zenobia asks leaning over and whispering in her girlfriend's ear.

"Round here they serve their beers in one of those weird little bags. It's kinda cool 'cause they don't drip or anything. I think it's weird but you know what they say...when in Rome," she laughs and calls the waitress over. Zenobia orders a Heineken and asks if they server Nuevo.

"Sorry ma'am; I don't think we have that in stock but I will check for you," the waitress responds.

"Hey can you bring three shots of Jager Bombs," the white girl tells the waitress as she nods a yes and dumps the ashtray in her trash bag.

"I want this to be the
Same as when we were young

Before all that made us
Fade out like shadows in the sun
We all live with mistakes
And we'll die trying to hide them
This world was never meant to take
Away the things we believe in
How does this all make sense
Where is the part that we
Says we'll be friends
Where's the boy I used to be
Stuck in past and present tense
My eyes are afraid to see
What waits at the end
To try and capture me
It's just your loss
It will never be this way again"

"Wow this is Trick Grenade. The music is a little scary but the lyrics are off the chain," Zenobia says to her girlfriend.

"I absolutely love this band. We partied with them at their house a few nights ago and they put that shit on youtube. They real cool down to earth guys," Zenobia's girlfriend tells her. The waitress brings the drinks to the table and they raise their drinks in the air.

"To one hell of a night," the white girl says.

"To prosperity," replies Zenobia as they all chug their drinks slamming them on the table.

"So I was told that you are Moorish American. What is that exactly?" the white girl asks.

"Well not to get too deep, but my religion is Islam. It's not what we are but who we are. We are ancient Moabites and my religion teaches us that we are more beneficial to earthly salvation and that our true nature has been withheld from us. Oh and by the way; I don't hate white people," she finishes and everyone bursts out laughing.

"Hey everyone I would like to welcome you all to the greatest band on earth…Whooooo…that's Wolf on the drum. (Wolf starts to give a beat on the drums) , That's Shane-O on the bass (Shane-O gives a deep chord), Tommy Guns on the guitar (Tommy Guns start thumbing his chords), and I'm T.J. Havik and only one of the rock stars tonight (T.J. begins playing his guitar in unison). We have to give a shout out to someone special that we all lost recently. Sing along if you know this song," he yells in the microphone as the band begins playing.

"I wanna rock with you
Allll night
Dance you into the
Sunlight
I wanna rock with you
All night
We're gonna rock the night away," the lead singer begins singing Michael Jackson's "Rock with You".

"Oh shit…yea baby…sing that shit," Zenobia yells raising her hand and bobbing her head allowing her braids to fall back and forth across her face.
"Let's rock," Zenobia says grabbing her girlfriend's hand and pulling her towards the dance floor.

"Girl
Close your eyes
Let that rhythm
Get into you
Don't try and fight it
There ain't nothing
That you can do
Relax your mind
Lay back and groove with mine
You gotta feel that heat

And we can ride the boogie
Share that beat of love," Zenobia begins singing and twirling her
girlfriend on the dance floor.

Yea...sing it T.J.," someone yells from the back of the
pub.

"We love you M.J.," someone else yells from the other
side of the pub as the band switches to a new song. They walk
back to the table and see their friend talks to some of her friends
at another table.

"Soooo...have you thought about what we've been talking
about?" Zenobia asks her girlfriend.

"Yes...I have and I am very strong and secure in my
womanhood to know that I am truly in love with another woman.
But it's scary. It's like letting the entire world look in my life.
That's scary to me but I see the strength that you posses and I
love that. I love the fact that you are so strong and committed to
your beliefs. I stand tall beside you because your light gives me
inspiration. The way you carry on a conversation with black
people is the same way you carry on a conversation with white
people and that shows strength and character. You know who
you are and that draws me to you more than anything else. You
give me the strength to want to tackle the world. With you-beside
you-I choose you-my answer is yes," her girlfriend says.

Chapter Forty-Nine

"Read Traces of You Again...
I wrote a Book...HAHA"

"Zokee"

Zokee looks through his playlist, presses play and tosses his phone on the bed.

"Yea I'm single
Nigga had to cancel that bitch like Nino
Ain't tripping on nothing
I'm just sipping on something
And my homeboy say he got a bad bitch for me tonight" he sings along   with   Lil   Wayne's   "I'm Single".

"Hurry up nigga," his brother calls out from the other room.
"Shut the fuck up nigga...I'll be out in five minutes," Zokee yells out. He stands in front of the mirror looking at his Raw Blue Meridian jeans and Roar Airborne t-shirt. He takes three pairs of shoes out of his bag and places them all on the floor in front of the mirror. He looks at his Kobe Bryant Zooms, Nike Zoom Oncore's, and his Air Jordan Fusions that he has purchased from the Post Exchange earlier. He chooses the Fusions and picks up his specially made S.I.O.B gold chain.
"The Set It Off Boys is in the house nigga," he says in the mirror. He picks up his phone and texts his girlfriend. *'Las Vegas baby...bout to het the base...I'll hit you later'*.

"She say she wish she could
Cut my dick off and take it with her
I said hold up
She say she just playing
Then I falls in that pussy like quicksand" Zokee raps to the song.

He puts on his gold watch with the red, blue and silver diamond in the face, walks out the room and sees his brother pouring a drink.

"You want some nigga?" Zokee's brother asks.

"Now you know I don't drink but let me taste it," Zokee says while his brother passes him a cup. "Goddamn…this shit is strong," he says coughing.

"Awww nigga you just can't drink," his brother says reaching for the cup.

"Hold up nigga," Zokee replies taking another sip before passing it back. They exit the barracks and walk towards Club Vibe bowling alley. Zokee points to the sign and reads it out-loud, *'Nellis Air Force Base…Home of the Fighter Pilot'*.

"When I was at camp they took us to the Virginia Aviation Museum. They let us get on the…the…I don't know who built it but it was the first plane ever built," Zokee says.

"Oh you mean the Wright Brothers stupid," his brother corrects him.

"Yea, the Wright Brothers and don't call me stupid," Zokee says agreeing with him.

"You should see the planes that they have in the museum here. It would put that one to shame. They got F/A 22's, Prowlers, Bombers, C-130's, F 16's, and a bunch of other shit. That would be a cool place to take mom when she comes down," Zokee's brother responds throwing his cup away as they enter Club Vibe bowling alley.

"We coulda worked it out, uh,

But I gurss things change
It's funny how someone else's success brings pain
When you no longer involved
That person has it
And you just stuck standing there
But I'm go need you to say something baby
Say something baby" Drake and Timbaland's "Say Something Baby" plays in the bowling alley.

"Yeaaaa baby…tonight we getting wasted baby," the D.J. yells remixing Gucci Mane's "Wasted".

"I'm so wasted
She so wasted
Tell the bartender send me twenty more cases
Rockstar lifestyle might not make it
President got him in the White House naked
Look at the clock
And it says right now
Get a pound
Break it down
Blow it like trial
Panatela Dutchy wine in my tall glass
Young money baby
Big shit like a horse ass
Stacks in my backpack
Shades on
Hat back
Bugatti Matte black
Where they do that at" Lil Wayne raps as Zokee follow his brother to rent bowling shoes.

"Let's order something to eat first. I'm hungry as shit," Zokee's brother tells him.

"Yea; I ain't ate all day. This place is like a club forreal. It's all types of bitches in here," Zokee replies following his brother to the bar.

"Mane it's like this every week. It be jumping in this muthafucker. What do you want to eat?" his brother asks.

"Shiiit…just get me a cheeseburger with extra pickles…Goddamn," Zokee says turning around to look at the girls walking past. His brother orders the food and a pitcher of beer for himself. The waitress hands him a card with a number on it.

"When your number is called you can pick up your food. I'm going to have to ask for his I.D.," the waitress says eyeing Zokee and withholding the pitcher of beer.

"Oh he's not drinking. You can bring him some mile," his brother says jokingly.

"Shut the fuck up nigga; let me get a Sprite," Zokee says as the waitress laughs and passes them the Sprite and pitcher of beer.

"You two must be brothers," she says laughing and walking away. They walk from the bar and his brother pounds up one of his Air Force friends.

"What's popping lil man…I got my lil cousin over there. Just sit at the table with us," he says pointing to the table. "I'm going to order another pitcher and I'll meet you there," his friend says walking away. They walk to the table and introduce themselves.

"Forty nine…Forty nine…your order is up," the waitress calls out. Zokee's brother gets up to go retrieve the food.

"Hey girl…what's your name?" Zokee asks.

"Hey girl…is that your best?...this girl do have a name," the female responds.

"Well; that's why I said Hey girl…what's your name?" Zokee responds sarcastically.

"You too funny…my name is Zia," she tells him.

"That's cool…my name is Zokee. I don't think I ever met a girl whose name begins with a Z," he says.

"Well you ain't met a lot of girls like me," she replies.

"Ooooh you funny and cute," he says.

"This must be your first time here 'cause I've never seen you before," Zia responds making an observation.

"Yep; my brother is in the Air Force and I'm visiting for the weekend," he tells her.

"Where are you from?" she asks. Zokee's brother and friend returns setting his plate of food down with a massive bowl of pickles.

"I hope you got some gum for that," she says pulling out a pack of Spearmint gum.

"Thanks," he responds taking a bite out of his cheeseburger. "Fuck," he yells out as the burger falls out the bun on the plate and she laughs.

"Fuck this…I'm gon' eat this muthafucker," Zokee says scooping the burger up with his bun.

"You are sooo funny…oh it's my turn to bowl. I'll be right back," she says laughing and getting up.

"Damn Zokee. She is fine as hell and you over here eating like a hobo," his brother says laughing and drinking his beer.

"Fuck that…this is America's favorite meal. I'll turn my swag back on when I'm done but right now I'm hungry," Zokee says picking up the sandwich to take another bite. His brother laughs and gets up to talk to his friends walking in the bowling alley.

"Did you see the spare I got?" Zia asks returning to the table.

"Yep…that shit was hot," he says.

"Oooooh so I see you're a liar too. I saw you murdering that sandwich. You didn't even look in my direction," she replies laughing.

"This here is on some truthful shit

It seem like everything I do you're used to it
And I hate hearing stories bout who you been with
That's when I gotta hide, what I'm feeling inside" Zokee puts the
sandwich down and begins singing.

"So you still think I'm confident and damn
Is this gonna last
You're up on a pedestal
Are we moving too fast
Feel like I'm in crazy competition with the past
That's why I gotta ask"

"This must be you're jam 'cause this is the first time I saw
you put that sandwich down for anything," Zia says as he
continues to sing.

"Is anything I'm doing brand new
Brand new brand new
Is anything I'm doing brand new
Brand new brand new" Zokee continues to sing along Drake's
"Brand New".

"Yea...I fucks with Drake," he tells her.
"Well I'm done playing. You want to walk around?" she
asks. Zokee takes one more bite of his sandwich, grabs his drink
and a napkin.
"Yea let's walk," he tells her getting up and they enter the
game room.
"Look...I'm kinda straightforward. I hope you don't
mind," she asks.
"Naw you good...what's up?" Zokee asks.
"What do you want to do when you get older?" she asks.
"I want to go to college, get a job and get married," he tells
her.
"So you DO want to get married," she says.

"Yes…you're kinda cool. The girls 'round my way don't talk like you do," he says.

"You never told me where you are from and what does S.I.O.B mean?" she asks pointing to his chain.

"I'm from Virginia and S.I.O.B stands for my squad the Set It Off Boys," he says cockily holding his chain up with his thumbs.

"Well; where I'm from they don't act like you. I hope you don't mind me being straightforward one more time?" Zia asks.

"Naw you good…what's up?" he replies. She looks around and leans over to kiss him.

"Is anything I'm doing brand new
Brand new
Brand new" Drake's song continues to play.

Traces of Raymond Goode

Website: www.Tracesofyou.org

Email: Raymond.d.goode@gmail.com
          Rd.goode@yahoo.com

Facebook: www.facebook.com/Raymond.Goode

Youtube: http://www.youtube.com/Gooderaymond

Blog: http://raymondgoode.wordpress.com

Twitter: @RaymondGoode